LOVE
REBORN

LOVE REBORN

a Dead Beautiful novel

YVONNE WOON

HYPERION
NEW YORK

For Paul,
who first walked this mountain path with me

Copyright © 2014 by Yvonne Woon

All rights reserved. Published by Hyperion, an imprint of Disney Book Group. No part of this book may be reproduced or transmitted in any form or by any means, electronic or mechanical, including photocopying, recording, or by any information storage and retrieval system, without written permission from the publisher. For information address Hyperion, 125 West End Avenue, New York, New York 10023.

First Edition

1 3 5 7 9 10 8 6 4 2

G475-5664-5-13288

Printed in the United States of America

This book is set in 13-point Garamond 3.
Designed by Marci Senders
Composition by Brad Walrod/Kenoza Type, Inc.
Reinforced binding

Library of Congress Cataloging-in-Publication Data
Woon, Yvonne.
Love reborn/Yvonne Woon.—First edition.
pages cm.
Summary: The soul that Renée and Dante share cannot sustain them both but Renée may hold the secret of eternal life which they must keep safe from the Liberum and a team of Monitors as they cross Europe seeking the Netherworld, a legendary chasm where souls go to be cleansed.
ISBN 978-1-4231-7120-1 (hardback)
[1. Soul—Fiction.   2. Immortality—Fiction.   3. Supernatural—Fiction.
4. Voyages and travels—Fiction.   5. Europe—Fiction.]   I. Title.
PZ7.W88723Lov 2014
[Fic]—dc23   2013034392

Visit www.un-requiredreading.com

contents

Whatever I have up till now accepted as most true I have acquired either from the senses or through the senses. But from time to time I have found that the senses deceive, and it is prudent never to trust completely those who have deceived us even once.

—René Descartes, *Meditations on First Philosophy*

CHAPTER 1

From the Depths of the Lake

I COULDN'T REMEMBER HOW I HAD GOTTEN THERE or how long I had been standing alone in the snow. A lake of ice stretched out before me, its water frozen into dark blue ribbons. The buildings of Gottfried Academy loomed around it, crooked and deserted. All was quiet save for a strange thudding. It echoed up through the ground as if something buried deep beneath the earth were trying to break free.

"Dante?" I called out. The winter air sucked his name from my lips before my voice made a sound.

I searched the horizon for him, but the snow was clean and unsullied by footprints. "Dante?" I said again, but I couldn't feel his presence. Had the Monitors found him? Had they buried him?

A dog barked in the distance. A deep voice echoed through the trees. "He's here! This way! I can feel him." It was my grandfather, the headmaster of Gottfried.

I turned toward the woods. Was he talking about Dante?

The thudding grew stronger until the ground seemed to tremble. I felt the earth vibrate beneath my feet. My gaze returned to the frozen lake. The sound was coming from beneath the surface. I inched toward it, watching the brittle ribbons of ice quiver.

The dogs were approaching, their barks sharpening, their feet scuttling through the snow. "Hurry!" my grandfather bellowed, his voice closer.

I covered my ears as the thudding grew louder, more desperate. The surface of the lake bulged. Dozens of tiny faults splintered toward the shore in jagged seams. Another thud, and it buckled. The air pulsed with each tremor until a sharp crack rang out through the cold.

The ice shattered. Then all went still.

I lowered my hands from my ears. My grandfather was closer now; I could hear him approaching through the snow, the footsteps of the Monitors following behind him, though I didn't dare turn. The black water pooled through the crack in the ice. It rippled. A pale hand reached up from the surface of the lake.

A boy's presence wrapped itself around my legs in a thin strand of cold air, beckoning me to move toward him. Water sloshed from the gash in the ice. His slick body rose from the depths, his lips a bruised purple, his auburn hair matted to his temples. He dug his fingers into the ice and dragged himself out. His eyes snapped open as the lake spilled off of him. He looked at me, his mouth forming my name. "Renée."

Noah. He was Undead.

I bolted awake, his name on my lips. I pressed them shut before the sound left my mouth, and sat up, the room coming into focus. I could almost smell the dried flowers bundled on the side table; could almost hear the water dripping off the icicles outside. Everything else—the lake, the thumping, the Monitors—had been nothing more than a dream. Noah hadn't burst through the ice, nor had he pulled himself out, his eyes rolling in his head as he faced me. Or had he? It had felt so real that his presence still seemed to coil around me—a stream of cold air tightening, pressing the air out of me—begging me to follow it back to that day, and relive Noah's death again.

I sank back into the cushions. How long had I been wandering through the woods? I thought back, trying to discern each gray morning from the next. Ten days since I had taken the train back to Gottfried Academy with Noah. Ten days since he had dived into the icy lake to retrieve the chest that the ninth sister had hidden at the bottom. Ten days since the Undead had surrounded us and dragged Noah back into the frozen lake, his palm pressing against the underside of the ice as the life left him. Ten days since Dante had whisked me away just before one of the Liberum had pressed his hollow mouth to mine to take my soul.

The Liberum. They were an Undead brotherhood so

elusive, so insidious, that many Monitors considered their existence a mere legend. There were nine of them, their faces shrouded with hoods, their bodies so gaunt they looked inhuman. They had been alive for centuries, taking the souls of innocent people to keep the decay of their bodies at bay. All for the sole purpose of finding eternal life and becoming human again.

The Liberum traveled with a group of Undead boys, who flanked them like an army. Many Monitors had spied the boys, but only a rare few had laid eyes on a Brother. Even fewer wanted to, for every Monitor knew that if you saw the Liberum, it was because they had been searching for you first. Their blue lips would be the last sight your eyes would see. I was the exception. Because of Dante, I was able to escape just before the Liberum took my soul, though that kind of luck wouldn't happen again. The Liberum had been searching for a way to become human for years, and now that they knew I had the chest of the Nine Sisters, which was supposed to contain the secret to eternal life, they would stop at nothing to find me and take it from my grasp.

Every so often, I thought I could feel their vacancy snaking through the mountains, moving toward us. Or was it just the winter chill? We had thrown them off our trail days before, and were spending nights wherever we could find shelter, Dante leading the way. An abandoned trailer, a deserted rest stop, the State Park Visitors' Lodge, an empty campground. Now we were in a cabin somewhere in the mountains between Maine and New Hampshire, navigating through the maze of icy ridges that belonged to no state or person.

Ten days. That was the amount of time it took for a person to reanimate. Maybe my dream had been real. Maybe Noah had reanimated.

I blinked, taking in the dusty sofa beneath me. I was sitting in the living room of a cabin that Dante and I had stumbled across while stealing through the White Mountains. A thin quilt was tangled around my legs. Instinctively, I reached for my bag. I had taken to sleeping with it for safekeeping, but when I patted the cushions I realized it was gone. I kicked off the blanket. The other side of the couch, where I had last seen Dante before I'd fallen asleep, was now empty.

Through the curtains, I could see the first hint of dawn peeking through the pines. "Dante?" I said.

"I'm here." His voice was so close that it startled me. He was hunched over the desk just a few feet away, his broad shoulders jutting out beneath the thin cotton of his shirt, his body so still it looked lifeless. And technically, it was. Dante had died seventeen years before in a plane crash, on the same day that I was born. His body had been lost at sea. Because he was never buried or put to rest, his body had reanimated ten days later as an Undead, pale and numb to all sensation. His soul had been reborn into a new person, from whom he could take it back with just a single, fatal kiss. Me.

His presence crept over me like frost blooming on a windowpane. With each day his face seemed to change, his handsome features sharpening and aging far too quickly for me to memorize them. His skin was still smooth, yet his face looked gaunter, paler; his eyes were still a rich brown, yet I could already see a cloudy haze creeping over their edges, threatening to engulf them in gray.

"It sounded like you were having a nightmare," he said.

I wanted to tell Dante about my dream. But how could I explain that although I loved him and my soul ached for him even when we were standing side by side, it also ached for Noah, and for what I had done to him? Why had I let him come with me to Gottfried that night? I felt responsible for Noah's death. Whenever I looked at Dante trudging ahead of me in the snow, I almost couldn't bear the shame of it—that we were still here and Noah was gone.

"You're lucky you never sleep," I said.

"No, I'm not," he said, pushing a strand of hair from his face. "The worst kinds of nightmares are the ones you have while you're awake."

My bag sat slumped by his feet. The chest that had been inside rested on the desk in front of him, its lid ajar, as though he had been studying it. It seemed to suck up all the air in the room, leaving Dante and me in a silence that never used to exist between us. I realized then that I didn't want to look at it. I preferred to pretend that we had never opened it, that its contents were still a source of hope.

"Did you find anything?" I asked.

Dante traced his hand around the rim of the chest. "Not yet."

It was made of a dark metal that was worn and uneven, as if it had been hammered into shape. Pinned to the underside of the lid was a preserved canary, laid flat as if in flight. Its plumage, though aged, had a golden luster; its tail feathers were long and sharp, two brilliant yellow streaks. Of all the creatures on earth, the canary was the most difficult animal for a Monitor to sense when it was dead. This was why the ninth sister had pinned it inside the chest before she hid it in the lake at Gottfried: so that only the most gifted of Monitors would be able to find it.

The canary's brittle body cracked as Dante unpinned it. When he set it aside, the bird's outline was still there. Engraved on the underside of the chest's lid was a constellation of five points: one at the head, one at either wing, and one at each of the two tail feathers. An elaborate collection of lines and shapes was etched into the metal around them, tangling into a strange sort of landscape.

Inside the chest sat a small black box, no larger than a bar of soap. It was such a little thing, so unassuming, and yet the mere sight of it gave me pause. It was carved bluntly out of a dull metallic rock. The shape of a canary was etched into its lid, along with the words: *Pour l'Amour Vrai*. For true love.

I lifted it from the recess, feeling its familiar heaviness in my palm. It had an unnatural gravity; its weight pulled away from me as if it didn't want to be held.

I turned it around in my palm, trying to see something I hadn't seen before. It had no latch or keyhole or hinge, not even a seam, and yet I could feel its contents shifting like dust. We still hadn't figured out how to open it; nor did we understand what the chest and the markings on its lid meant. They were supposed to contain the secret to eternal life—yet all I could see was another question mark.

"The answer is probably staring at us," Dante said. "We just don't see it yet."

I was about to respond when a dog's bark rang out through the woods. "Did you hear that?"

"Hear what?" said Dante, reminding me how muted his senses had become.

I crept to the window, hoping I had imagined the sound. A flock of crows scattered from a tree nearby. Behind it, the snowy mountains glistened in the early morning sun. All was still. Too still. Where were the rest of the birds? I cracked open the window, listening as the wind carried the sound of dogs barking, followed by a shout, so distant it could have been from my dream.

"Monitors," I whispered. People who could sense death just like I could, and were charged with hunting the Undead and burying them. But how had they found us? We had lost them over a week ago, the snowfall masking our footprints, the woods so quiet that it felt like we were the only ones for miles.

The chair scraped the floor as Dante stood. "We have to leave."

I stuffed the chest, the canary, and the small black box into my bag, then followed Dante to the back of the cabin. A white gust swept through the room as he opened the door.

I sank up to my shins in the snow. The cold shocked my lungs. Trees filled the landscape around us, making every direction I turned look the same, but Dante seemed to know the way. He set off toward where the brush was thickest. I stole into the woods after him.

The sound of the dogs grew closer. The echo of their barking clapped against the trees. The metal chest thudded against the back of my ribs like a second heart as I ran in Dante's footprints. They were larger than mine, and spread so far apart that it was hard for me to keep up. Reading my thoughts, he turned around, his gaze the only trace of warmth in the woods. He said nothing—neither of us did—but as he continued onward through the woods he slowed, shortening his gait until I was right behind him.

The tags of the dogs clinked behind us, growing louder, louder. I could hear their feet crunching in the snow, their panting heavy as they emerged through the trees. I glanced over my shoulder and they were almost upon us, leaping through the branches in a snarl of fur and teeth and saliva. Two, three, four German shepherds, their mottled coats caked with ice.

"Stay in front of me," Dante shouted, slowing until I passed him.

The dogs snapped at the air, skidding to follow us as

we took a sharp turn through a thicket of trees. Breaking a branch from a tree, Dante swiped at them while we zigzagged through the woods, shouting at me to turn left, then right. But the snow was too thick; I couldn't run fast enough. Behind me, I heard Dante's footsteps slow.

"What are you doing?" I shouted.

"Go," he said. When I hesitated, he spoke louder. "Go!"

He turned to face the dogs just as they leaped through the thicket, their breath reaching out to him in clouds of fog. I looked back only once, just in time to see him swing his branch through the air and strike one of them aside by the muzzle.

The branches of the pines whipped against my arms. I ran, listening to the scuffle behind me: a growl, jaws snapping at wood, an animal thrown across the snow; a whimper. Then I heard feet padding over the ice. I glanced over my shoulder to see a dog break free from the others, its lean body bounding through the brush toward me. My legs sank so deep that I stumbled. The ice stung my cheeks. Picking myself up, I backed away and searched the pines for branches thick enough for me to climb, but they were all too thin or too high.

The dog leaped at me, its eyes sharp and yellowed, its jowls wet with spit. I steadied my arm, ready to strike, but just as its whiskers grazed my neck, Dante burst through the woods, his body colliding with the dog's in a tangle of fur and ice and blood. They fell to the ground, a flurry of white billowing up around them. All I could hear was panting and the guttural growl of the dog as it struggled, digging its feet into the snow. Through the flurry, Dante's outline hardened. He kneeled over the dog, pressing his knee into its chest to hold it down. His hands gripped its skull, ready to snap its neck. The dog whimpered beneath him.

"Don't!" I shouted, as the crack rang out through the trees.

Its head fell limp in Dante's arms. All went still. The lifelessness of the dog crept toward me, the air rearranging itself until the forest felt hollow.

A lock of hair dangled in front of Dante's face as he looked up, his eyes clouded and cold, void of the deep brown gaze that belonged to the boy I knew. His cheek was smeared with blood. As he took me in, his eyes came back into focus; the haze over his irises receded. The muscles in his face softened, his shoulders relaxing, until he was back to the Dante I had come here with. The Dante who was gentle and kind, who had never killed anything in front of me before.

He hesitated before walking toward me. He must have seen the fear in my eyes. "Are you okay?"

I nodded, willing my lips to stop quivering. I reached out to his cheek, but let my arm drop. "You have blood," I said. "Here."

He wiped it away. "It's not mine."

Though of course, I already knew. Dante healed too quickly to have left such a brazen trace of red.

The snow fell around us in thick clumps, like shreds of

cloud falling from the sky. It clung to his hair, his shoulders, preserving him in white as he trudged toward me. Gently, he brushed the snowflakes from my eyelashes, sending an icy prickle up my skin. At his touch, I could suddenly smell the sharp pine of the trees around us, the wind whistling through the branches in a melancholy key.

The first time I had felt the prickle of his touch it had frightened me; now, though, it was a comfort. The Undead have only twenty-one years to roam the earth, their bodies decaying, growing hungrier and more desperate until they die again for good.

Feeling the cold tug of Dante's presence reminded me that he was still here, that we still had time; though how much, I wasn't sure. He had four years left as an Undead, but how many as the Dante that I knew? How long did we have until he succumbed to darkness? Until his skin withered and the hunger within him surfaced, the hunger that would urge him to take my soul? He had already begun his decline; I could see it in the coldness that came over him when he was angry. He could barely hear the dogs until they were upon us. He couldn't feel the slick of blood on his cheek, or any other sensation except for my touch. He couldn't smell the woods around us unless I was close to him, nor taste anything but the salt on my skin, nor hear music—to Dante, everything was noise, except for the sound of my voice.

With every day that I lived, Dante was dying.

I tried to imagine what it would it be like when all

of this was over, and we could walk down a snowy street hand in hand, like any other couple—never having to worry about who might see us, or how much time we had left together. A muffled shout brought me back to the woods.

"This way—he feels stronger than any other Undead I've ever known!"

My body went rigid. I recognized the deep intonations of my grandfather.

"They're coming," I said, and turned to Dante, confused. "They can feel you more than any other Undead."

But why? Dante's presence couldn't be that much stronger than it was weeks earlier. I knew that the presence of an Undead grew more potent as he aged, but my grandfather had been hunting Dante for months, and had never had this response. Something must have changed in the past ten days, but what? My hand tightened around the strap of my bag. "The canary," I said, feeling its subtle tug on my back. Could its presence be somehow heightening Dante's vacancy? I had never heard of such a phenomena. It didn't make sense—the canary was supposed to be the most difficult corpse to find—but nothing else did either. "Maybe . . . maybe it's drawing the Monitors closer?"

Dante didn't question me. "We have to leave it behind."

"What if we need it?"

"Need it for what?" Dante said. "It was probably only pinned inside the chest so that you could find it."

I hesitated. "I'm not sure."

Dante had no answer. "If you're right that it's adding to

my vacancy, and we keep it, there's more of a chance that they'll find us. If that happens, they'll bury me. And there will be no use for the chest at all."

In the distance, I could hear the muffled cries of the Monitors.

"Okay," I said, and fumbled through my bag until I found its brittle body. Before I could change my mind, I tossed it far into the woods.

A swirl of snow followed us as he led me deeper into the white woods. It was a place where everything looked alike; one tree seemed identical to the next, until I felt like I was running in circles. Everything had an eerie hollowness to it here, as if the forest around us was sleeping, waiting, watching. All the while, the sound of the Monitors crept up on us, their footsteps crunching in the snow, their voices carrying on the wind like the murmurs of ghosts.

"Hurry!" my grandfather said, his baritone voice silencing the others. "His presence is stronger than ever."

I slowed. "It didn't help," I said, realizing then that my instinct had been right—the canary had never been the problem. "They can still sense you more than ever before."

Dante stopped in his tracks. "It's because we're together," he said, the realization making his face drop. "We feel stronger to them. That's how they were able to find us so quickly...." He met my gaze, his eyes already apologizing for what he was about to say. "We have to split up."

I shook my head, already knowing my answer. I had only just found him; I couldn't lose him again.

"If we stay together, they'll be able to follow us wherever we go. Our only chance is to go in separate directions, and hope that they can't sense me as strongly. Once we gain some ground, we'll find each other."

The thought of leaving him made my insides collapse. "No," I said. "I can't leave you." But he slipped his hand from mine.

"Then you might as well bury me now."

My grandfather's voice cut through the woods. "He's killed the dogs!"

Dante's eyes implored me. *Please,* they seemed to say.

What choice did I have? I lowered my bag, my fingers nervous and clumsy as I unlatched the hinges on the chest and took out the small black box within. I felt its weight pulling away from me as my fingers closed around it. I thrust it into his hands.

"Take this, then," I said. "So I know I'll see you again."

Dante hesitated.

My eyes stung in the wind. "I won't leave until you take it."

He nodded and tucked it inside his coat. "Now, go." He pointed up to the two mountains that rose above us. "In the valley between them is a town. You should be able to make it there in a few hours. There's a bus station and an inn, which should be safe. They mind their own business."

"And then what? How will I find you?"

"Meet me tomorrow night in Pilgrim, Massachusetts. When you get there, you'll know where to go."

"What?" I asked, unable to hide the desperation in my voice. "But how——"

Through the trees, I heard the sound of footsteps crunching in the snow.

"Trust me," Dante said. "Now, where are you meeting me?"

"Pilgrim, Massachusetts," I whispered, my voice cracking. "Tomorrow night."

He nodded. *I love you*, he mouthed, and disappeared into the white.

CHAPTER 2

The Quiet Pilgrim

V ACANCY, BLINKED THE MOTEL SIGN. I STOPPED to catch my breath. The afternoon sun waned in the sky. Had anyone followed me? My grandfather's voice had faded away hours ago, along with the Monitors, the footsteps. Our split had only slowed them down briefly; after a few miles, they had veered off my trail to follow Dante. I felt his presence slip away as he traveled farther south, quicker than he ever could have with me. Had he lost them? He was too far away for me to tell. There was nothing I could do to help. Unless...

I ran across the street to the motel. The inside was colored in shades of brown—the carpet, the wood siding, the curtains, the furniture. I rang the bell on the counter, and a woman shuffled in from the back room. The sound of a television floated in behind her. She eyed my clothes, which were caked with snow. "From out of town?"

I nodded. "I was wondering if you had a map of Maine that I could look at?"

She paused. "You mean New Hampshire?"

So that's where I was. "I'm just passing through," I explained.

"Sounds like you need this," she said, and slid a road map of New England across the counter. I unfolded it and scanned the web of lines until I found a small dot near the southern coast of Massachusetts. Pilgrim.

"And where are we now?"

The woman squinted at me, then pointed to the mountains in western New Hampshire. I felt her watching me, and quickly folded it up. "Thanks," I said, sliding it back to her. "Is there a bus station nearby?"

"On the other side of town. Swing a left at the light and keep walking till you hit the end of Main Street. You can't miss it."

When I reached the small booth on the edge of town, I quickly found the schedule posted on the window and scanned down to Pilgrim, which was leaving in an hour. But that wasn't my first destination. I had one more place to go before meeting Dante.

"A ticket to Amherst," I said through the glass. "One way."

A white canopy of trees led us into Western Massachusetts. While dusk set over the rooftops, I took a taxi to a lonely road that wove out to the foothills.

"Are you sure this is the right way?" the driver asked.

I gazed out at the long barren landscape passing by the window, nothing but naked trees and snow for as far as the eye could see. Yes, I was sure. When the road narrowed, I asked him to let me off.

"You're certain?" the driver asked again.

"Yes."

The walk was short. After just a few paces, I could make out a slant of black shingles through the trees. A few steps more and a spire cut into the sunset, followed by a chimney, cold and smokeless; a line of diamond-paned windows flanked by shutters; and a heavy wooden door. My grandfather's house loomed over the pines. The topiaries were covered in burlap bags for the winter, the lampposts off. A long driveway packed with snow rolled out before the mansion. I crept closer.

All of the windows were dark, except for one. A shadow moved behind it. I stood in the snow and peered through the gap in the curtains. Dustin, my grandfather's estate manager, paced back and forth in the kitchen rubbing the bald skin of his head, his brow furrowed. After a moment, he picked up the phone and bent over a pad on the counter, dialing a number. He waited, then spoke into the phone, his words deliberate, though they were lost on me. Before the person on the other end of the line could have possibly had time to respond, he hung up.

He paced. After a few moments, the phone rang. He picked it up immediately. *Hello?* his lips said. He listened, his shoulders growing tight, and began to talk. He turned his back to me and leaned over the counter. I watched him until he hung up for the second time. He hovered over the phone, deep in thought, as if the conversation had had no closure. Then, without warning, he turned to the window.

I ducked out of the way and crouched in the snow beneath the sill, pressing myself against the side of the house. *Swish*, went the curtains. A bar of warm light stretched out over the lawn, Dustin's shadow cutting through the center. The fog of my breath billowed in front of me. I covered my mouth and eyed the rectangle of light. The snow was a smooth white, unmarred by my footprints, except for a heel mark at the very edge. Had Dustin noticed it?

No. He backed away, his shadow moving out of the light. After he closed the curtains, I stood up and peered through the gap as Dustin disappeared into an adjacent room. My eyes followed him to the next room over, where he pulled a weekend travel bag out of the closet and ran upstairs. When he came back down he wore a wool cap and an overcoat, and carried a long shovel. Was it his? His bag looked heavy. He set it down in the foyer and pulled a handkerchief from his suit pocket. He patted his upper lip, then folded the cloth into his coat and opened the door. I hid behind a hedge and watched through the branches as he walked down the icy steps toward the spare cars, threw his bags in the back of my grandfather's Roadster, and sped away, his taillights disappearing into the night.

When I was sure he wasn't coming back, I fumbled through my bag for my keys, and snuck inside.

The house was quiet and dark. The heat creaked through the radiators, and the faint smell of dinner clung to the air. The other members of the mansion staff were probably in their quarters by now, though I still had to be careful. I tiptoed down the hall and into the kitchen, where Dustin had stood minutes before. Leaving the lights off, I picked up the phone and pressed redial. It rang and rang. Finally, a woman picked up.

"We still haven't recovered him yet," she said. I recognized her voice as my grandfather's secretary at Gottfried Academy. "They're searching the lake now, but so far there's no sign of him."

I pressed my lips shut just before the gasp left my mouth. She had to have been talking about Noah. He was the only person who would have been in the lake.

"Dustin?" the woman said. "Dustin, are you there?"

Quickly, I hung up. She must have been in contact with Dustin while my grandfather was away, updating him on the status of Noah's body. Which apparently was gone, just like in my dream. I gazed out the window, wondering. Had Dustin packed his things in order to go to Gottfried himself in my grandfather's stead? If so, he wouldn't be back tonight. He had been dressed like he was going on a trip, but I couldn't be sure. He could return at any moment.

I crept down the hall to my grandfather's study. He

was an organized man, his desk decorated sparsely with a telephone and a jar of odd objects: a magnifying glass for reading, a spare set of spectacles, a few pens, a compass. I turned the compass until the needle inside trembled and pointed north. I followed its direction out the window to the snowy pines outside, imagining Dante trudging through the woods. They couldn't have caught him yet. He was still out there.

I walked straight to the hutch behind my grandfather's desk and unlatched its doors, behind which hung his entire collection of shovels, gleaming in the light. I picked them up one by one, testing their weight and sharpness, before choosing a small silver shovel. Its handle was just long enough for me to wield it like a sword, but just short enough that it would fit, concealed, within my coat. I then opened the bottom drawers of the hutch, where my grandfather kept his Monitoring supplies, and stuffed as many rolls of gauze as I could fit into the front pocket of my bag.

While the staff slept, I crept into the kitchen and snuck food from the pantry. A triangle of light stretched over the tiles as I peeked into the refrigerator at the pots of leftovers. I spooned myself a plate of mushroom stew and sweet potatoes and carried it upstairs to my room. There I packed a small bag with clothes, a light blanket, and all of the money in my dresser drawer. A little over three hundred dollars. It was all I had left from what I'd saved at my job in California. Only two years had passed since then, though it felt

like a lifetime had gone by. Leaning against the bea,
at my bedroom, which had once belonged to my mot...
She, too, was a part of a different life. She and my father
were fading in my memory to something hazy and distant,
their faces stuck in time. I glanced around the room at all of
her things. They were my things now, though as I studied
them, I realized I didn't care that I might never see them
again. I felt no attachment to the mansion, to this place,
to *any* place. My parents had been my home, and now that
they were gone, all I had left was Dante. I glanced down
at my bag, the chest heavy at the bottom. Where would it
lead us? And would I meet my parents there?

I turned off the light and pulled a blanket into the
closet, where I made a bed beneath my mother's clothes.
I couldn't chance being caught. And with the hems of my
mother's dresses tickling my arms, I closed my eyes and
prepared myself for what I had to do in the morning, before
I left the mansion for the last time.

I woke before the sun rose and called a taxi from the phone
in my grandfather's office, telling the driver to meet me
by the end of the lane. While I waited for him to arrive,
I picked up the phone again and dialed my grandfather's
mobile number. It rang three times before he picked up.

"Dustin, yes?" he said, static crackling through his
voice. So he didn't know that Dustin had left. Strange.

"Dustin?" my grandfather repeated. "Are you there?"

e weak connection, I could hear the exhaus-
ce. He hadn't caught up with Dante yet; I

ed. "I'm here," I said. "But not for long. Come
."

I heard my grandfather shout just before I hung up. All my grandfather wanted to do was protect me from the Liberum, and from Dante, whom he had been hunting ever since Dante and I exchanged souls. Maybe my phone call would make him change his course.

The phone rang, but I didn't pick up. As the house stirred with the sound, I slung my bag over my shoulder and slipped outside. I ran toward the road, the zing of the morning cold making my limbs move faster. My taxi was waiting to take me to the bus station in Amherst. The driver nodded as he pulled away from the road, and I watched the last trace of my grandfather's mansion disappear through the pines.

Pilgrim, Massachusetts, was a quiet fishing town, the shores rocky and the water dark. The slant of the afternoon sun made my shadow stretch as I walked down Main Street, trying to figure out what to do. Souvenir shops and fish shacks lined the sidewalk, though almost all were closed for the winter, and the streets were empty save for a few stray seagulls perched on the awnings. I was supposed to meet Dante somewhere in town, but I felt no trace of him. That had to have been what Dante had meant when he'd told me I would know where to go—that I would be able to sense him—but all I could feel now was the salty sea breeze rolling in over the ocean.

The shops on the street grew sparse as I made my way toward the end of town, the chest heavy against my back. I tried to keep my mind from wandering, but all I could think about was: what if? What if my grandfather had caught up to Dante? What if the Monitors had decided to bury him? What if I never saw him again? The seagulls cried overhead, circling like vultures, while the waves crashed against the rocks. I slowed, about to lose hope, when something caught my eye.

The street rose up a hill. At the top stood a rickety brown house with a wooden sign hanging off its awning. It swung, creaking in the wind. THE OLD SOUL, it read in a mariner's typeface. Before I knew it, I was walking, then jogging toward it, the air sharp in my lungs.

At the top of the hill, I stopped to catch my breath. The Old Soul stood only a few paces away: a weathered colonial with screen doors, a wraparound porch, and shutters flanking its windows. TAVERN AND RESTAURANT, the sign read.

I peered through the windows, looking for Dante even though I knew he couldn't be there—not without me feeling him. On the other side of the window stood a rustic dining room with long wooden tables set with mugs and dinnerware. No sign of guests or waiters. I scanned the chairs, looking for some clue as to why Dante would have told me to come here, when I saw something move.

I jumped back. An elderly man stood behind the bar,

listening to a portable radio. He didn't seem to see me. I squinted, watching him sneeze, then pat around the counter for a stack of napkins as if he were blind.

I leaned forward to get a better look, when I noticed someone peering in through the window on the opposite side of the building. I cupped my hands over the glass. It looked like a girl, though she was too far away to make out the details of her face. All I could see was the top of her hair, which was dyed a deep, unnatural red. I paused. The color looked shockingly familiar.

"Anya?" I whispered.

Just before my breath fogged the glass, her eyes darted to mine as though she'd heard me. But no, it couldn't be. I wiped the condensation off the window; she ducked out of the way. Anya had been one of my closest friends at St. Clément last year. But the school and her home were both in Montreal—why would she be here, in this country, in this state, in the same exact town, peering into the same exact window on the opposite side of the restaurant where I was supposed to meet Dante? No one knew we were meeting here; in fact, even I hadn't known until a few minutes before. I must be seeing things, I thought, and backed away.

"Renée?" It was a high-pitched voice with a Russian accent.

Before I knew it, Anya Pinsky had wrapped her skinny arms around me with an excited squeal. I breathed in her tangy perfume. It reminded me of winter in Montreal, of the cozy smell of smoke and incense that had enveloped me every time she'd opened the door to her dorm room; of the scratchy blanket she'd thrown over me all those times I'd fallen asleep on her sofa, the candles on her windowsill flickering while the snow fell over the city. Suddenly everything felt like it was going to be okay.

We parted quickly, an awkwardness coming over us as Anya brushed herself off. She normally wasn't one for hugs. I couldn't help but smile when I took in her tight black ensemble, which was more urban than rural, and made her look at odds with the rocky natural landscape of Massachusetts. She wore heavy black eyeliner and nail polish to match.

"What are you doing here?" she demanded, eyeing my wet jeans, my windswept hair, my coat, which was stained at the hem with flecks of mud. "And what are these shoes?" she said with a frown.

I looked down at the tall shearling boots, which I had taken from my mother's closet. "What's wrong with them?" I asked.

Anya raised an eyebrow. "Nothing," she said. "They're just ugly."

I rolled my eyes, though a part of me wanted to squeeze her. After our flight through the woods, after the dogs and the Monitors and the mysterious chest from the lake, it was a relief to hear Anya criticize my fashion choices—to be reminded that normal life still existed somewhere. "What are *you* doing here?"

She dug around in her pocket and handed me an envelope. I opened it and unfolded the note inside. It was written on a thick piece of paper with an expensive grain.

Dear Ms. Pinsky,

You do not know me, but I know you. I am writing to you on a matter of utmost urgency. Enclosed is one ticket to Pilgrim, Massachusetts. Go there immediately, and wait at the Old Soul Tavern on Main Street. Once you arrive, you will know what to do.

Sincerely,
Monsieur

I stared at the swirls of black ink. The handwriting was neat but elegant. "Monsieur?" I murmured to myself. It was French, though all it meant was *Mister*. "Monsieur who?"

Anya shook her head, her pale cheeks flushed from the cold. "Maybe that's just his name."

I flipped the envelope over. It was addressed to her home in Montreal. There was no sender or postmark. It must have been hand-delivered.

"It was sitting in our mailbox a few days ago," Anya said, reading my thoughts. "But it doesn't look like it came by the normal post."

Was it a coincidence that someone had sent a letter to Anya telling her to come to the same town Dante had told me to meet him in? He was the only other person who knew we were coming here, but the handwriting didn't belong to him. Plus, there was no way Dante would have had time to send Anya a note. He'd been with me for the last ten days.

I gazed at the first line. *You do not know me, but I know you.* It felt threatening. Had someone been watching her? I studied the signature. *Monsieur.* It couldn't have been a coincidence.

"How did he know I was coming here?" I asked, almost to myself. "And why did he tell you to come, too?"

Anya furrowed her brow, which was a delicate shade of brown. Her natural color. "Didn't you get a letter from him, too?"

"No."

"So why are you here?" she asked, and glanced behind me. "And where's Noah?"

My face dropped. The last time I had seen Anya was in Montreal, just before Noah and I had left by train for Gottfried Academy. She didn't know that we'd found the chest beneath the lake, or that the Liberum and their Undead boys had followed us. She hadn't heard that they'd taken Noah and pulled him beneath the ice, or that Dante had come and saved me. Did anyone outside of Gottfried know what had happened?

My expression must have betrayed my thoughts because Anya stepped back, her chest collapsing.

"He can't be..." she whispered. "But you only just left school. He was fine then."

I bit my lip, wishing I could tell her what she wanted to hear. Instead, I told her what had happened, starting with my train ride with Noah from Montreal to Maine. We had been following clues left by the Nine Sisters, a Monitoring sisterhood that had claimed to have found the secret to eternal life. The sisters had vowed to destroy their secret, but before they could, they were murdered by the Liberum—all but one. The ninth sister, Ophelia Hart, survived. She defied her sisters by hiding their secret with three clues, which she planted throughout Montreal, the historic city of Monitors. I had found the final clue at St. Clément, an academy for Monitors, where I had met Anya and Noah. But Ophelia's clue had led me back to Maine, to Gottfried Academy: the school where I had first learned of the Undead; where I'd discovered that I was a Monitor, predisposed to bury the dead; and where I had first met Dante. It was there that Noah dove to the bottom of the lake to retrieve the chest Ophelia Hart had buried. The Liberum had caught up to us, and their Undead boys dragged Noah back into the frozen lake. Dante had whisked me away just before one of the Brothers lowered his withered face to mine to take my soul.

When I was finished, Anya's gaze was distant. She said nothing for a long while. When she finally looked at me, her face was firm, wiped free of any grief. She wasn't one for crying. She believed in karma and superstitions; that everything happened for a reason.

"It was unlucky from the start," she said. "I should have known. I felt that from the beginning."

She didn't seem to be talking to me, but to some force in the air around us. "What happened next?" she said.

I told her about the Monitors from Gottfried Academy, about how they had come running from the school, my grandfather leading the pack as they chased Dante and me into the mountains. I told her about how we'd split up. "Dante told me to meet him in Pilgrim, Massachusetts. He said that I would know where to go." I glanced up at the wooden sign creaking in the wind. "So I found my way here...."

"But Dante isn't here," Anya said, finishing what I couldn't say.

"Yet," I said, trying to ignore the fact that the sky was already folding into a dark orange sunset. Had the Monitors caught up to him? No, if they'd buried Dante, I would have felt it somehow. It had to work that way; our connection was too deep. I couldn't lose my soul mate without realizing it, could I?

"So what happened to the chest?" Anya pressed, the spaces in between her words asking me if it had been worth the price of Noah's life. "Do you still have it?"

I bit my lip. "Only half of it."

"Half?" Anya asked. "I don't understand."

"Dante has the contents."

"What do you mean? What was inside of it?"

"We're not totally sure—" I began to say, but before I could continue, the screen door of the tavern opened and the old man stepped onto the porch. He looked a sturdy seventy; his white hair was thinning at the top, and a pipe was tucked into the breast pocket of his sweater. He held a walking stick, which he used to feel his way a few paces forward. He *was* blind.

A hush fell over us. Had he heard us talking about the chest?

He grasped the porch column beside him. "You girls still out here?" he asked in a grizzly, kind voice. He squinted in our general direction. "It's getting late. Isn't it about time you both came inside?"

Anya and I exchanged a perplexed glance. Had he known we were here the entire time? Neither of us spoke.

"Now, don't go and pretend you're not there," he said with a harmless smile. "I may be blind, but I'm not dead yet. You've been standing out here in the cold for almost an hour. Besides, I've been expecting you."

I froze. What did he mean?

"My grandson told me," the man said simply, and opened the screen door. "Are you coming in or not? The draft is getting to me."

Grandson? I looked to Anya, hoping she might know what he was talking about, but she looked as dazed as I felt. I watched the old man feel his way inside. His grandson was probably the same age I was, though I couldn't think of anyone I knew who resembled him. I gazed down at the storefronts that lined the street. They were all closed, the dusk settling over them. We had nowhere else to go. Anya must have been thinking the same thing, because she shrugged, slung her bag over her shoulder, and walked toward the porch. I followed her.

Two mugs of mulled cider and a set table were waiting for us inside. A fireplace crackled in the corner of the room, giving the tavern a country glow.

"Do you girls want stew or bisque?" the man said from behind the bar.

I frowned. What was the difference?

"Bisque," Anya said, as if she had strong feelings on the matter. She turned to me.

"I'll have the same."

"Excellent," the old man muttered.

I watched as he struggled to reach the top shelf, stacked with an assortment of plates, glasses, and bowls. His arms trembled as he patted around, tenuously close to knocking everything over. "Should we help him?" I whispered to Anya.

"He's fine," a voice said over my shoulder.

I spun around. A boy stood behind us, so close it seemed impossible that neither Anya nor I had heard him coming.

He looked like a well-bred boy who had spent too many years lurking in corners, his brown hair lush yet unkempt, his eyes mischievous as they darted between us. He could only have been a few years older than I was. A grin spread across his face—impish, as if he were in on some practical joke.

"See?" he said, nodding to his grandfather, who was now gracefully picking out two bowls and two water glasses from the mix of plates and snifters and wineglasses, as if he could see them. "He taps the shelf so he can tell what the shape of each dish is. He can tell by the way the sound reverberates off of them."

I watched the way the boy spoke, looking for something familiar about him that would explain why Dante had told me to come here.

"I'm Theo," he said. "Or Theodore, to my grandfather. Or Theodore Arthur Healy to my aunt, when she's angry with me, which is most of the time. Or That Healy Kid to the cops. Or Case Number 5418 to the Monitors, but I guess you don't really need to know about that." He paused, studying us as if to see if we were familiar with any of the things he'd just said. But they all sounded foreign to me. Case Number 5418? Monitors? Was he a Monitor?

"And you are—wait, let me guess." He glanced between the two of us, pretending to think hard. "Renée and Anya."

"How did you know that?" I demanded. "And how did you know we were coming here tonight?"

"I was actually expecting you earlier this morning," he said, and pulled up a chair, straddling the back.

"How—?" I let my voice trail off. Beside me, Anya said nothing. She studied Theo, squinting as if she could see through him.

"He received a note from Monsieur too," she said thoughtfully.

He raised an eyebrow. "I did," he conceded. "Though that isn't how I knew your names. And I have to say, my

34

note is a little better than yours." Before either of us could ask how he knew what Anya's note said, he pulled a slip of paper from his pocket and began to read. "Dear Ms. Pinsky—"

Confused, Anya patted her pocket, looking for her note, but it wasn't there.

Theo grinned, pleased with himself, and emptied the contents of his pockets, which included both of our wallets, one of Anya's bracelets, and the silverware from my place setting. "Sticky fingers," he said with a shrug. "Sorry."

That was how he knew our names, I realized. I took back my wallet, the clasp loose over my license. I wasn't sure if I should be angry or awed. Then I remembered the chest. I glanced down at the floor, hoping he hadn't somehow looked inside without me knowing, but to my relief it was still there by my feet, the outline of the chest barely visible through the canvas.

Theo must have noticed, because he gazed at my bag with curiosity. I shifted my weight, scolding myself for being so obvious, but he didn't ask me about it. Instead, his eyes met mine. A glimmer of understanding passed between us. Then he reached in his pocket and took out his own note.

Dear Mr. Healy,
    You do not know me, but I know you. I am writing to you on a matter of utmost urgency. In a few days' time, three strangers will arrive at your

35

doorstep. They will need your help. Do not turn them away.

When they arrive, you will know what to do.
Sincerely,
Monsieur

When he finished reading, he dropped the note on the table. "So who's the third?"

Dante. A draft seeped in through the window, mimicking his presence, but it was nothing more than the night closing in around us. I took it as a sign. "He's coming," I said, hoping it would make it true.

Theo crossed his arms over the back of the chair. "That's not what I asked."

"His name is Dante," I said softly, and glanced up to see if any glimmer of recognition passed over Theo's face, but he only frowned.

"What's holding him up?"

Anya answered for me. "He's just running a little late."

I picked up Theo's note. It was written in the same handwriting as Anya's, the same ink. Monsieur. How did he know so much? And why did he think that this boy could somehow help us?

"Did this come in the mail?" I asked.

Theo shook his head. "Someone slipped it beneath the door when I was out. But my grandfather was here," he said, just as the old man felt his way to our table, carrying two bowls of bisque.

He lowered them onto the table, his hands trembling. "Heavy footsteps," he said, his dull eyes gazing off toward the side of the room. "Three of them. Like he had a third leg."

Anya frowned. "A mutant?"

"A cane," I murmured. "Monsieur is old."

"Or crippled," Anya said.

"And tall," I said.

"Or fat," Anya added.

Theo clapped his hands together. "Mystery solved. He's a tall old fat crippled mutant with a cane." I rolled my eyes as he turned to me. "So where's your note?"

"I never got one."

"So why are you here?"

I hesitated. Had Dante received a note, too, or had someone been watching us? I imagined the dark shadow of a man following us through snowy woods, a withered face peering through the window of our cabin. The thought of it made me shudder. "Dante told me to meet him here. Today."

"Dante," he said, turning the name around in his mouth. "The third stranger. So he's the one with all the answers."

I stared at the bowl of bisque getting cold in front of me. "Look," I said. "We don't need your help."

Theo's eye twitched. "Who said I was offering?" He stood up, casting a fleeting glance at the bag by my feet. I closed my legs around it. "So I guess that means you don't need a room?"

Anya gave me an uncomfortable look.

"I hate to break it to you, but today is almost over. What if your friend doesn't show up?"

"He's coming," I said, because he had to; without him, I was lost.

CHAPTER 3

The Spade

DANTE DIDN'T ARRIVE THAT NIGHT. WITH nowhere else to go, we found ourselves following the old man up the back stairs of the tavern to his apartment, which occupied the second and third stories of the building. Anya and I shared a small guest room overlooking the street, with two twin beds and a stack of dusty sheets. If we needed anything, Theodore was just down the hall, his grandfather assured us, his dull eyes staring off into the distance. The moon glinted off of them, and I shuddered, remembering the Undead children from last fall—the way their eyes blurred to gray just before they decayed. Soon Dante's eyes would grow cloudy, too.

Once we were alone, Anya folded herself onto the tiny bed. "Do you smell that?" she whispered. She sniffed the air, then bent over and held her nose to the coarse blanket by her feet. She winced. "Smells like farm."

I sniffed mine, but didn't notice anything off about it.

"I'm descended from peasants," Anya reasoned. "My nose is extremely sensitive to this sort of thing." She kicked her blanket aside and pulled an extra sweater from her bag.

Outside, the trees trembled in the wind, the shadows of their branches stretching across the street like a tangle of legs. How I wished to see Dante emerge from the night. "I'm glad you're here," I said.

"Me too," Anya said.

Who was Monsieur? We considered the facts. He was a man, probably French, and walked with a cane and a heavy gait. He was familiar with each of us, which meant he'd been watching us for a while. He knew that Dante and I would come to the Old Soul, and he'd assumed that when we did, we would need help—which is why he'd sent Anya and Theo notes.

"But why Theo?" I said. "And why you?"

Anya went quiet. "Perhaps because we're friends? And Theo—perhaps he has some skill that we don't."

"Like what?" I said. "Stealing?"

Anya shrugged. "That can be useful in the right situation, too."

"Maybe," I said, though I wasn't convinced. Theo, I knew, was a mistake. And Anya—though I was happy to have her with me now, her being my friend wasn't a good enough reason to send her on this journey. Monsieur must have chosen her for a reason.

But the question that really bothered me was: Why would Monsieur want to help me in the first place?

My eyes rested on my bag at the foot of my bed. It couldn't be a coincidence that Monsieur was intervening now. He must have known about the chest. "Maybe Monsieur isn't trying to help me. Maybe he's just pretending to because I have something he wants."

I pulled my bag into my lap and unzipped it. "This—" I began to say, when I heard the floorboards creak in the hallway. I held a finger to my lips, and crept to the door. I pressed my ear against it, only to hear footsteps. I cracked it open and watched Theo disappear around the corner. He'd been listening.

"It isn't safe to talk about it here," I said. "When Dante gets here, we'll leave. Then I'll tell you everything."

Anya nodded and, after taking off her bangles, earrings, a mood ring, a pendant, and a choker, and piling them in a mound on the bedside table, she slipped beneath the sheets. "Do you feel him?"

I shook my head, trying to swallow around the knot in my throat.

"Don't worry," she said, her red hair coiled across her pillow. "He's probably just too far away for you to sense. I have a good feeling about him. He'll come."

Even though I never believed in Anya's superstitions, that night I stayed awake, repeating her words in my mind and listening to the sound of her breathing as she fell asleep.

It calmed me, watching her thin body rise and fall beneath the sheets. The sign outside creaked in the wind. I curled up beneath the blankets, my bag nestled safely in my lap. I wasn't alone. Not yet.

But I couldn't sleep, and in the middle of the night, I slipped out of bed and into the hallway. I meant to go downstairs to the kitchen for a glass of water, when I noticed a light on at the end of the hall. A door was ajar. I tiptoed toward it and peered through the gap.

Theo was sitting at his desk, his back turned to me. Tinny music blared from his headphones. I inched closer. His room was stark: dingy white walls, a naked bulb hanging from the ceiling. Theo leaned over something in his lap, sweat soaking the back of his T-shirt, his hair dangling about his face as he worked. The sound of sandpaper scraping wood. His arm moved back and forth, back and forth. A mess of sawdust lay scattered around his boots.

A bad feeling crept through me. Maybe it was the heavy sound of his breathing, or the way he clenched his neck, his muscles red and tense. Finally, he stopped and sat up, wiping the sweat from his brow. He brushed the sawdust from his lap and held the object up to his desk lamp.

The sharp tip of a shovel glinted in the light. I could see a sliver of it through the crack in the door, yet even from my vantage point, I could tell it was a beautiful instrument. Its face was crafted into the shape of an inverted heart, and was made of thick metal that had been polished until it gave off a brilliant luster. Elegant fluting ran down either side of the head, meeting at the tip. Engraved there was an elaborate letter *M*. I recognized it. The official seal of the High Court of Monitors.

I had heard about shovels like it in passing; older Monitoring students at St. Clément had whispered about them in awe. It was a sanctioned Spade, the kind that the High Court issued to Monitors who had completed an elite apprenticeship, after which they had to pass a rigorous physical examination, a character assessment, and what the Court called a "demonstration of specialized skills." All of the Monitoring students had dreamed of wielding one in the future, though I had barely gave the notion any thought. I had never wanted to be a Monitor, and I certainly never planned on earning a Spade.

I gazed at Theo. Had he stolen it? The only other way he could have gotten the Spade was to have earned it. But he couldn't have; he was too young. It took most people years of training to earn their Spades. Then I noticed two documents framed on the wall behind him, each stamped with the seal of the High Court. The font was too small to read, but it didn't matter. I already knew what they said, for a pair of identical documents hung in my grandfather's office, deeming him an official Monitor and servant of the High Court.

Theo had trained and apprenticed. He had passed the exams and the character check. He had been licensed by the Court: a certified Monitor, able to hunt and bury at his own discretion, without supervision or direct orders from the Court. Other Monitors were only allowed to do so on their own when acting in self-defense.

Theo passed his fingers down the handle, feeling the smooth blond wood. As he did, I caught my breath. Half of the handle had been scoured down to the natural wood. The other half had been dyed a deep red.

I realized what he had been doing. A red handle. That could only mean one thing: he had been disbarred, banished by the High Court and forbidden to bury any Undead, his Spade dyed red in a mark of disgrace. And now he was sanding it down so that no one would know. So that he could use it again without shame.

He picked up his sandpaper and went back to work. I crept into the shadows and tiptoed back to my room, all the while remembering his words. *I'm Theo. Or Theodore, to my grandfather. . . . Or Case Number 5418 to the Monitors.* Who was this Theo, who had earned his Spade at such a young age? And what had he done to lose it?

I wanted to leave, but I couldn't. Not without Dante. So with nothing left to do, I crawled back into the hard twin bed across from Anya and fell asleep, cradling my bag to my ribs as if it were an external heart.

The next morning I woke to something tickling my arm. *Dante,* I mouthed in my sleep, feeling the warmth of his hand as he wrapped his fingers around my wrist. But no—it couldn't be. Warmth? Dante's skin was cold to the touch, pale and thin as ice. This hand didn't feel like his at all.

44

I opened my eyes to find Theo standing over me, his face startlingly close to mine, his hand perched over my bag as if he were about to slip it from my arms.

I jumped back, pulling my bag out of reach. "What are you doing?"

His face softened and he recoiled. "Nothing," he said with a confused laugh. "Just bringing you breakfast."

He turned to the desk, where two plates of scrambled eggs, bacon, and toast sat. He wore the same gray T-shirt as he had last night. Although the sweat stains and sawdust were gone, I could still picture them, as real as if I were crouching in that dark hallway.

I narrowed my eyes. "You were trying to steal my bag."

He feigned innocence. "Me? Steal? Why would you think that?"

"You were touching my arm. You were trying to lift it so you could take my bag."

Theo acted like he had no idea what I was talking about. "I was trying to wake you up."

"You're lying," I said, incredulous. "You've been eyeing my bag ever since you saw it by my feet last night."

Theo hesitated, then leaned closer, his muggy breath beating against my cheek as he whispered, "Does that mean there's something inside worth stealing?"

Before I could respond, Anya sat up and rubbed her eyes. "What's going on?"

I stared at Theo, challenging him to answer.

"I brought you breakfast," he said.

Anya yawned and kicked off the sheet. "It smells delicious."

"See," said Theo, clearly pleased. "That's the appropriate response."

The ease of his smile disturbed me. He lied so effortlessly. I didn't like it. When I said nothing, he gave me a wink—a *wink*, the audacity—and slipped out the door.

Anya rolled out of bed and nibbled on a piece of bacon. "He has a strange demeanor, don't you think?"

"That's an understatement," I murmured and pushed past her. I followed Theo down the hall to his room, catching the door just before he swung it shut.

"I know what you were doing last night," I said. "I saw you sanding down your Spade."

Theo froze, his face surprised. I thought I had finally trapped him in a corner, when he spoke. "How did you know I had a Spade?"

"Because I saw you last night. You were sanding off the red dye from its handle."

"Red dye?" he said, narrowing his eyes. "Are you calling me a criminal?"

I gave him a steady look. "Aren't you?"

Without responding, he opened his closet door and removed a tall shovel, almost the same height as him. I recognized its face—the polished metal, the fluting, the official seal of an *M* etched just before the tip—but the handle, I didn't. It had a smooth finish, with no signs of red dye, or any irregular marks from sandpaper. Theo held it out to me.

I turned it around in my palms, inspecting the handle. No matter how hard I looked, I couldn't find a trace of what I had witnessed last night.

I backed away, confused. "But I saw you last night. You were sanding it away."

"No, I wasn't," he said plainly.

I traced the seal of the M on the Spade's face. His name was etched into the metal beneath it. THEODORE ARTHUR HEALY. It really was his.

"No," I rationalized. "You must have finished it last night. You sanded all of the red away and oiled the wood."

"Last night? As in a few hours ago?" Theo laughed. "How would I have been able to get it this smooth so quickly? Wood can only get this worn feeling from being handled over years."

I thought back to the scene I had witnessed last night. It had felt so real. Could I have dreamed it?

"But you were wearing those exact clothes. How would I have known that?"

He looked down at his worn cotton shirt and pants. "Because I was wearing them yesterday."

Had he been wearing the same clothes yesterday? I couldn't remember. "But how would I have known that you had a Spade?" I countered. Surely he couldn't have an answer to that.

Theo's eye twitched. "You tell me. Maybe you went to the bathroom and saw my certification hanging in my room. Or maybe you saw me polishing it, which I do most nights before I go to sleep. Or . . . maybe you went through my things."

I took a step back. "What? Are you accusing me of—?"

"Maybe I am," Theo said. "How does it feel?"

He was smart; he had to be, to have earned a Spade at his age. "What about Case Number 5418? The one you mentioned yesterday."

Theo let out an amused laugh. "So that's what's been eating at you," he said and leaned against his desk. "That case was nothing. I got caught Monitoring without my partner. The Court gave me a petty reprimand, then sent me on my way."

It didn't make sense. Just yesterday he'd said that the Monitors knew him only by Case Number 5418, as if he'd done something awful that had forever tainted him. But now he was saying it was nothing more than a reprimand? Why would he have even mentioned it before if it had been something so trivial? He was lying. He had to be.

"So you expect me to believe that you earned a Spade and then just moved in here with your grandfather to help him run his tavern instead of moving to Montreal and working for the High Court."

Theo went silent for a moment. "Yes. I had a rough childhood. And my grandfather is blind. He needs me."

"What about your parents?" I said.

Theo hesitated. "My mother died when I was a baby."

"And your father?"

He averted his eyes. "He died as well."

I waited for him to elaborate, but he merely took his Spade back from me. "Now if you'll excuse me," he said, his voice cold. "I'd rather not spend my morning reliving the harrowing parts of my past."

"What if I looked it up in the records?" I said as he turned.

I almost detected a moment of hesitation in his face, though when I blinked, it had passed. "Go ahead," he said coolly. "But you won't find anything of interest."

What was that supposed to mean? He smiled as if reading my thoughts. Before I had a chance to respond, Anya appeared in the doorway. "What's going on?"

I backed into the hallway, whispering in her ear: "I don't trust him."

After that I kept my bag with me at all times, and Theo kept his distance. Maybe I had made it up. Maybe I had walked past his room in the middle of the night, caught a glimpse of his Spade, and then dreamed the rest.

"It's possible," Anya said while we wandered around the tavern grounds. Her curious gaze lingered on him through the window. His brow was heavy as he mopped the floor of the dining room. To my bewilderment, she didn't seem to mind Theo; actually, she seemed fascinated by him.

"There must be a reason Monsieur sent him a note," she said. "Maybe he has something that can help you. Maybe I do, too."

The sticky ocean breeze blew through my hair. Anya had always been one to think that things happened for a reason; that when fate showed her a sign, she shouldn't ignore it. But I didn't want Theo's help, and though it pained me to think it, I didn't want Anya's either. I had learned my lesson with Noah. The chest was my burden, to be shared with Dante only.

But Dante didn't arrive that day, or the next. It wasn't until the following night that I felt a stream of cool air drift in through the seam of the door. Beneath the blankets, goose bumps prickled up my arms. I opened my eyes. Anya tossed in her sleep and didn't wake. I felt an icy strand of air wrap itself around my wrist and pull me out of bed. He was here.

I let it coax me out into the hallway, down the stairs, through the restaurant and to the front door. I held out my hand, feeling the vacant draft coil itself around my fingers.

"Dante?" I whispered, when I heard the sound of some-one breathing behind me. Before I could turn around, a hand closed over my mouth and pulled me away from the door.

"Don't move," an old man whispered in my ear, his breath sour with sleep. Theo's grandfather. "The Undead has come to call."

He was a Monitor, too. I tried to shake myself free from

his grasp, to tell him that it was only Dante; that I knew him; that he wasn't dangerous; but he only clamped my mouth tighter. He was stronger than he let on. In his free hand he held a tall, rusty shovel. The old man had a Spade, too. I could barely make out the seal of the High Court through the corrosion. He wielded it like a cane, its metal tip barely grazing the floor as he felt his way through the darkness and thrust open the door.

A rush of cold swept through the room. The curtains billowed. The dark silhouette of a boy filled the frame. The old man pushed me aside, his leathery hand sliding off my lips to grasp the handle of his Spade. I called out to Dante, trying to warn him, but it all happened too quickly—the sound of rusty metal banging against wood, a grunt, the thud of a body dropping to the ground, the old man wheezing as he pulled Dante inside, Dante's heels scraping against the wood floor as he tried to free himself of the man's grasp.

Upstairs, a light turned on, casting a warm glow over the room. The light tap of footsteps sounded through the ceiling. The commotion had woken the rest of the house.

Finally, in the dim light, I saw him. His long hair was damp from the rain. His face was leaner and more mature than I remembered, though still as striking as the day I had first seen him at Gottfried Academy. Could he have aged in the mere days we had been apart? His eyes met mine, his irises warm and dark like the last embers of a fire.

The old man pushed him against the wall, pressing the tip of his Spade into his chest.

"Wait!" I said. "He's with us. I know him." But the old man ignored me.

"I can sense everything about you," the old man whispered to him. "You've been dead for seventeen years. You're still strong, still clinging on to whatever life you have left, but your body is beginning to decay. Your eyes are clouding. Soon they'll be blind, just like mine. I can sense everything about you."

"Tell me more, then," Dante said, his voice steady.

The old man tilted his head. "Something is keeping you alive. Something external. You're preserved better than you should be." His wrinkled mouth trembled. "You've been taking lives to extend your own. You've been stealing the souls of others—"

"No," Dante said, cutting him off. "I don't do that. I won't."

The old man pushed his Spade into Dante's chest. "Then how?" he demanded. "How are you so . . . human?"

Because of me, I realized. Because we had exchanged souls a year ago, extending his life ever so slightly, while shortening mine. But Dante divulged none of that. "I'm far less human than I appear," he said, his voice rife with regret.

The old man tilted his head. "Why have you come here?"

"I received a letter." Dante looked at me when he said it, and finally I understood. Dante had also been summoned to the Old Soul.

Anya appeared in the stairwell, her makeup smudged

from sleep. The old man's dull eyes turned to her as if he could see, then to me, and finally, back to Dante. "You're the third stranger from Theodore's note," the old man realized, as if he had never expected the final visitor to be Undead.

"Yes," I said. "I know him. His name is Dante. He doesn't mean us any harm."

The old man hesitated before lowering his Spade. "Very well," he said carefully, though his voice remained skeptical.

"Thank you," Dante said. I ran to him, expecting him to fold me into his arms, but he held me back.

"Do you still have it?" he asked. The urgency in his voice startled me.

"Of course I do."

"Where?"

I glanced over my shoulder, where I usually slung my bag, but soon realized that I didn't have it with me. I must have left it in my bed when Dante's presence woke me in the middle of the night.

"Upstairs. Why? Is something wrong?"

"Show me."

I led him upstairs, past Anya, whom he barely registered. She followed us. When I opened the door to our room, I found Theo huddled over my bag, the chest open in his hands.

"Hey!" I shouted. "Put that down!"

But this time, Theo didn't seem to care that I had caught him going through my things. Instead, he looked at me in awe. "Where did you find this?"

"Get out!" I yelled and ran toward him, but Theo held the chest out of my reach.

"Why didn't you tell me you had the Cartesian Map?"

"The what?" Dante said, narrowing his eyes as he stepped toward him. The warmth drained from his face. Suddenly he was no longer the boy I had fallen in love with two years ago, but just another Undead close to expiration, cold and merciless.

Theo fell silent, as if he had only just noticed Dante's presence in the room. He eyed him as if he were a wild animal and backed away. "The Cartesian Map," he repeated. He held up the open chest and pointed to the underside of the lid, where I could just make out the five points etched into the shape of a canary. "Do you have any idea what this means?"

Cartesian? As in René Descartes, the philosopher who first wrote about the existence of the Undead? I had read his *Seventh Meditation* two years ago after finding it in my grandfather's mansion, but I had never heard of a map. I gazed at the chest in Theo's hands, as if seeing it for the first time. The five points in the shape of a canary suddenly made sense. The elaborate tangle of lines etched around each of the points had always vaguely looked like a landscape: a twist of etchings that looked like three rivers braiding together; a collection of straight lines that almost looked like a forest; a series of triangles that mimicked the jagged peaks of mountains. How could we not have realized?

"How do you know so much about this chest?" Dante asked in a voice so steady that it was frightening.

Theo took a step back. "Just stumbled across it in my studies."

"Oh?" Dante said. "Is that why you felt you had the right to go through our things?"

"It's not yours either. You only found it," Theo said, though his voice didn't have the same confidence it normally did. "As far as I'm concerned, it's still up for grabs. And this is my house, you know. I received a letter from Monsieur, too."

Dante's face hardened. He walked toward him, saying nothing, and placed his hands on the chest. Theo glanced at Anya's small shovel leaning against her bag on the opposite side of the room, as if the only way he knew how to deal with the Undead was with a weapon between them. It was too far away now. Dante's cold hand brushed his, making him flinch. Theo shrank in his shadow and let go.

A look of relief passed over Dante's face as he felt the weight of the chest in his hands. He stepped forward, pushing Theo back into the hallway. When he was out of the room, Dante shut the door.

"And who are you?" Dante said, gazing at Anya curiously.

"Anya," she said. "I received a letter from Monsieur, too. I've heard a lot about you."

Dante looked to me, as if to ask if she were okay. I nodded, and Anya stepped toward him, studying his face. "You're the first Undead I've met up close." She squinted at something I couldn't see. "Renée was right about you. You have a complex aura."

I pressed my ear against the door, making sure Theo wasn't listening, then turned to Dante. "What happened? I thought they found you. I thought..."

"They were close," Dante said. "They split up the next morning. Half of them went south toward Massachusetts."

My phone call, I thought.

"Still, your grandfather was on my trail for days. If I hadn't stumbled past the camp of the Liberum and their Undead boys, who distracted the Monitors, I never would have gotten ahead of him. We can't stay here long," Dante said. "The only way I could get away from the Monitors was to make sure that the Liberum saw me and followed me most of the way here. That way, if the Monitors caught up, they would first have to face the Undead. I lost them both early this morning, but they weren't far behind. They'll be able to find us. Your grandfather, he's figured something out. He knows why you came to Gottfried in the first place, and that you found the secret of the Nine Sisters in the lake. I heard the other Monitors talking about what it could be before they turned back." Dante paused, as if parsing what he was about to say. "They mentioned something called the *Netherworld*."

"The Netherworld?"

"It's some sort of underworld," Anya said. "I've read about these things. A mythic place. A place you can't get to by normal means."

"Eternal life," I murmured, echoing the promise of the Nine Sisters. "Maybe we'll find it there."

Dante looked like he was about to say something, but when he met my gaze, he stopped himself.

"There's something else," I said, studying him. "Tell me."

"I was just worried about you," he said, though he didn't look me in the eye. Before I could ask him again, he reached into his coat pocket and removed a creased envelope. I immediately recognized the handwriting on the address. Monsieur.

Dear Mr. Berlin,
You don't know me, but I know you. Should you ever need a place of refuge, you may find one in Pilgrim, Massachusetts. When you arrive, you will know where to go.
Sincerely,
Monsieur

"I received it a week ago, wedged in the door of one of the cabins we stayed in. No postage. I first assumed he was a Monitor, trying to trap me, but that didn't make much sense. The only way he could have known where I was staying was to have followed me; if he wanted to bury me, he could have done it far earlier."

"Why didn't you tell me?"

"I didn't want you to worry. I never planned on coming here, but when the Monitors were upon us in the woods, I didn't know what else to do. We needed a place of refuge. The letter was all I had left."

I touched the signature, feeling the indentation of Monsieur's pen on the paper. Why was he helping us?

"And this one is for you," Dante said, handing me an envelope identical to all the others. Written across the front in Monsieur's neat handwriting was my name. No postage or return address. "It was wedged in the door of the tavern when I arrived."

"He was here?" I said. "Today?" I ran to the window and pulled back the curtains to search the street, even though I knew that I wouldn't find him. The town was empty, the buildings lining the road dark.

"He could have left it hours ago," Anya murmured behind me.

The letter felt heavier than the others. I ripped it open, wondering if my note was longer. To my surprise, an airplane ticket fluttered to the floor. Anya picked it up.

She gasped, her eyes widening. "Paris?"

My heart skipped. I glanced down at the envelope in my hand. There were three other tickets, each leaving the next morning for Charles de Gaulle Airport. I flipped through them, checking for an accompanying note, but none was included.

"Is this real?" I asked, not sure if I should be excited. Every time I glanced at Monsieur's handwriting, a wave of apprehension passed over me. What did he know that we didn't?

"If this really is a map," Dante said, holding up the chest, "it's possible that it starts in France. After all, René Descartes was French."

"So were the Nine Sisters," I added. "The entire Monitoring society began in France." Suddenly, the tickets started to make sense. Everything in the Monitoring community went back to Europe; that much I remembered from school. But what would we do once we got there? Paris was a huge city. Even if the chest was a map, it was only comprised of five points in the vague shape of a bird, with no other physical markers. The points could be anywhere.

Anya interrupted my thoughts. "You know who else is French?" she said somberly. "Monsieur. And these tickets are only one-way."

The room fell quiet, all of us realizing that the trip, the tickets—even the fact of our gathering there, in that creaky room in Massachusetts—had been orchestrated for reasons we didn't understand, and by a person we weren't certain we could trust.

I felt my pocket, where my passport sat. Anya must have had one with her, too, since she had come from Montreal just as I had two weeks before—but did Dante?

"Do you even have a passport with you?" I said.

Dante nodded at the side pocket of his bag. "I came to see you in Montreal, didn't I?"

My shoulders relaxed with relief.

"I think we should go," he continued. "What other option do we have? We can either go to Paris tomorrow and face whatever it is that's waiting for us there, or we can stay here, and do nothing while our time runs out."

On the other side of the door, Theo cleared his throat, letting us know that he had been listening.

"We could ask him," Anya whispered. "He might have an answer—"

"No way," I said. "He's a liar and a con man. Besides, this doesn't involve him."

"There are four tickets," Anya countered. "One has his name on it."

"And we don't have any better ideas," Dante added.

I turned to him in disbelief. He couldn't be serious.

"The plane leaves tomorrow morning," Dante said softly. "We don't have much time."

I let out an incredulous laugh. "We just caught him going through my things. If we hadn't found him, he probably would have stolen the chest. I know he's lying to us about who he is. He could be anyone. He could be wanted for murder—"

"He isn't a *complete* stranger," Anya said. "We've already stayed with him for three days, and nothing awful has happened yet."

I looked to Dante for help, but he leaned against the windowsill. "He did know about the Cartesian Map."

"What if he's lying?" I couldn't understand why they weren't listening to me. "What if he has no idea? Or worse—what if he does, and is trying to take the chest from us?"

Dante considered my point, then said in a calm voice, "So what?"

I blinked. Had I heard him correctly?

"He already knows we have the chest. He knows where we're heading. He could try to take it from us either way. I think it's better to keep him close. Keep an eye on him."

"I agree," Anya said.

Dante studied me. His eyes begged me to say yes. To trust in things I didn't understand or have any reason to trust—just like I had trusted him, just like he had trusted me. To walk into the future with him and face what was coming, because that was our only hope. "Okay."

When Anya opened the door, Theo was leaning against the door frame, polishing a bit of wood with sandpaper. He quickly slipped it into his pocket.

Sandpaper, I thought, catching my breath. But before I could point it out, Dante spoke.

"Does Paris mean anything to you?" he said.

A mischievous smile spread across Theo's face. "Yes."

CHAPTER 4

The Magician

RENÉ DESCARTES DIED ON A FRIGID WINTER'S evening in 1650. Candles flickered in the chambers. He wasn't at home; he no longer had a home. Instead, he found himself far from his birthplace, in the house of the French ambassador to Sweden. He tossed in the guest bed, sweating through the sheets, his body weak with pneumonia. The bustle of the staff—pots clinking in the kitchen, the footsteps of the maids on the stairwell— was absent. They knew what was about to happen. But he didn't look frightened; not of dying.

His thin hair was matted to his forehead. He coughed: a spatter of blood. Someone stepped forth from the shadows. A French nursemaid leaned in to blot his temples with a damp washcloth. While she was close, he uttered something in her ear.

"*Quoi?*" she whispered.

He coughed again. She pressed a handkerchief to his mouth, patting it dry.

"What, to you, is a second soul worth?" he repeated in French, his breath sour.

The nurse hovered over him. *"Je ne comprends pas,"* she said.

He blinked, his gaze trained on the ceiling. He was nearly blind, nearly deaf; his mouth was so parched he could barely speak. He had been traveling for months, but to where, no one knew. A farmer had discovered him weeks prior, wandering the French countryside, lost, confused, and speaking in tongues. When the French authorities realized who he was, they turned Descartes over to his friend, the French ambassador to Sweden, who whisked him away to his guesthouse in Stockholm, where Descartes could recover in peace. But his illness was persistent, and mysteriously untreatable. A strange lifelessness had overtaken him.

"An early death, a wombless rebirth?" he continued, his voice weak.

The nurse set down her rag and reached for the ink and paper on his bedside. *"Que voulez-vous dire?"*

He wheezed, his chest heavy beneath the sheets.

"The way follows the soul's path after death,
With each step it is cleansed, with each point one less
*   breath.*
The nethers first call from their hollows by dark,

In the shape of a bird, with each sense the route has been
*   marked.*
Sounds, they fade to the ground, the earth's music
*   unsung,*
Then taste, until food is but dirt on the tongue."

His lips were dry. He pressed them together, resting his voice, while the nurse transcribed his verse.

"The nose, it next decays, death the only stench to stay,
The eyes follow, the jaws of the mountains a colorless
*   gray;*
Touch, the noblest, is last to decline,
The final remainder of life in this soul of mine."

He swallowed and closed his eyes, as if he were traveling back into his past.

"In its world it is dust, in the hand it is coal,
At long last I found it, the ephemeral soul."

The scrawl of the nurse's quill grew still as he sank back into his pillow, a calm passing over him. She didn't know what his verses meant; perhaps they were just the last musings of a man on his deathbed.

"Please," he said, his voice cracking. *"A glass of water."*

She set the pages down on his nightstand and picked

up the metal pitcher, which was nearly empty. *"Bien sûr,"* she said, and left the room.

Five minutes passed.

She returned to an unnatural silence. His body lay twisted and limp on its side, the sheets tangled around him as though he had tried to reach something by the candle. Water sloshed out of the nurse's pitcher as she rushed to him. His face was wan, its warmth already fading. A smudge of black grazed his cheek. Nothing more than a stray bit of ash, she thought. She checked his pulse, then ran to get the doctor.

According to legend, the nursemaid gave the doctor the verses she'd transcribed, and the doctor gave them to the French ambassador who had taken him in, and then to Descartes's family. Word trickled down to the staff, and out to the circles in which Descartes had traveled. His last words were whispered at dinners and parties, in small groups behind closed doors. Those close to him knew he had spent the latter part of his life writing about the Undead—about how, after the body died, the soul left it and traveled to a mythical underworld, where it was purified before being reborn into a new body. The *Netherworld*, he'd called it.

In his *Seventh Meditation*, he'd described what he believed the Netherworld would be like: a hollow in the earth where millions of souls traveled to after they were cleansed, waiting in a swirl of particles to be reborn into a new human. He'd believed that if he could only find the way into the Netherworld, he would be able to then capture one of the purified souls, breathe it in, and live a second life. It didn't matter whose soul he took, for once they entered the Netherworld, they belonged to no one, to anyone.

His deathbed verses were curious.

In its world it is dust, in the hand it is coal,
At long last I found it, the ephemeral soul.

To many of his friends, those final lines seemed to imply that he had found the Netherworld and taken a second soul. But his death contradicted them. He hadn't disappeared; he hadn't burst into life again. He had died in bed of pneumonia, and had been buried the following morning, per his wishes. Or so they thought.

Not long after his burial, rumors began to circulate. There were sightings of him. One person claimed they saw him in France. Another in the Netherlands. Another in Sweden. Another in Belgium. They dug up his grave, but all that was left inside was dust.

Had his bones dissolved in a trick of disease or parasites? Perhaps someone had robbed his grave. Or perhaps his final verses had been true. Perhaps he had found the Netherworld, and after burial had reanimated and dug himself out to live a second life.

Scholars and fellow philosophers scoured his belongings, but found nothing they didn't already know. So instead, they took to decoding his final words.

It was a map in riddles, they realized. If solved, it would lead to the Netherworld: a place where anyone could claim a second soul and live another life.

The way follows the soul's path after death,
With each step it is cleansed, with each point one less
* breath.*

The path to the Netherworld follows the path the soul takes when it leaves the body and is cleansed.

The nethers first call from their hollows by dark,
In the shape of a bird, with each sense the route has been
* marked.*

The route lay in the shape of a bird, each point representing one of the five senses that is washed from the soul to purify it.

Sounds, they fade to the ground, the earth's music unsung.

The first mark on the path represented sound.

Then taste, until food is but dirt on the tongue.

The second mark represented taste.

The nose, it next decays, death the only stench to stay.

The third: smell.

The eyes follow, the jaws of the mountains a colorless
*   gray.*

The fourth: sight.

Touch, the noblest, is last to decline.

The fifth: touch.

Or at least that's what Theo claimed.

"People have been trying to locate the five points in his riddle since the eighteenth century," Theo continued. "Over time, it came to be called the Cartesian Map, though no one believed Descartes had ever written it down. The riddle was all anyone had, and even that is a matter of belief. Maybe it never existed in the first place, and all Descartes did was ask for water. No one ever found the nurse's transcript. Even more strangely, the French version is so similar to the English one that it, too, rhymes, as do many versions in other languages. To me, that makes the riddle all the more believable. Descartes always paid extreme attention to detail; that he would arrange his riddle to make even the rhymes translatable into many different languages is something I can imagine him doing," Theo said. Then he added, "Though I suppose almost everything in French rhymes, since consonants at the end of French words are typically not pronounced."

His eyes lit up as he gazed between us. "But now we

know. Don't you see? The shape of a bird? The five points? It's just like the markings on your chest."

I felt my heart stammer as I lifted the lid of the chest just enough for the light to catch the five points engraved inside, each surrounded by strange swirls and shapes, forming a dramatic and foreign landscape. The Cartesian Map. Could it be?

"But Descartes didn't hide this chest," I said, remembering the trail of riddles I'd followed in Montreal that had led me to the chest, which was at the bottom of the lake at Gottfried Academy. Riddles that sounded oddly similar to Descartes's final words. "It belonged to the Nine Sisters. And they were going to destroy it, if the ninth sister, Ophelia Hart, hadn't betrayed them and hid it for someone to find."

"The Nine Sisters supposedly found the secret to eternal life," Theo said. "Right?"

I nodded.

"What if they decoded Descartes's riddle and found the Netherworld? After they were murdered, the last remaining sister, Ophelia, carved it on the inside of a chest. She could even still be alive."

The Cartesian Map *was* their secret. As I traced the engravings on the inner lid, I felt Dante's breath on the back of my neck, cool and thin. I walked my fingers through the strange landscape etched into the metal. The sweeping lines and symbols that marked the path made me shudder. They didn't look like they belonged to this world.

"So what was inside the chest?" Theo said.

My eyes flitted to Dante's.

"Nothing," Dante said.

Theo gave him a curious look. "It seems awfully strange that the ninth sister would have etched the map into a chest, of all things, without wanting to put anything inside with it."

"Does your legend say there's supposed to be something included with the map?" Dante countered.

Theo's gaze drifted to Dante's bag. "No," he said thoughtfully. "It doesn't."

Anya broke the silence that followed. "So what exactly does Paris have to do with all of this?"

Theo pursed his lips, a silent acknowledgement that if we were going to keep our secrets, he was going to keep his, too. "I'll show you once we get there."

"We?" I said. "Who says you're invited?"

"I do," Dante said, surprising all of us. "Under the condition that once we get there, you'll show us what you know. In exchange, I'll show you what was inside the chest."

A crooked grin split across Theo's face. "Deal."

We landed in Paris at night, its skyline covered in a swirling winter flurry like a city enclosed in a snow globe. While Theo hailed a taxi, I stood on the curb with Dante and gazed out at the rooftops in the distance—the city so bright that it set the horizon aglow, as if dawn were approaching. I was about to turn around when I felt a wisp of cold air tickle my neck. I froze.

"Do you feel that?" I said.

"What?" said Dante.

"The Undead," I said, and looked to Anya and Theo to see if they had sensed it. They followed my gaze toward the dark field that flanked the airport.

"I don't feel anything," Anya said after a moment.

"Me neither," said Theo. "Probably just a draft."

"Yeah," I said, as Dante picked up my bag. "It must have been in my head."

I tried to shake the feeling as we squeezed into a tiny taxi, Theo in the front, Anya, Dante, and I in the back, the aroma of vanilla and sweet tobacco clinging to the seats. It was exactly what I had imagined Paris to smell like. Tinny Christmas music played from the radio.

Theo leaned toward us over the passenger's seat. "So where are we going?"

I stiffened. Wasn't he supposed to know?

"This was your side of the deal," Dante said, his voice losing its warmth. "I think you'd better figure out quickly what exactly we're doing here, because if turns out you lied to me, I'm not going to be generous." His tone was so callous that it sent a chill through the car.

"Relax," Theo said, swallowing. "I was just joking. Of course I know where we're going. But it's closed now. We have to wait until morning."

My stomach sank as I realized that even though I didn't believe him, I wanted to, for without Theo, we were already lost.

Dante ignored him and spoke directly to the driver. *"Pourriez-vous nous amener—"* he began to say. I was so used to hearing him speak Latin that I didn't realize the deep voice belonged to Dante until Theo interrupted him, giving the driver conflicting directions.

"Menez-nous à la rue Chartreuse, s'il vous plaît," he said, in an immaculate accent.

The driver shot Dante an impatient glance in the rear-view mirror.

Theo turned to Dante. "I'm not lying to you, okay? So let me do the talking."

After a moment, Dante nodded.

As we pulled away from the curb, I turned and cast one last glance at the darkened field by the airport. Had the sensation just been a chill? I focused on the field, searching for that cool wisp again, and I thought I noticed headlights blink on in the distance, pull away from the curb, and drive after us. Was it just another taxi? I watched the lights bob behind us until we turned onto a highway, where they got lost in the sea of cars zipping around us.

We drove in circles, whizzing through roads crowded with tiny European cars that looked like toys, down winding streets lined with cafés, and finally through cobblestoned alleys crowded with pigeons, our car splashing through slushy puddles. Every so often I gazed over my shoulder, unable to shake the feeling that we were being followed.

"What are you looking at?" Anya asked as I studied a car behind us, its driver nothing more than a dark silhouette beneath a hat. But before I could point him out, he turned down a side street. I must have been seeing things.

"Just the city," I said.

"It's beautiful, isn't it?" Anya said.

I realized then how long it had been since I had taken a moment to admire the beauty around me. "I suppose it is."

We turned down an alley off the main road. There, the streetlamps looked dimmer, the buildings run-down and dark. A shudder passed through the car. The air suddenly felt colder, the strands grasping at my neck as though we were driving past a cemetery. But there was none in sight.

"What is that?" Anya said to me.

Death. It enveloped the street, seeping up from the ground, down from the buildings, in through the alleyways. There had to be a tomb nearby. A church, a graveyard—something.

We pulled up in front of a crumbling hotel, its facade streaked with water stains. I immediately didn't like it—the cracked windows, the blown bulb in one of the decorative lamps out front, the rat scurrying in front of the door. Death reached out from its walls in long, cold tendrils.

Theo leaned into the backseat. "Don't worry," he said. "I know this place. The owner owes me a favor. And the bad sensation you're feeling? That is what's going to muffle our presence," he said, looking pointedly at Dante.

"Where did you get that?" Anya asked, as Theo took out a wad of euros from his pocket and counted out a few bills for the driver.

"*Merci*," Theo said, and opened the door. Once we were outside, he explained. "I nabbed it from the woman standing in front of us in the customs line."

"You stole it?" Anya said, but I only rolled my eyes. I had warned them about what Theo was like, and they chose not to listen.

"How else were we going to pay for the cab?" Theo asked with a shrug, and without waiting for an answer he picked up his bag and walked into the hotel. It was a musty old place that might have looked decent decades ago but had since fallen into disrepair. A few sagging couches lined the lobby. Anya collapsed onto one of them and fiddled with the chess table beside her, a half-finished game abandoned on top.

Theo and the rest of us approached the front desk and rang a small bell. An attendant in a red uniform appeared from the back room. "*Bonsoir*," he said. "*Comment puis-je vous aider?*"

Theo began to tell him that he knew the owner and needed a last-minute room. The attendant asked for his name.

"Theodore Healy," he said.

The attendant squinted at him, then removed an envelope from beneath the desk and handed it to him.

Surprised, Theo opened it. I could just make out Monsieur's familiar handwriting. He skimmed the words, the smile fading from his face.

"What is it?" Anya asked from the couch, but Theo looked too stunned to answer.

The hotel attendant called out to us, and asked if we wanted our luggage taken upstairs.

Theo barely registered the question. Instead, his eyes darted to the window as though he were suddenly aware of someone watching us. Dante slipped the note from Theo, who didn't seem to care.

After reading it, Dante folded it up and turned to the attendant. *"Pardonnez-nous pour un moment,"* he said, his voice calm, and nodded to us. "Let's go," he said under his breath, and led Theo and the rest of us toward the door.

"What was that about?" Anya asked.

"Act normal," Dante said. "We have to leave." As we stepped into the night, he handed me the note. I read it, Anya's chin perched on my shoulder.

They are on their way. They know you are coming here. Do not let them find you.
Monsieur

The cold bit at my cheeks as I lowered the page. Dante stood beside me beneath the awning of the hotel, his face barely visible in the shadows.

"Who is he talking about?" I asked. "The Monitors or the Undead?"

Dante ripped the note to shreds and threw it in the waste bin. "We'll find out soon enough."

He led us across the street, stealing through the darkness toward a run-down boarding house, where he asked for a room overlooking the street. The attendant grunted in response and disappeared behind the counter to produce two rusty keys. Our room was cramped, the air smelling faintly of an ashtray. Two metal bunk beds stood against either wall. The neon sign outside flickered, casting a red glow over the floor.

Our window overlooked the hotel we had just come from, a pair of decorative lamps flanking the door, one bulb blown, the other flickering, threatening to go dark. We took turns sitting on the sill, waiting for whoever was looking for us to come and collect. But the hours wore on, and save for the occasional passing car, the street remained still. Then it was my turn.

Dante sat beside me in the dim light, sketching in a pad while his eyes shifted between two things: the map on the inner lid of the chest, and me. Behind us, Theo sat sideways on an armchair, his legs slung over the armrest while he whittled away at a bit of wood. Anya sat on the floor, nervously shuffling a deck of tarot cards. I heard her murmur to herself while she laid them out on the floorboards and practiced reading them.

Dante studied me in between strokes of his pencil, sketching my face on the page in his long scrawl. I watched as he drew me, the blunt lines slowly forming my eyes, my hair, my lips. I looked sad, I realized. Older. Without looking up from his work, Dante touched my hand, his cold fingertips tickling mine, as if we were just a normal couple waiting for the sun to rise over Paris. I tried to hold that image in my head when I heard Anya sigh.

Blowing the wood shavings off his pants, Theo leaned toward her. "What are you doing?"

Anya furrowed her brow as she studied the cards laid out before her. "I'm perfecting my tarot readings."

"Tarot?" Theo said. "What, like palm reading or something?"

"No," said Anya. "It's a lot more precise than that. The cards can tell us what lies behind us, what lies directly in front of us that we may not be able to see, and what lies ahead of us. It depicts one version our lives can take."

Theo swung his legs to the front of the chair, suddenly interested. "One version? What do you mean?"

"All of our possible futures are imprinted on our souls," Anya said. "They change depending on the choices we make. When done correctly, a reading of the tarot cards is supposed to reveal the path your life will take based on the state of your soul at this very moment. But what the cards tell you isn't written in stone. The future isn't fixed; it can always be changed, but that requires a choice." She fanned the cards out over the table until they formed the shape of a crescent. "It's all here," she whispered, staring at them. "Waiting to be turned over."

"How do you know they work?" Theo said.

"Before I came here, I had a reading of my own. They told me I was going to go on a journey that would change my life forever. The next morning I received the note from Monsieur."

"Really?" Theo said. "All right, let's give it a go."

Anya eyes brightened.

"It can't hurt, right?"

Anya looked like she was about to disagree, but then changed her mind. "I suppose not," she said. "Though only the cards can say." She stacked the deck and held it out to Theo. "Choose a card, and without looking, press it to your forehead."

Theo leaned back, an amused grin on his face. He chose the card at the bottom of the deck and held it to his head. It was upside down, and decorated with an elaborate illustration of a robed man holding a divining rod over a cup. *The Magician* it read.

Theo glanced at each of us, trying to make out from our reactions what it read. But Anya barely blinked. "Good," she said. "Without looking, place the card back into the deck and shuffle it."

The cards fluttered together.

"Cut the deck three times."

After he was finished, Anya stacked them back together and sat up straight. "I'm going to lay out your cards in a lifeline. They will move from past to present to future. Okay?"

"Got it."

Starting with the top of the deck, she placed the first card onto the table with a satisfying slap. To everyone's surprise but Theo's, it was the same card he had pressed to his forehead just moments before. It was even upside down. *The Magician.*

"This card represents who you are," she said. She traced the edge of it. "The Magician is very talented, but doesn't make use of his skills. He has a difficult time making choices, and for that reason he often backs away from challenges instead of making a hard decision. He isn't trustworthy."

Theo let out an uncomfortable laugh. "Are you calling me a coward?"

Anya pursed her lips. "I'm not calling you anything," she said. "I'm reading the deck."

She flipped the next card, revealing an image of a white fist holding a leafy torch. *Ace of Wands*, it read. "You were a young talent," she said. "A prodigy. You had a brilliant start to your career. Everyone thought you were going to shine."

She turned over the next card. *Two of Swords*, upside down. It depicted a woman sitting on a beach, her eyes closed. She held a sword over either shoulder, each facing opposite directions. They looked strangely similar to Spades. "But you were deceived. You didn't realize it at the time, but someone was playing a trick on you. They tried to use you for something else."

Theo seemed to hold his breath when he saw the next card. It was a dark image. At its center lay a man stuck with dozens of swords. *Ten of Swords.* "A death occurred. Perhaps it was an accident."

The color drained from Theo's face.

Anya frowned. "Or murder? The cards do not say."

Theo relaxed a little, as if the ambiguity relieved him. Anya flipped over the next card. It depicted an old man in a tattered cloak. He faced the distance, which looked gray and bleak. *The Hermit.* "You were cast out."

Theo averted his eyes. Anya continued, laying down a card with an image of a beautiful woman, her long hair flowing down her shoulders. *The High Priestess.* "You will meet a girl and fall in love."

Theo's cheeks blushed ever so slightly, but he quickly laughed it off. "Right, well, she's not my type," he said, nodding to the woman on the card. "I hope the cards take that into account."

Anya didn't respond. She laid out the last card. *The Knight of Swords.* A valiant man riding a horse, wielding his sword fearlessly in front of him. Anya passed her hand over the cards, her eyes darting down the line as she took them all in. "You have a choice ahead of you. You will leave your path and walk on another. You will have to choose to return or go back. The lives of those around you will be sealed with your decision."

Theo gazed at the cards without saying anything. Finally, he let out a laugh. "You're some sort of witch."

Anya studied him with curiosity. "Thank you."

Theo looked to Dante. "His turn."

But before Dante could respond, through the curtains I saw something move. I pushed them back just in time to see the shadows on the street shift. Everything inside me tensed. Dante must have noticed because the scratching of his pencil stopped. "What do you see?" he whispered. I didn't dare turn around lest I miss it. Dante turned off the lamp behind us, leaving us under the cover of darkness.

I leaned closer, watching a shadow shift in the alley. The night seemed to unfold in its wake. One by one, a wave of figures emerged from the darkness, each wearing a long gray overcoat and a gray suit. The only flashes of color among them were their crimson scarves, tucked into the lapels of their coats. They walked quickly, each carrying what looked like a long staff. I could only catch glimpses of their faces. A hooked chin; an old sunken cheek; a bit of gray beard; a pair of lips, thin and elegant; a wisp of long white hair.

"Who are they?" I asked, watching still more of them seep from the darkest corners of the street.

"The Court of Monitors," Theo whispered beside me. "Their gray coats and suits are meant to help them blend into a crowd, though I'd recognize them anywhere."

The Court of Monitors was the supreme power in the Monitoring world. They made all of the decisions—which Undead to follow, which to bury, which to watch over, which to try in the court of the land. It was made up of two factions—the elders of the High Court, and the junior Monitors of the Lower Court. The elders had the final say on all matters regarding Monitoring. They deemed who was worthy of a Spade and who wasn't. Every Monitor wanted to become them; to sit on the High Court; to have their power and talent. Except for me.

They were here now to find Dante. My grandfather had been hunting him for a year and a half, ever since the headmistress at Gottfried Academy was killed by an Undead. My grandfather had blamed Dante, though I knew the truth—Dante had tried to save her life that night, and had saved mine as well.

The elders of the High Court surrounded the hotel across from us, blending in with the night until it looked like no one was there. All I could see was a bit of light reflecting off the metal bottoms of their staffs, which I realized were Spades. Two of them stepped inside, the gray tails of their coats disappearing into the lobby. They marched past the front desk without explaining themselves and began to search the premises.

Dante's hollow presence beside me struck a sudden worry in my heart. The High Court of Monitors were the best, wisest, and most senior Monitors—which meant that it was only a matter of time before they sensed Dante's existence, and realized they had chosen the wrong hotel.

"There are so many of them," Anya said, her hair dangling over my shoulder as she watched the hotel across the way light up. "There's no way we can get past them if they find us."

"How *did* they find us?" I said.

All of our eyes drifted to Theo.

He backed away, holding up his hands. "Don't look at me. I didn't tell anyone," he said, reading our thoughts. "Maybe they found their way to my grandfather's tavern and forced it out of him. Or maybe your grandfather went to the airport and got our flight information out of one of the attendants. You are still a minor. There are plenty of ways to find people; believe me, I know."

Despite myself, I believed him.

"Besides," Theo continued, "I chose this part of the city for a reason." He motioned to a cross jutting out between two buildings. "There's a cemetery on the other side of that church. The Paris Catacombs are below us. And all those boarded-up triple-deckers? Well, who knows what kind of filth is rotting in there."

Anya grimaced, but I couldn't help but feel relieved. In the hotel across the street, the lights in the upstairs windows flipped on one by one, the stiff shadows of the Monitors stalking past the shades.

"This neighborhood is a place that Monitors who work in Paris often find themselves searching," Theo said. "Especially that hotel, mostly because of its unsavory clientele and the... *baggage*... they leave behind."

Human baggage, he meant.

"You used to Monitor in Paris?" Anya asked.

"How else did you think I knew the owner?" he asked. "He owes me a lot of favors for helping that place keep a low profile. Anyway, they won't be sensing you tonight," he said to Dante. "Not with the rest of the death around here. You can thank me for that."

I flinched at Theo's choice of words. "*Thank* you? If it weren't for Monsieur, we'd be at the mercy of the High Court, and Dante would be halfway in the ground."

"Without me you wouldn't have even left Pilgrim," Theo scoffed. "Besides, he's Undead. You better get used to the idea of him being gone, because it's coming soon. I can sense his age just as well as you can."

I bolted out of the chair, ready to tell Theo how Dante was more of a person than he would ever be, but Dante held me back. "Don't," he said to me. "We need him now." He turned to Theo and spoke, his voice so steady it was frightening. "Though we may not need him later."

CHAPTER 5

The Cartographer

AFTER SEARCHING THE PREMISES AND FINDING nothing, the Monitors of the High Court trickled out of the hotel, their dark overcoats melting together, a spill of gray over the pavement. They huddled together as if speaking, then peered up at the buildings around them. I shrank back from the window, catching the curtains just before they swished shut. For a moment, I thought I saw one of the Monitors look up at our window, his skin such a dark shade of brown that I couldn't make out his face. But he looked away, flipping up the lapel of his overcoat as he scanned the rooftops.

The Monitors fanned out over the street, tucking themselves into its darkest corners. There they stood as still as lampposts, surveying the streets, the moonlight glinting off their eyes. They were waiting for us. They were here to bury Dante.

We stayed up into the early hours of the morning,

preparing ourselves for the moment when they noticed Dante's presence and swept up through our boarding house, but it never happened. I woke curled up in the chair by the desk, Dante watching over me from the windowsill. Behind him, grainy rays of sun split through the curtains, illuminating his body with a thin seam of light. I leaned toward him and touched my hand to his, making sure he was real, that he was still here with me.

"They're gone," he said, then added, "For the moment."

When the others woke, we packed our things and snuck outside, Theo leading the way. The street was bright and empty, save for an old woman sweeping a stoop and a flock of pigeons pecking at crumbs by the curb. It bore no trace of the Monitors who had stood watch the night before. Their somber stance was echoed only in the stone gargoyles chiseled onto the corners of every building, watching over us with hard eyes.

Theo led us through a maze of side streets, careful to stay out of sight. The sounds of the city waking up snuck through the cracks between the buildings—trucks delivering barrels of fresh produce, shop owners cranking open the awnings over their storefronts, the Métro rumbling beneath our feet. Down an alley, I heard a bicycle bell ding. I peered back into the distance just as a girl jumped out of the way. A familiar girl.

She had deep brown skin, which made the whites of her eyes look all the more sharp. Her short hair was combed to one side and held in place with a barrette. *Impossible*, I thought. Could I really be staring at Clementine LaGuerre, the girl who had lived in the dorm room next to mine in St. Clément? The girl who had done everything in her power to make my life hell last year, and the only girl I knew who was as good of a Monitor as I was.

Clementine glared at the cyclist and wiped the mud off the side of her skirt. Seeing that scowl was almost comforting; it made me feel like I was back in the St. Clément dormitory, listening through the walls to her friends gossiping about me. If only that were my biggest problem now.

She called out to someone in the distance, though I couldn't see whom. She must have come with her father, the headmaster of St. Clément.

I gripped Dante's arm as she disappeared into the crowd. "My old roommate—she's here." I wasn't sure if I should be spooked or relieved. Clementine wasn't on our side, and yet despite our fraught past, a part of me wanted to believe that she wasn't against us, either.

"Clementine?" Anya said, a few steps behind me. Her eyes narrowed; they hadn't gotten along either. "Where? I'll bury her myself."

Dante tightened his hand around mine. "We have to move faster."

Theo stopped in front of a sleepy storefront with books and maps displayed in its window. LA FIN DU MONDE, its sign read.

"This is it," he said. "One of the oldest mapmaking shops in Europe. The owner has been trying to plot the

Cartesian Map for decades." Theo paused before he opened the door. "Just don't show him the chest unless I say it's okay. Got it?"

"Why?" I asked.

"He's . . . well, you'll see. Just remember, I know what I'm doing."

A bell on the door jingled as we stepped inside. The store was warm and yeasty like a museum, the dust settling on the books that lined the shelves. The walls were covered with maps. A few customers browsed through them, quiet, barely acknowledging our entrance. Theo led us past them toward the rear of the shop.

At a desk in the corner sat a stout, greasy man with a puff of hair. His mouth was stuck in a grimace, as though he'd just eaten something sour. He nibbled on a piece of bread and jam while reading the newspaper, a pair of glasses perched on his nose. He pressed them to his face when he saw us approach.

"Monsieur Pruneaux," Theo said with a smile.

A look of surprise passed over the man's face. He recognized Theo, but didn't seem happy to see him. "Theodore?" he said, his neck stiffening. *"Es-tu venu ici pour proposer vos services à nouveau? Parce qu'ils ne sont pas les bienvenus."*

He spit the words out, his voice so full of vitriol that I wondered if coming here with Theo was a good idea.

"Actually, this time I was hoping you could help us," Theo said, barely ruffled by his anger.

Monsieur Pruneaux's eyes darted to me, Anya, and

finally Dante, where they rested. He could feel Dante's presence, too. I could tell by the way he clenched his jaw. Pruneaux was a Monitor.

What was Theo thinking, bringing us to a place where Dante could be in danger? But before I could turn to leave, Theo caught my eye, the cautionary look on his face telling me to wait.

"I'm nothing more than a humble mapmaker," Pruneaux said, his throaty French accent exacerbated by a smoker's cough. "I do not know what kind of trouble you are in now, but I'm afraid that unless it has to do with my work, I can't be of service to you." He cast one last nervous glance at Dante, as though he were about to pick up the phone and report us. Instead, he settled back in his chair and raised his newspaper.

"That's exactly why we came to you," Theo said. "Because of your work. And not just the humble kind."

Pruneaux lowered the newspaper until his eyes were visible over the top.

Theo gave me a slight nod. I set my bag down on the desk. I could feel Pruneaux's focus sharpen as I unzipped it and took out the metal chest.

"*Qu'est-ce que c'est ça?*" he asked, glancing between the chest and the door.

"Go on," Theo said. "Open it."

He cast a suspicious eye at Theo, then lifted the lid. It took him a moment to notice the map. I watched him search the empty recess of the box, adjust his glasses, and tilt it forward until the light shined on the points engraved into the underside of the lid. He traced them with his fingers, counting. *One. Two. Three. Four.* At the fifth, he pulled his hands away, as if he had just realized he was touching something delicate.

"*Non,*" he murmured in awe. "*Ce n'est pas possible.*"

"You know what it is?" Dante asked.

Pruneaux looked up at him as if the question were absurd. "Where did you get this?" he said in a throaty accent.

"That doesn't concern you," Dante said. "Do you know what it is?"

"*Bien sûr,*" Pruneaux said, his voice trembling with anticipation. "The Cartesian Map. What every Monitor dreams of finding. When I was younger I always imagined what it would be like to find it, but I never thought it would just stumble into my shop—"

A creak in the floor stopped him, and we all turned as a customer walked in from the front of the store. "*Pardonnez-moi,*" he said, a bushy mustache sweeping his lips as he spoke. "*Combien ça coûte?*" He held up an antique nautical chart of the European waters.

Pruneaux shut the lid of the chest and gave him a startled look. "*Err—il n'est pas à vendre,*" he said. *It's not for sale,* I translated.

"*Quoi?*" the customer asked, his mustache emphasizing his confusion.

Pruneaux snatched the chart from his hands, and amid

the man's protests, he escorted him to the door, telling him in French that the store was now closed. He shooed the other customers out behind him, then locked the door, hanging a sign in the window that read FERMÉ.

While he pulled the shades down over the shop windows, we lingered by his desk.

"He's not going to report us, is he?" I asked Theo.

"No," he said. "We have something he wants. If he were going to call one of them, he would have done it when we first walked in."

"That's a comfort," Dante murmured while he leafed through a stack of charts on Pruneaux's desk.

Anya picked up a map of the ancient world. It looked at least two hundred years old, the pages yellowed, the continents dominated by empires, their colors fading as if they were disappearing into time. When she saw the price marked at the corner, she gaped and set it down with care.

"Five thousand euros," she whispered to us.

"Yours is worth a lot more," said Pruneaux, making us all jump.

He was standing behind us, a bit of crumb from his toast clinging to the stubble on his chin.

I stepped between him and the chest. "It's not for sale."

The phone rang. Instead of answering it, he unplugged the line.

"Un moment," Pruneaux said, and reached beneath the mess of papers on his desk. In spite of his messy office, he seemed to know where everything was. He pulled out a pair of magnifying bifocals. *"Bien,"* he said, securing them over his regular glasses. "Open it."

I lifted the lid and he leaned in. He didn't speak for a long while. Instead, he ran his palm over the chest, barely allowing himself to touch it as he inspected each of its surfaces, its hinges, its latches. *"C'est magnifique,"* he said under his breath. *"C'est incroyable. Je ne peux pas en croire mes yeux. . . ."*

He passed his hand over the five points, tracing their path until his hand rested in the center. His fingers trembled. In a cracked whisper he said, "The Netherworld."

"How do we read it?" I asked.

Pruneaux didn't seem to hear me. He held a finger to his lips, then jumped from his seat and opened one of the dented filing cabinets that lined the far wall. He thumbed through one drawer, then the next, pulling out rolls of paper until his arms were full. He stumbled back to the desk. Pushing the rest of his things aside, he unrolled the first sheet.

Sprawled across it was a meticulous, hand-drawn map of Europe, colored in the most delicate shades of green. Five towns spanning the continent had been darkened to points, and a line connected them, forming an odd geometric shape. It looked vaguely like the outline of the canary that the points on our map formed, though positioned at a different angle, the head facing upward, the wings narrow and long.

"I've spent decades drawing maps of where the five points might be," Pruneaux said, admiring the sketch work. "I assume you are aware of the myth of the Netherworld?"

"Of course," Theo said, his voice impatient. Anya elbowed him in the side. "We know about Descartes's riddle," he added. "If that's what you mean."

Pruneaux looked up at him wearily, then continued. "The riddle is important, but it is not the entire story," he said. "You must already be well-versed in Descartes's writings of the soul. He believed that after the body died, the soul left the body and traveled to a distant land, where it was cleansed before being reborn into a new body." Pruneaux lowered his voice. "That distant land is the Netherworld. A place where millions of souls travel to once they leave their bodies, drifting to each of the five points to cleanse themselves before they gather in a lake of mist. Descartes believed that if he could follow that path of the soul back to this, its place of origin, he would be able to take one and live a second life."

"Take it how?" I asked.

Pruneaux pressed a finger to his lips. "Ah, that is the question, isn't it? Many have interpreted the final lines of Descartes's riddle, trying to find the answer. Some believe you can take a soul from the lake in the form of coal. Others believe you have to breathe a soul in, or drink it like water. No one knows. All we are certain of is that the path contains five points arranged in the approximate shape of a bird. It is important to remember that the Nine Sisters did not create this map; the points have existed since the beginning of time. Many scholars believe that one of the reason why the Sisters chose the canary for their crest is because of the shape they saw in this map.

"We also are certain that each point represents one of the five human senses. To find them you must use your sense of hearing, of taste, of smell, of sight, and finally of touch. You must follow the points one by one, in the order that Descartes spoke them in the riddle; you cannot merely skip to the end."

Why couldn't we? I wondered, but before I could ask, Pruneaux continued.

"Aside from a few physical features—the mention of the smell of death in the third point, and the mountains in the fourth point—the riddle says nothing about where the points may be, so I was left to guesswork."

Pruneaux turned to the map he had drawn. "I assumed that if Descartes had discovered the five points, he would have done so through his travels and work. In his entire life, he never left Europe—they must be here somewhere, the trail buried in his life and writing. Over the last three decades, I have been compiling a list of all the places Descartes traveled to or lived in—all of the places that seemed meaningful to him in some way—with the hope that they would lead me to the Cartesian Map." He patted a worn notebook resting on his desk. It was stuffed with papers and notes, its top edge puckered and stained brown from a coffee spill. "All in here."

Theo's eyes lingered on it, his interest piqued, while Pruneaux leaned over his map. "This was my first attempt."

He pointed to a dark dot on the map in the west of France. "Descartes grew up *ici*." He traced his hand across the map. "*Ici* is where he attended university." He pointed to another dot. "*Et ici* is where he wrote his first essay." He slid his finger to the fourth dot. "*Ici* is where he published his *Seventh Meditation*, his essay on the Undead." He let his hand drift to the fifth dot, in Stockholm. "And here is where he died."

Pruneaux compared his map to the one inside our chest and shook his head. "All wrong."

He threw it aside and opened the next map. It had a larger scope, and was colored a pale brown, with mountains winding up the center like vertebrae. The Alps. Black dots marked five new towns, but they didn't form the shape of a canary, either. He opened another, then another, comparing them to the chest and to each other, but none of them matched. Finally, he opened a map that spanned the entirety of Europe. It looked rougher than the rest, the edges half colored in, the lines on the border only lightly sketched. Dozens of black dots studded the page—far more than five.

"This was one of my last attempts, but I gave up before I finished, as you can see. I was trying to map Descartes's entire life, along with all of the places in Europe where extraordinary natural phenomena had been reported. I had the idea that if each of the points can only be discovered by using one of the five senses, then they must exist in the midst of a unusual phenomenon of nature. I thought if I could map all of the places where people have reported strange sightings, smells, sounds, then I would be able to see where they overlapped with Descartes's travels. But I soon discovered that it was useless; there weren't enough places of natural wonder, and those that were reported didn't match any of the landmarks of Descartes's life." Pruneaux shook his head. "No," he said. "The points on the Cartesian Map are not places that anyone would report; they are places that are hidden in plain sight."

He leaned over his map, tracing the dots that littered the countryside of France, then turned to the chest. He swept his finger over the etchings that led from what he believed to be the first point to the second. "I've been plotting the points chronologically in his life, the first corresponding to a place Descartes visited earlier in his life, and so on. These three lines right here look *un peu* like three rivers, intersecting just before the second point." He slid his fingers over the triangles between the second and third points. "These look like a jaw of mountains, with a pair of twin peaks in the distance." He traced a staircase leading up to a billowing tuft of circles, inside which lay the fourth point. "This could be a ridge climbing up into the clouds." He followed the path over three circles chiseled into the map, positioned like stepping stones. The fifth point was circumscribed in the last circle. "And, *peut-être*, these could be lakes." Pruneaux frowned. "But there are dozens of these kinds of landmarks all over Europe," he muttered to himself. "It would take ages to try and find a location where all of these matched up exactly as so."

I shot Dante a worried look. What would we do if Pruneaux couldn't figure out where the points were? I didn't have any ideas, and judging from the way Dante was frowning as he watched him, and the way Theo was tapping his foot nervously against the floor, they didn't either. Anya was the only one who didn't look concerned. In fact, she wasn't even watching Pruneaux. Her eyes wandered about the store, resting on a map of the world from the 1700s that hung in a frame by the window. It was a magical thing, with mermaids and sea creatures sketched in the blue waters. It seemed like the Netherworld belonged more to that map than to ours.

Pruneaux lowered his glasses and collapsed into his chair with a sigh. *"Je suis désolé,"* he said, blinking through his bifocals. *"Je ne sais pas.* I have to study this. It is not something that can be done in mere minutes." He wrapped his hands around the edges of the chest greedily. "I could keep it here, work on it. I would have to draw a copy for myself, of course, as payment for my help."

"No," Dante and I both said immediately, but before we could go on, Theo interrupted.

"How long would it take?" he asked.

Pruneaux ran a hand through his greasy hair, his eyes darkening with calculations. "Two, maybe three weeks." He wiped the sweat from his upper lip. "It would be safe. I assure you."

The crack in his voice made me uneasy. "Weeks?" I said. The Monitors were already here, searching for us. "We don't have that kind of time."

Pruneaux leaned over his desk, his stout fingers tracing the rim of the chest. "Why?" he said, giving Dante a curious look. "Are you in a rush?"

"That doesn't concern you," Theo said.

Pruneaux wrung his hands together. "Tell me again, where, *exactement*, did you find this chest?"

"Let's just say it found us," Dante said.

Pruneaux squinted at him. "How lucky you must be," he said. "The most searched-for map in the history of Monitoring, and you happen to stumble across it?"

"I never said we stumbled," Dante countered.

"And when it found you," Pruneaux continued, "what was inside this chest?"

"Nothing," Dante said.

Theo looked at me and mouthed, *We should go.* I nodded and turned to Anya, but she wasn't paying attention. She was still staring at the ancient map by the window. But when I nudged her, she held up her hand.

"Look," she whispered.

I followed her gaze to the ships and sea monsters that

flitted through the oceans, to the mountains and castles that studded the land, until I saw it—a yellow bird flying right over the western side of what was now Europe.

I felt my breath go thin. What if our map didn't just seem like it belonged to this world; what if it actually did?

I searched the modern map of the world that hung right below the antique one, trying to figure out where that bird would have been drawn in today.

NEDERLAND.

"It can't be," I said, though the excitement was already prickling up my skin.

"Why not?" Anya challenged. She was always the first to believe. She turned to the others, interrupting their argument. "Did Descartes ever spend time in the Netherlands?"

Pruneaux leaned on his desk. Damp patches of sweat stained the underarms of his shirt. *"Oui."*

Dante immediately saw what I did. "The Netherlands," he said. "Just like the Netherworld."

Pruneaux's eyes twitched as he made the connection between the names. *"Non,"* he said to himself. *"C'est trop facile. Je l'aurais vu. . . ."*

"Does that mean that the entire map could be in the Netherlands?" I said.

"I doubt it," said Anya. "The border of the Netherlands and the surrounding countries has changed significantly over the years; it would be too perfect. I bet it spans Europe."

"So how do we know where to start?" I said. "The point in the Netherlands could be the last point."

Theo groaned. "This is making my brain hurt. Can't we just go to the Netherlands, find the point that's there, and if it's the last point or a point in the middle, we can just skip ahead?"

"No," Dante said.

"Maybe we do know where to start," Anya said, and closed her eyes. "Remember Descartes's riddle? *The nethers first call from their hollows by dark, / In the shape of a bird, with each sense the route has been marked,*" she recited. *"First,"* she repeated. "It's subtle, but it could mean that the first point is in the Netherlands."

"Could?" Theo scoffed. "It has to. Descartes prided himself on his subtlety. Every word in that riddle was intentional."

"Where exactly was he in the Netherlands?" I asked, but Pruneaux was too absorbed in his thoughts to answer.

"Pruneaux?" I repeated.

When he finally turned, his face was guarded. He wasn't going to tell us.

"How much does that Descartes map cost?" Theo said.

The question caught him off guard. He wiped the sweat from his temple. "It is not for sale."

"Everything can be bought. It's just a matter of price," Theo said. "Name yours."

Pruneaux looked at Theo with disgust. "I am interested in collecting information, not giving it away to those who do not even appreciate it. People like you think that mapmaking is only about simple geography, about finding

100

places on a map and going to them," he said, his jowls trembling. "You don't understand that locating a place on a map like this one is not the same as getting there in real life, and that navigating the expanses of the Netherworld takes a lot more than just cleverness. Do you have any idea what kinds of unnatural forces shape its landscape? The depths of darkness you will be plunged into? There is a reason why no one has found it yet, and it is not just that it is hard to find. Many do not *want* to find it, for fear of what it will do to them."

Our silence was enough of an answer.

"You claim you are familiar with Descartes's riddle, but you are like everyone else. You have only paid attention to half of his words. You think his verses merely tell you where the points are, and how you will find them. But what of the beginning? *What, to you, is a second soul worth? / An early death, a wombless rebirth.* There is a price to following the path of the soul as it is cleansed of each of its senses." Pruneaux gave us a level look. "Your soul will be cleansed of its senses, too."

Cleansed of its senses? That couldn't mean what I thought it did. . . .

"What are you saying?" Theo asked. "That our souls are going to get purer as we get closer?"

"No," Anya said quietly. "He's saying that at each point we will lose one of our senses, until they are all gone, and we are vacant."

"*Oui,*" Pruneaux said.

I swallowed, understanding why we had to go through each of the points; why we couldn't skip to the end.

"Descartes speaks of each of his senses fading as he travels from each point, until the only sense he has left is touch," Pruneaux continued. *"Touch, the noblest, is last to decline. / The final remainder of life in this soul of mine.* That will happen to you, too. There is a reason why Descartes died so suddenly. Why he was nearly blind and deaf; why his nurses reported that he didn't eat or sleep. Point by point, he lost each of his senses. You cannot merely walk to the Netherworld. You have to give up your soul in order to find it."

CHAPTER 6

La Fin du Monde

WE WALKED BACK TO THE BOARDING HOUSE in silence. I trained my eyes on the slushy streets, unsure of what to say. My heart told me not to turn back. I had to go with Dante and find the Netherworld, otherwise I would lose him again. He would never be able to find the points on his own; his senses were already muted. And yet I was scared. What would it feel like to die slowly, to waste away, my senses withering one by one until I was crippled and vacant? I imagined the world darkening around me, Dante's voice fading as I lost my hearing, his face growing blurry as my eyes went dull. I never thought I'd be frightened of death, being so near to it all the time; but now that it was waiting for me, close enough that I could almost feel its wisps pulling at my throat, I was terrified.

But what would the world be without Dante? My parents had already been killed; my grandfather was nothing more than a cold outline of a patriarch; half of my friends were Undead and wasting away, and the others were all Monitors, a talent I never wanted in the first place. I had no interest in burying people. Their world didn't belong to me, and yet neither did any other. Dante was the only thing in my life that felt like home. Being with him made me alive. Without him, what would any of it be worth?

A woman in a stained apron stood in front of a *boulangerie*, scattering rock salt over the sidewalk. I touched my hand to Dante's until the sweet aroma of baking bread wafting out the front door grew stronger, enveloping me in its warmth.

"Renée," he said, his voice steady. "We can't—"

I could already guess what Dante was thinking by the heaviness in his gait: that I had to turn back, that he wouldn't let me surrender my soul to save him. "Don't say it," I said. "Not yet." He was about to protest when I cut him off. "Please."

With his fingers grazing mine, I looked up at the shop fronts, suddenly brimming with life under his touch. I saw the sun glinting off the windows, the people passing by: a blink of brilliant blue silk beneath a heavy coat, a flash of red beneath a pair of high heels. Soon, it would all fade. I pressed my palm to his, feeling the roughness of his skin, the cool tingle it sent up my arm. That, too, would soon be lost to me.

I reminded myself that I knew what it felt like to die, for I had given my life to Dante once before. Ever since our kiss, my senses had dwindled, the world coated in a dreary gray film unless Dante was by my side. Even now, the blue sky peeking through the rooftops seemed slightly duller than it used to, the ornate buildings plainer and charm-less, their awnings muted into wan shades of yellow, red, and blue. Life without him would be even worse—a vast expanse of gray, void of beauty and feeling. Without Dante to share it with, the world meant nothing.

Anya walked a few paces behind us, absently picking at the chipped polish on her nails, her eyes distant, as though her thoughts were as dark as mine. Theo was the only one of us who looked chipper.

"What's with the dour faces?" he asked as we reached the lobby. "Did we or did we not just figure out where the first point on the map is?"

"That's not funny," I said.

Theo frowned. "I wasn't trying to be."

"Were you not paying attention when Pruneaux was talking about the riddle?"

"Of course I was. I mean, it's not going to be a walk in the park, but . . ."

His nonchalance baffled me. "This might seem like a big joke to you, but it isn't to us." I lowered my voice as we walked up the creaky staircase to our room. "This chest is all we have. We're giving up everything for it. And if we reach the end and there's nothing there, then . . ." I let my voice trail off, unable to finish the sentence. Behind me, Dante was conspicuously silent.

Theo only shrugged. "What did you think would happen? That you would be able to just walk up to the Netherworld, knock on the door, and ask for a new soul? Of course it involves sacrifice. Everything does."

"What does it even matter to you?" I said to Theo. "You're not coming with us. Neither of you are. You have no reason to go to the Netherworld."

Anya looked like she was about to speak, but then changed her mind.

Theo traced his finger along the brass railing. "How are you so sure of that?"

I was about to respond when a boy walked toward us in the hallway. He wore a red cap and uniform, as if he were a bellboy. He hurried past without looking up. Were there bellboys in this boarding house? I couldn't remember ever seeing one.

"Besides," Theo continued. "If I were you, I wouldn't uninvite me yet. I might be able to help you. After all, I was the one who brought us to Pruneaux. Without me, you never would have found the first point."

I let out a cold laugh. "We haven't found anything yet," I said. "We *think* it's in the Netherlands. But that's an entire country."

"So all we have to do is figure out where Descartes stayed in the Netherlands, and go there," said Theo as he fiddled with the keys to our room. "Bingo. Easy. The question is, how will we get there?" He pushed open the door and was about to step inside when he stopped.

Lying on the floor was the answer to his question: an envelope with Monsieur's handwriting sprawled across the front, spelling out my name. I bent down and picked it up before Theo could snatch it. Dante must have been thinking the same thing I was, for he ran down the hallway, calling out to the boy who had passed us. *"Garçon! Attendez!"* But it was too late.

I slipped the note out of the envelope. Tucked inside were four train tickets, each leaving the next morning for Amsterdam.

Be careful. They are watching you.
Sincerely,
Monsieur

His words sent a prickle up my spine. I lowered the page and looked out the window, searching the blank buildings for eyes. But whose? The Monitors, the Undead, or both?

Theo grabbed it from my hand and read it, Anya peering over his shoulder.

"I guess that answers it," he said, and tossed the note on the nightstand. "The four of us are leaving tomorrow."

"But where do we go when we get there?" Anya asked. "I couldn't see any of the towns on that map in Pruneaux's office."

I paused, wondering if I had heard her correctly. "You— you still want to come too?" I said in disbelief. "Even after Pruneaux's warning?"

Anya bit her lower lip, trying to decide the best way to answer. "Monsieur asked me to help you," she said, then averted her eyes and played with a lock of her hair. "I don't want to go against the signs."

"The signs?" I laughed. "You must have a better reason than that," I said. "You're risking your life—your soul—to find a place only corroborated by a legend."

"I know that," she said softly.

I didn't understand. "Then why—?" But judging from the look on her face, she wasn't going to answer me. "This is our burden, not yours—" I began to say, when Dante cut me off.

"*My* burden," he corrected, his eyes pleading with me to understand. He ran a hand through his long hair, which was tied back in a knot. "And I don't want any of you coming with me." He was speaking to everyone, though he was staring at me. "I've already put you in enough danger. I can't let you give away your soul for me."

"You can't just send me home," I said, unable to believe what I was hearing. "This is my choice, not yours. And I choose you, at any cost."

Dante's chest expanded, as if my words made his heart ache. "You don't know what it means to be like me," he said. "I can't let you waste away. I wouldn't be able to bear it."

"It's already happening," I said, no longer caring that Anya and Theo were listening. "There's nothing for me without you."

"Don't say that," Dante said, his voice low.

"I don't know how else to make you understand."

His muscles flexed as he leaned against the desk, a lock of hair falling in front of his face as he lowered his head. "I'm sorry," he said, as if that explained everything. But all I heard was *Good-bye*.

"I don't care if you're sorry," I said, trying to stop my words from wavering. "I've made my decision, and you can't change it. I'm a Monitor. I can take care of myself. I'm following this map, with or without you, though I think we'd both be better off together."

"You might want to listen to her," Theo said, surprising us both. He drummed his fingers along the bedpost. "First, she has the chest, and thus the map, and thus the power. Second, you're Undead. How are you going to find all of these points, which we're supposed to find through our senses, if you have none? Third, Renée is a Monitor. Without her, you won't be able to tell where the Liberum are until they're upon you. And, of course, she'll be safer if we're around, too, seeing how we're Monitors and all, and can help protect her." He began to pace around the room. "Fourth," he said, raising an eyebrow, "as a former student of St. Clément, she understands the mindset of the Monitors far better than you do. And, of course, if I were to come along, I would understand even more, since I'm the only one among us who has earned a Spade."

Anya rolled her eyes, but I barely moved. My gaze was trained on Dante, who listened, arms crossed, his face unreadable.

"And fifth," Theo continued, "even if you do go on your own, you don't know where in the Netherlands to start. Yes, you could go to a library and research all of the places Descartes had ever been to, but that could take weeks, maybe months. And then, of course, you'll need to do the same for the next four points, which could take years, if you ever even figure it all out."

"And how does Renée coming with me change that?" Dante said.

"Because if she doesn't come," Theo said, winking at me, "then I don't, either, and it seems like you need *me* right now, more than anyone else."

I tilted my head, curious. What kind of trick did he have up his sleeve this time?

Dante squinted at him. "Enlighten me."

Theo collapsed onto the bed, pulled a notebook from his coat pocket and began flipping through it nonchalantly, as if he was barely paying attention to us.

I stepped closer. "Is that—?"

Theo looked up, feigning surprise. "What?" he said. "Oh, this old thing?" He swung the cover shut, the beginning of a grin spreading across his face. "It's just Pruneaux's notebook."

"The one he had in his shop?" Anya asked.

"*Oui,*" he said, pressing his fingers to his chin in his best Pruneaux impression.

"The one with all of his notes on Descartes?" I asked. "The one with all of the places he'd visited written inside?"

"*Oui.*"

"How did you get it?" I said.

"I nabbed it while the old man was lecturing you. Something about evil forces and creatures lurking in darkness. Anyway, while he was off on his tangent, I figured he wasn't going to help us, so I had to help myself. I just slipped it off his desk. It was easy."

I wanted to touch it, to make sure it was real, but Theo held it away from my grasp. "Ah ah ah," he teased. "It's mine now." He turned to Dante. "And it doesn't go anywhere without *all* of us."

"Why do you even want to go?" I asked Theo.

He tilted his head as he studied me. "Do you think you're the only one who wants a fresh start?"

"A fresh start from what?" I asked, but Theo had already turned away, avoiding my question.

Even though I suspected that Theo was only helping me for his own benefit, I couldn't help but feel grateful, a sentiment I never thought I'd have toward him.

"There are four tickets," Anya added. "Monsieur is putting us together for a reason. Maybe he knows something we don't."

But Dante's attention was focused only on me. His body seemed to reach toward me, its cold tendrils wrapping around my arms, coaxing me toward him.

"This is the life that I want," I said to him. "Let me live it with you to the end."

His lips parted; they were a pale pink, as though they'd

111

frosted over. He took me in as though he were looking at something that would soon be gone. "That's all I've ever wanted to hear you say, and yet now I can't bear to hear it."

Choose me, I pleaded with him. *Choose me like I chose you.*

Dante lowered his head and ran his hands through his hair. "It isn't a second life that I want," he said, succumbing to my pleas. "It's you. You're the only reason any of this matters."

"So that means that I'm coming with you?" I said.

Dante bit his lip, as if he didn't want to let the words out. "I guess it does."

I wanted to run to him, to wrap my arms around him and bury my face in his hair, but Theo's voice reminded me that we weren't alone.

"Seeing as how I've held up my side of the deal," he said, "I think it's your turn. Show me what was inside the chest."

Dante slipped his bag off his shoulder and took out the small black box.

Theo's expression changed when he held it, his anticipation fading to bewilderment. I could see its weight straining to pull away from him as he turned it around in his hand, feeling its heaviness, its unwillingness to be held.

"A box?" he said, tracing the striations in the rock, some smooth to the touch, others uneven like seams. He passed his hand over the top, where the tangle of grains in the rock had formed those same words I saw when I clutched the box: *Pour l'Amour Vrai.* Theo paused as his hand touched them. "For true love," he said, translating the inscription. He looked between Dante and me. "How romantic."

"It doesn't feel that way," I said.

"Love can come in a lot of different forms," Anya said. "It doesn't necessarily mean romantic love. You can love a friend purely. A family member . . . a parent." She paused. "A mother—"

"I know," Theo said bluntly, as though he had been thinking the same thing. He searched the box for an opening. Theo dug his nails into the grooves in the stone, to no avail. "So what's inside?" he said. "A love letter?"

"We haven't figured out how to open it," I admitted.

Theo gripped the top and bottom and twisted, attempting to unscrew it. When that didn't work, he tried to pry it open from one of the seams with his nails.

"We tried that," I said. "It doesn't work."

Theo leaned against the bedpost, stumped. He held it up to his ear. "It feels so heavy," he said. "And yet—"

"It sounds hollow, like a vast empty space," Dante said, completing his thought. "Odd, isn't it?"

Theo lowered it from his ear. "Yes."

Anya twirled a lock of hair around her lips, her gaze fearful but curious as she watched him handle the box. "Let me look at it," she said.

Theo tightened his grip around the box.

"Give it to me," Anya said, an edge of concern in her voice.

Theo quickly released it, letting it drop into her hand.

She held it lightly, rotating it with her fingers, as though she wanted to minimize the amount of her skin that touched it. When her hands passed over the lid, she paused, as though she, too, could see letters forming in the stone. Their words seemed to startle her, but she hid her surprise. She quickly set the box down on the side table by Dante and backed away from it.

"What if there isn't anything inside?" she said, eyeing it with suspicion.

Theo snorted. "Why would anyone hide a box without putting anything inside it?"

Anya didn't share his humor. "Who knows," she said. "It's possible that it isn't even a box."

A silence fell over the room.

"I guess we'll just have to wait and see," Dante said, and slipped it back into his bag.

Theo stood up and zipped his coat. "I guess so," he said. "Well, I'm out for the day."

"Where are you going?" I asked.

He shoved his hands in his pockets. "Oh, here and there. I have some business to attend to. Our train doesn't leave until tomorrow. Which means we have the entire night to kill. I'll see you squares back here later tonight."

"What kind of business could he possibly have tonight?" I asked as he left the room.

"I actually have something to do, too," Anya said.

"What?" I said with a laugh. "But we only just got here.

114

How could you...?" my voice trailed off when I realized she was serious. "Where are you going?"

She bit at her chipping nail polish. "I just have some errands to run," she said vaguely. "I'll see you guys later tonight." Before Dante or I could ask her anything more, she left.

"What was that about?" Dante asked.

I pushed back the curtains of the window. "I don't know."

Her hair blew in front of her face as she stepped out of the lobby into the street below us. She peered at the buildings around her to make sure no one was watching, then turned right and stole down the sidewalk until she was nothing but a flounce of red hair melting into the dusk. For a moment, I wanted to be her. I had almost forgotten what it felt like to do whatever I wanted, to pick up and go anywhere I pleased without worrying that anyone was following me. Paris was sprawled out in front of us, waiting to be discovered, yet Dante and I were imprisoned in this dirty hotel.

Outside I heard a bottle smash against the ground. A drunk man shouted a slurry of words to no one, then kicked a garbage can. It was strange to think that this part of the city was the safest place for us, but it was. The cemetery behind the church, the catacombs beneath us—all of the long-dead people were now drowning out Dante's presence. The moment we left the area, the Monitors would be able to sense us. We couldn't wander the city or see the Eiffel

Tower at night. We couldn't eat at a fancy restaurant or sit at a café, sharing a buttery pastry. Dante couldn't even eat. Being confined here, forced to embrace the death that surrounded us, made me feel like we were already doomed.

Dante slid his hand down the back of my neck. "Come on," he said softly, as if he could read my thoughts. "Let's go out."

"How?" I said.

His eyes glimmered. "The catacombs."

The sun was setting. A light snow fell over the city, but I couldn't enjoy it. Every time I looked up at the buildings, I swore I could see the glimmer of eyes watching us through the dusk. We snuck beneath the awnings, avoiding the streetlights as we crept from alley to alley. I led the way. I didn't know where the catacombs were, I only knew what I could feel: the dead lurking all around us, beneath us. Were they watching us now? As we approached an intersection, I thought I saw a gargoyle move, but when I looked again, it was still.

I shook my head, laughing at myself, and was about to cross the street when Dante clamped his hand over my mouth and whisked me into a dark alley. I gasped, but his arms tightened around me, muffling the sound. A maze of fire escapes zigzagged above us.

"Shh," he whispered in my ear and peered out at the sliver of street. I fell quiet. A lone streetlamp cast a cone of yellow over the sidewalk. A shadow stretched into it, followed by another, then another.

Three men walked through the light, all dressed in somber gray overcoats and caps, which shrouded their faces from the snow. I didn't dare move. Were they Monitors of the High Court, or just a group of men going to the opera? The tallest one turned. Beneath his cap, I could make out the heavy wrinkles in his cheeks that could only have belonged to a man close to death. He walked with a cane. Or was it a Spade? I couldn't tell. Something caught the street light beneath his hand. The metal end of a shovel, hidden from view, perhaps. Or was it nothing more than a cuff link?

Dante inched deeper into the alley, pulling me with him. *No*, I wanted to whisper to him. Movement would give us away. I gripped his arm to stop him, but not quickly enough. The smallest of the three men glanced over his shoulder, and while the others continued down the street, he paused, his eyes lingering on the alley.

A stray pigeon cooed behind us. I begged it to be silent. I tried to catch a glimpse of the small man's eyes, but as he stepped outside of the dim light from the streetlamp they were reduced to nothing but dark sockets. Even his skin dissolved into the night. I squinted into the shadows, trying to make out the silhouette of his face beneath his cap, but it vanished, in its place nothing but darkness. The pavement crunched beneath his feet.

I felt Dante's chest against my back, his irregular heartbeat so loud that I was certain the Monitor could hear it, too. This couldn't be how it ended. I closed my eyes and willed blood to pulse stronger through my veins, to make up for his lack of life, but the sound of the Monitor's footsteps only got closer.

Then I heard a gasp. It was so soft that the wind swallowed it almost immediately. I opened my eyes, surprised. That voice—it didn't sound like it belonged to a man.

The Monitor had stopped walking and stood only a few feet away. He slipped off his cap, revealing a head of short black hair, combed to one side and pinned with a barrette; a sliver of skin, dark and buttery; and a pair of sharp eyes, their whites shining through the darkness. He wasn't a man at all, but a girl. Clementine LaGuerre.

She looked at me, then at Dante, her eyes widening with intrigue as she realized what she had discovered. Suddenly, I felt like I was standing in the hallway of my dormitory from last fall, caught doing something illicit with a boy in the middle of the night. Except we weren't at school anymore. She didn't have her friends standing behind her, only the two Monitors of the High Court loitering on the street in the distance. And instead of spitting an insult at me—a public embarrassment that would fade over time—with one word, she could bury us.

She parted her lips as if she were going to call out to the others. Unable to help myself, I sprang forward. I didn't know what I planned to do, only that I had to stop her, but Dante held me back. He was right. The Monitors behind her were too close; they would hear a scuffle, or if they didn't, they would quickly notice she was gone.

Clementine's face sharpened. *Don't test me*, she seemed

to say. I saw the ambition flash through her face. If she told them we were here, she would get the credit. She'd be honored by the High Court, and would probably get her Spade soon after, not to mention that she'd be getting rid of the only Monitor her age who had ranked higher than she had. Me.

I knew all of those things because despite our history, we weren't that different. She had a natural talent for Monitoring, one of the best in our school's history, until I came around. We had both liked the same boy, Noah, and I could tell from the heaviness in her shoulders that she mourned his death just as much as I did. We both wanted, more than anything, for other people to stay out of our business. And, most important, we were both—by instinct and by trade—killers. We were drawn to the Undead by a single urge: to bury them. If Dante and all of the other Undead were dangerous, then we were no better.

I tried to communicate all of that to her while we stood locked in the alley, the snow collecting on our shoulders. *Please*, my eyes begged. *We are more similar than different.*

That's when I felt a lick of cold against my legs. At first I thought it was the wind, a gust of snow wrapping itself around me. But when the breeze died down, the wisp of air was still there, coiling itself around my ankles, willing me to follow it. Undead, dozens of them, stealing through the night.

Clementine must have felt them, too, because she glanced over her shoulder in the direction of the vacancy.

One of the Monitors shouted to her. Clementine's eyes lingered on me, still deciding if she should tell the others.

Please, I begged her.

She curled her fingers as if something was prickling them. I knew that sensation. Dante's presence was coiling itself around her, pulling her closer. She clenched her fists, forcing the sensation away. "I'll be right there, Dad," she said, her voice cool, controlled.

I followed the direction of their voices to the dimly lit street, realizing that her father, John LaGuerre, the jovial headmaster of St. Clément, was standing just beyond the buildings.

"I found you," she whispered, a teasing smile spreading across her face. "In this round, you lose. Lucky for you, I want to see where this game goes." She slipped her cap back on. "Go," she mouthed and slinked back through the alley, disappearing around the corner.

It wasn't until Dante wrapped his hand around mine that I realized I was shaking. I curled my fingers around his. We were still here. Though next time, Clementine might not be so forgiving.

Dante gazed down at me, the reflection of the streetlamp in the distance making his eyes glow a pale white. He pulled me back to the side of the building, where he leaned toward me, pressing me against the brick. I felt the cold metal against my neck, the damp railing pressing into my skin. His shadow enveloped me. His fingers felt like icicles as they crept beneath my coat, counting the vertebrae of my back. I trembled, feeling everything within me begin to unravel. His hollowness wrapped itself around me in frigid tendrils. He buried his hands in my hair and pulled me closer, his cool breath tickling my throat until I couldn't tell the difference between him and a gust of winter wind.

Then his lips grazed mine. Too close. They drew the breath from me, making it twist up my throat in a thin wisp of air. I pressed my lips shut before it could escape, and pushed him away, his body stiffening as he realized how close he had let his mouth come to mine. Had it been an accident, or was he losing control? I searched his eyes for an answer. They were dulling with age, a hint of gray creeping over his dark irises like clouds obscuring the night sky.

He pressed his hands to his lips, realizing what he had almost done. "I'm sorry," he whispered, the words curling around me like an icy strand of air. "I would never..." But he let his voice trail off, as if he wasn't sure anymore if it was true. I felt my heart skip. Or was it his? I could no longer tell where his life ended and mine began, and suddenly the space between life and death seemed impossibly small. A cold hand. An irregular heartbeat. A pair of cloudy eyes.

I didn't realize until I backed away that I had been gripping the handle of my shovel within my coat. My voice quivered. "And I would never let you," I said. I knew then that I had to be careful.

As I finished speaking, a man and woman from the street stumbled into our alley, laughing and holding hands. When they saw us, they jumped, then apologized and ran back into the street in a huddled whisper. To them we were just two people kissing beneath a fire escape. Except we couldn't kiss.

Dante held his fingers just above my lips, as if he were afraid to touch them. Guilt filled his eyes. "Let's go," he said.

We walked in a somber silence as I led him through the streets. We didn't have a destination; just a path that we could walk along, marked invisibly by the maze of catacombs lying beneath the city. The tombs under the earth pulled one foot down, then the other. Their presence felt heavy, as if gravity was stronger along the path we were taking. The trail of the dead. I followed it blindly, taking a right, then a left. To anyone watching us, we looked like we knew where we were going—like we had chosen this route—but the constant tugging at my feet reminded me that our path had been set a long time ago. We couldn't veer off it now.

We stopped when we reached an empty street corner. The streetlamp overhead flickered until it switched off, as if it knew we needed cover. Between the buildings, we could just make out a bridge lit up in the distance. "The Seine," said Dante, keeping his distance beside me. "Hundreds of years ago, the Catholics massacred the Huguenots. They threw the bodies into the river. There were so many people that the water ran red with blood."

I shivered.

"People claim that some of that blood is still there,

staining the banks, and if you stare into the water while it ripples, you can see the way you're going to die."

I already knew what Dante would see if he looked into the river. I remembered his death as if it had been my own. I remembered his little sister, wrapped in a blanket and shivering with fever while Dante and his family boarded a small plane headed for the closest hospital. I remembered how quickly the pressure in the cabin had changed, the way his stomach flipped as they plummeted, the sound of his father's voice while he prayed, the sheer force of them hitting the ocean as if it were a cement wall, and finally the water—first blue, then a deep, endless black.

"What do you think I would see?" I asked him.

"Long, gray hair," Dante said, touching the ends of my locks as they fluttered in the wind. He traced the smooth patch of skin on my temple. "Wrinkles here," he said, and slid his finger down the side of my cheek. "And here," he said, pointing to the edge of my mouth, "from smiling." He passed his hands over my eyes, his fingertips grazing my lashes. "You'll fall asleep. It will be easy, painless, like drifting into a dream."

The richness of his voice drowned out the street around us, until I could almost see my future self through his eyes.

"And I hope," he continued, "that if I am given a second chance to die, it will be with you."

"Me too," I whispered.

In the distance, the lights of the city at night gave the horizon a brilliant glow. I imagined all the people beneath it, strolling down the snowy streets arm in arm; laughing at the end of a long dinner, a plate of cheese getting soft on the table; sitting in their apartments, sipping wine and staring up at the sky, just like I was. We weren't there yet, but maybe one day we would be.

A gust of wind interrupted my thoughts. It swirled around my legs, picking up the hem of my coat and sending a shiver up my skin. It was the same sensation I'd felt just before Clementine's father had called out to her, though this time it felt even stronger. The Undead, a lot of them, all moving away from us to the east. Their presence grew stronger, pulling at me with a strength I could barely resist.

"The Liberum," I said.

The wail of a siren pierced the air. We both turned just in time to see flashing blue lights crest over the hill. A rush of air pushed me back from the curb as police cars sped past us. An ambulance trailed behind them, slowing as it rounded the bend. They headed in the same direction as the vacancy. Their lights flashed in the night, giving the street an eerie blue glare. I followed the drone of their sirens until they faded behind the buildings. "Are they—?"

"Going in the direction of Pruneaux's shop," Dante said, my thoughts slowly becoming his. Without saying anything more, we started to run.

The narrow street that led to the map shop was blocked off by police cars, their lights cycling through the falling snow. Two men in uniform stood in the intersection, directing cars to a detour. I crept past them and leaned over the barricade. Shattered glass was strewn across the sidewalk. I followed its trail up to the window, now jagged with shards, a dim light still on inside; to the maps fluttering out of the gash, their edges already damp from the snow; to the tiny fingerprints pressed into the white flakes collecting on the sill. There were dozens of them, all so small that they could only have belonged to children.

The Undead. As soon as I realized what had happened, I started to see signs of them everywhere. The footprints were scattered across the sidewalk, like dozens of children had run barefoot through the snow. In the midst of them were two wobbly lines scraped into the ice. A chill wrapped itself around me as I imagined the heels of a man's loafers cutting through the snow, the Undead dragging him away.

I turned to Dante, whose face had hardened into one I barely recognized. It was fierce and wild. The face of an Undead.

A task force of people was busy closing off the area with tape and sheltering it from the weather with a tarp. Two bodies lay in the street, the snow already accumulating on the sheet pulled over their faces. All I could make out was one limp hand peeking out from beneath the tarp. It was so pale it blended in with the ice. My heart began to race. It reminded me of my mother's hand, lying delicately in the dirt. Of my father's hand a few feet away from hers. Of Dante's hand. I reached out and touched the back of my hand to his. His cool skin comforted me.

"Who are they?" I whispered, just as the paramedics

rolled a stretcher past them with a third body strapped to the top. It was already zipped in a black bag. The wind swallowed my gasp.

A few feet away, two police officers spoke. I listened in, trying to translate their French, but they were speaking far too quickly for me to catch everything. I turned to Dante. "What are they saying?"

Dante leaned in and began to whisper. *"Found on the scene: three people. One elderly woman. A business man, middle-aged. A woman in her thirties. Bystanders, I'm guessing. None of them connected to each other."* A car honked behind us. Dante strained to hear. *"Cause of death: unknown. No wounds or internal damage, only a few slight scratches around the mouth."*

I could feel Dante's cold breath against my ear as he spoke, his words transporting me back to two years before: my sixteenth birthday, when I had found my parents dead in the redwood forest.

Dante continued. *"The paramedics seem to think they all died of heart attacks. I don't see how that is possible."*

A heart attack. That was what the coroner said my parents had died of. It was what they always listed as the cause of death when an Undead had sucked away someone's soul.

"We believe that the shopkeeper, Monsieur Jean Pruneaux, was there at the time of the burglary. His wallet, coat, and personal belongings are still in his office. The mug of coffee on his desk was still warm when we arrived. The cash register was left untouched, as were many of his high-worth items. Judging from the scratches

in the snow, he was dragged into the street while he was alive. He may still be. His body has yet to be found."

An officer bent down to survey the zigzag of little footprints in the snow. He shook his head, confused. Beneath his feet, charts and maps lay matted to the pavement, turning to pulp. He nudged one with his foot, then stood and adjusted his hat.

One of the police directing traffic approached us. *"Excusez-moi, mademoiselle, mais vous n'êtes pas censée être ici."*

A lump rose in my throat. I couldn't speak. The Liberum and their Undead boys must have followed us to the map store that morning. They had taken Pruneaux.

"Mademoiselle?"

Dante touched my arm. "Come on," he said. "Let's go home."

"Home?" I said. "Where is that?"

CHAPTER 7

The Soundless Gap

a THUDDING REVERBERATED THROUGH THE AIR. It made the ground shudder and the crows disperse. I had been here before. The frozen lake at Gottfried Academy was gray and hazy like the eye of an Undead, the black water seeping up through the cracks beneath in thin veins. A hand pounded against the underside of the ice, trying to break through. *Thump thump thump thump:* like an irregular heartbeat. The naked trees lining the campus trembled with each blow.

The ice buckled, a force pushing upward until a loud crack rang out through the morning air. It clapped off the buildings, their windows dark and vacant. Then an ashen hand shot up through the gash.

A boy pulled himself out from the hollow, black water spilling off of him as his shoulders uncurled toward the sky. Noah. His cheeks were ashen, his auburn hair dripping around his face. His eyes sharpened until they were in focus.

Noah looked up at the sky, at the sunlight peeking through the clouds, his face bewildered, as though the world looked foreign to him. The playful glimmer in his eyes was now dull. All traces of joy had vanished from his face. He was no longer the Noah that I knew.

With a blink, he was running through the woods faster than I had ever seen him move, the branches of the evergreens snapping against his legs. He looked lost, desperate. His feet were bare as he trekked through the snow, yet he didn't seem to notice the cold. He stopped when he reached a cabin, one that I recognized. The same cabin that Dante and I had slept in, just before we had been forced to split up. The windows were dark, the front door ajar, from when the Monitors had thrown it open to search for us.

Noah stepped toward it, inspecting the muddy footprints tracked through the entryway. "Renée," Noah said, his lips so pale they looked blue. "I'm coming for you."

I gasped and opened my eyes. I was sitting in a smooth felt seat, my hands gripping the armrests. The green, hilly landscape of the European countryside whizzed past the window. Relieved, I slumped back against the headrest, and let out a long breath. The train hummed softly beneath me, rumbling slightly as we crossed a bumpy patch of rail. *Thump thump thump thump.*

"What's wrong?"

Dante's voice shook me out of my thoughts. He sat beside me, his shoulder touching mine. He was reading Pruneaux's notebook on Descartes, which Theo had only agreed to let him read after the train left the station with all of us inside it. He shut it and studied me.

I could still see Noah's eyes, as handsome as they were before but now dull, the spark behind them extinguished by the icy depths of the lake. I realized then that I owed Noah my life as much as I did Dante. I pressed my eyes shut. "Nothing," I said. "Just a nightmare."

It had to have been a dream. Though I'd had visions like it before, of Dante's past, of his death, of him searching for the clues left behind from the ninth sister, those were different. I had been seeing into Dante's life because we shared a soul, because a part of me had been planted within him. I had no such connection with Noah. Now, it was just my memory and my guilt that were haunting me.

"About what?" he asked.

Across the aisle sat Anya, her face nestled into a sweater while she slept. Beside her, Theo fiddled with a bit of rope from his backpack, tying elaborate knots and then unraveling them. His eyes shifted to me as if he had been listening in on our conversation.

I swallowed. "I—I can't remember."

Dante didn't believe me; I could tell by the way he studied me. "You can't change the past," he said, reading my thoughts.

"I know," I said, though I couldn't help but wonder what I was supposed to do if my past caught up to me, and became my present.

• • •

The Netherlands met us like the start of a new day. A brilliant swath of sun broke through the windows at Amsterdam Central Station. It was a beautiful old place, lined with arched metal beams that made it look like an industrial cathedral. Birds chirped from the ceiling. Every so often three chimes sounded over the station intercom, followed by a woman's voice speaking in melodic Dutch.

We lingered on the platform, unsure of what to do next. A rush of people pressed past us, coloring the station in tweed and khaki and wool. Through the wall of windows behind them, I could just barely glimpse the blue sky reflecting off the glassy waters of a canal.

According to Pruneaux's notes, Descartes had lived in or visited dozens of places in the Netherlands, any of which could be the first point on our map. "Or none," Theo added, though if that was the case, we had no hope. So we decided to believe.

This was what we knew: Descartes first came to the Netherlands when he was twenty-two, to fight against Spain. After the war was over, he was stationed with his army in various other countries, where he claimed to have had strange dreams and visions that influenced his later writings. Before returning to France, he completed his first philosophical essay. Yet for some reason, a few years later, he moved away from his homeland and went back to the Netherlands, where he stayed for over twenty years.

While he was there, he led a secretive life. He enrolled at one university, but soon quit, and much of his life during that time was a mystery. He later emerged as a professor at Utrecht University. By then he had a daughter from a maid he had met in his travels, but in a cruel twist of fate, the girl died when she was only five years old, of scarlet fever.

The grieving Descartes spent the rest of his time in the Netherlands wandering from place to place, haunted. As time passed, his peregrinations became almost obsessive. He moved to one town, only to pick up and leave less than a year later. Was he running from his past, or searching for a future?

Dante flipped through his notes. "Out of all of the spots Descartes traveled to, three stand out to me. The first is the city of Leiden, where he quit university and dropped out of society for a while. He returned far later in his life. There has to be a reason why he chose to disappear while he was there, why he decided to return years later.

"The second is a town called Oegstgeest, where he purportedly finished writing *Seventh Meditation,* his essay on souls and the Undead.

"And the third is a small village in the countryside called Egmond-Binnen, his last residence in the Netherlands. It was the last place he lived before disappearing for months. When he later resurfaced, wandering the French countryside, he was taken to Stockholm, where he died. It seems significant that after his twenty years of traveling within the Netherlands, he decided to stop at Egmond-Binnen. Maybe he found what he was looking for there."

The intercom chimed in the background.

"I think we should start with Leiden," Dante said, lowering his voice. "It seems too suspicious that Descartes continued to return there. He must have been there looking for something that he didn't want anyone else to find."

But Anya didn't agree. "Theo, you said that Descartes had a daughter who died in the Netherlands. What about the city where he buried her? Don't you think that if he had discovered the path to the Netherworld, he would have taken her there first?"

"If he had discovered it by then, yes," Dante said skeptically. "But then he never would have buried her in the first place. And thus, there would be no tombstone."

Anya shot back. "Of course there would be. It would be a symbolic tombstone. And anyway, it's not like you have any more proof that it's at Leiden."

"You're both idiots," Theo said. "It's obviously in Oegstgeest. How else would he have had the idea for his *Seventh Meditation*? He probably discovered something there, and then sat down and wrote about it. It's the clearest clue. And we know he wanted to leave clues behind. Why else would he tell the nurse a riddle with his dying breath? He could have easily taken the secret with him. He *wanted* people to know."

"That's too obvious," Anya said. "And anyway, *Seventh Meditation* isn't about the Netherworld, it's about the Undead."

"Shh," Dante cautioned.

They argued back and forth, neither actually listening to

the other. Anya took out her deck of tarot cards, announcing that she was going to ask the fates. Finally, they turned to me. "What do you think?" Dante asked.

Leiden intrigued me, though if Descartes had found the first point on the path to the Netherworld there, why did he keep leaving, then returning? It seemed to me that he might have had a strong suspicion that it was there, which was why he kept going back, but in the end, he found it somewhere else.

Anya's idea seemed plausible, too, though no more so than Dante's, and with just as many flaws. The town of Oegstgeest, where Descartes wrote *Seventh Meditation,* also seemed hopeful. Though if Pruneaux was right when he warned us that each of the five points was shrouded in shadows that no earthly being had encountered before, then it seemed unlikely that Descartes would have settled down and written a treatise in such a dangerous place. Which left only one option.

"I think it's in Egmond-Binnen," I said. "The town where Descartes last lived in the Netherlands."

Dante studied me. "Why?"

"If Descartes was in the Netherlands to search for the path to the Netherworld, he would have left once he found it. So it can't be Leiden or Oegstgeest. If either of those were where the path began, then why would Descartes keep going back to them? Why would he keep searching?"

Dante considered my argument, then nodded. "Okay," he said. "Let's try it."

Anya bit her lip. "Fine," she said. "Though if you're wrong, we're asking the cards." She stuffed the tarot deck back into her pocket.

I was so absorbed in our conversation that I didn't even notice that Theo had gone missing until someone bumped into my shoulder. I spun around, thinking it was Theo. "Knock it off," I said, but it was only a passing traveler.

"*Pardon,*" the man said, adjusting his bag.

I scanned the station. "Where's Theo?"

"Did I hear my name?" Theo said from behind me.

"Where were you?" I demanded. "I thought something had—"

"Happened to me?" he said, finishing my sentence. My worry seemed to amuse him. "While you three were here talking about what we should do, I was out getting us a car." He dangled a set of keys.

"How—?" Anya began to ask, but Theo cut her off.

"I have my ways."

"Did you steal it?" I said.

Theo placed his hand on his chest, as if we had wounded him. "Me? Steal?" he said, feigning innocence. He shook his head. "No trust," he said, and threw me the keys, which were attached to a polished metal ring. "A gift from Monsieur. Now, who knows where we're going?"

We must have looked confused because he explained. "I was hungry. So while you guys were talking, I dropped by the concession stand to grab a bite. That's when a boy tugged on the sleeve of my shirt. 'A message for you,' he

135

said, and handed me an envelope. Inside was a set of keys and a note."

He pulled the folded piece of paper from his pocket to show us. All that was written on it was a license plate number, along with the following message:

The Undead are coming. They will take two things from you. Let them.
Sincerely,
Monsieur

We all froze, suddenly aware of our surroundings. I reached behind me to pat the bottom of my bag. The chest was still inside. Dante did the same, his shoulders collapsing with relief when he felt the smooth corners of the box.

"How do they know where we are?" Anya wondered aloud.

"Pruneaux," Dante said. "They broke into his store and took him. He knew we were heading to the Netherlands. He could have told them. Or maybe they brought him along. He has valuable information in his head."

"'*Let them*'?" I said, reading the note again. "We don't have anything worth stealing except for the chest and the box, and all of us know that we can't part with either of them."

My eyes darted to the people walking past us. I couldn't feel the Undead around us yet.

"Maybe it's something else," Theo said. "Something we aren't thinking of now."

"What would that be?" I asked, and held up my white canvas backpack, which was heavy with my shovel and the chest. "All of my things fit in this bag, and Dante's things in another. I'm not overlooking anything. Unless one of you has something you're not telling us about?"

I searched Anya and Theo for an answer, but they only stared back at me with blank looks.

"I have nothing but this," Anya said, motioning to her suitcase. "Just clothes, jewelry, makeup, my shovel, and my burial gear. Oh, and of course my tarot cards. And a few candles. And some teas and vitamins, and a few tonics and elixirs from my father's store."

Theo raised his eyebrow. "Tonics and elixirs?"

"Why do you laugh?" Anya questioned. "Isn't that what we're all here for—to find the ultimate elixir?"

"Touché," Theo said, and lowered his pack, which was attached to his Spade and its sheath. "Other than this," he said, nodding to his weapon, "I don't have anything of worth."

My eyes couldn't help lingering on Anya. I still couldn't figure out why she wanted to find the Netherworld or why Monsieur would have asked her to come in the first place. What would she want an elixir of life for?

"All I'm saying is that so far, Monsieur has turned out to be helpful," Theo said. "So we'd better prepare ourselves."

By the edge of the concourse, two patrol officers peered in our direction. "Keep your voice down," I said. "We don't know who's watching us."

"Monsieur, it seems," Dante said. "How else would he know where we're going before we even get there?" He motioned to the note in Theo's hand. "A boy gave that to you?"

"Skinny, dirty blond hair. A street kid. Couldn't have been older than ten. I thought I saw him following us when we got off the train. I asked him who gave him the note, but all he said was *a man in a long overcoat with a cane.*"

I spun around. Was Monsieur here, at this very moment, watching us? The others turned with me, all searching the train station. But for what? It was winter. Everyone in the train station wore long, heavy coats.

"An overcoat?" Dante said. "Like the ones the Monitors of the High Court wore?"

Theo shrugged. "It's possible. Considering how much he knows about the Undead and about where we're going, he's probably a Monitor. And a good one."

"Maybe it wasn't a cane he was carrying, but a Spade," I said, remembering the glint of metal I had seen beneath the Monitors' coats on the night Clementine had found us. "How do we know that he's not working for the High Court?" I asked. "He could be leading us into their grasp. We already know he's been following us."

"All of our cards are on the table, but his hand is still a

mystery," Anya said. "Though that doesn't necessarily mean he's holding a winning hand."

I bit my lip. "I still don't like it."

Judging from the silence that followed, neither did anyone else. Then again, Monsieur had told us that the Monitors were coming to find us in Pilgrim, just like he had warned us about them raiding our first hotel in Paris. He had yet to give us any reason to distrust him.

"Without him, we'd be stuck in this train station," Dante said.

"Or worse," Theo added. "Still in Pilgrim, Massachusetts."

Dante nodded in agreement. "If there's anything I've learned from Monsieur thus far, it's that we have less time than we think. Let's go."

A sleek vintage car waited for us in the parking lot. It had just two doors, a low dashboard, and nostalgic round headlights—the kind that belonged in a smoky noir movie, switching on in the night to follow someone on a winding road through the mountains. Except here, we were the ones being followed. *Lancia,* the badge on the rear hood read. On the dashboard sat a road map of the Netherlands.

Theo whistled when he saw the car, then ran his hand over its glossy angles. After admiring it for a moment, he stepped back and looked at the field in the distance. Slowly, he smiled. "I think it's safe to say that regardless of what kind of coat Monsieur is wearing, he's on our side, at least for now."

I didn't understand what he meant until I looked at the car against the snowy field in the background. Its white paint blended into the wintery landscape almost perfectly. If Monsieur was trying to give us away to the Monitors, he definitely chose the wrong color car, for any Monitor or Undead who tried to spot us in the distance would have a hard time.

Anya narrowed her eyes. "And it's also safe to say that he's a criminal."

That silenced all of us. "What?" I said. "How do you know?"

"Don't you recognize it?" Anya said, as if it were obvious. When no one seemed to know what she was talking about, she glanced over her shoulder, and said, "Get in. I'll tell you on the way."

Theo approached the driver's seat, but Dante intercepted him, grabbing the keys from him before Theo could unlock the doors.

"What are you doing?" Theo asked, incredulous. He tried to take them back, but Dante held them out of reach.

"I'm sorry," Dante said. "But you're not driving."

"Says who?" Theo shot back. "The kid gave the envelope to *me*. Which means the keys are mine."

"Let me see the envelope," said Dante.

Theo went quiet. "It's in my bag."

"No it's not," Dante said. "It's in your pocket."

Theo hesitated, then pulled the crumpled envelope out of his coat. On the front was written a single name. *Dante Berlin.*

"That's what I thought," Dante said, and opened the front door, relegating Theo to the backseat. He drove us out of the city and onto a winding country road that led us through the rolling hills, following the map toward Egmond-Binnen. The Dutch countryside was dotted with farmhouses, windmills, and wooden bridges pressed with snow, their crooked planks making our car rattle.

"A little over thirty years ago, there was an attack on the High Court," Anya said from the backseat. "There was a big trial going on with a group of Undead children who had supposedly worked for the Liberum. All of the top Monitors were there. But just minutes after they had gathered in the grand assembly room, a loud rumble shook the floor. The walls trembled, the windows shattered, and the building began to collapse in on itself."

She paused. The sound of the ice crunching beneath the tires filled the car.

"A fire raged up from the furnace, scorching the walls and filling what was left of the courthouse with smoke. A handful of Monitors on the High Court died that day, trapped in the rubble. Others were badly injured. My father has a permanent cough from the debris, and he was one of the lucky ones. He wasn't even in the courthouse when it happened, but on the street."

"My grandfather was there, too," Theo said. "That's how he lost his vision. He doesn't like to talk about it."

"Neither does my father," said Anya. "He only brings it up at family gatherings, after he's had too many drinks.

He gets especially animated at the part where he bursts through the doors into the smoky lobby and carries the receptionist outside to safety." Anya rolled her eyes. "Every year his story gets more elaborate."

"Your grandfather was there, too," Theo said, looking at me.

"Mine?" I said.

"He wasn't a sitting Court member at the time. I think he was on leave or something, but he was definitely there when it happened. Afterward, he rose to become to Head of the High Court."

"He's never mentioned anything about it," I said.

Theo's eyes lingered on me. "Why would he?" he said. "It was an awful day. He's probably trying to forget it."

I turned to Anya. "Outside of the train station, you implied that all of this has something to do with the car. How?"

"In the investigation afterward, they found the source of the explosion. A car parked in the lot beneath the building, or what was left of it—a bit of leather seat, a dented segment of the door, a hood ornament. It had been filled with explosives. And it wasn't just any car, but a custom Lancia, pure white." She ran her fingers along the edge of the window. "The exact same model and color as this one.

"They never found out who did it, or why. Only that it was probably a Monitor. They were the only ones who knew when trials took place. Plus, the car was parked in the basement lot, which means it couldn't have been an Undead."

"A Monitor with a vendetta," Theo said.

Anya ran her hand down the leather interior. "It isn't the sort of car you see every day. It seems too much of a coincidence not to mean something. . . . I suppose Monsieur could have been there at the time. He could just want to send us the message that he doesn't care for the Monitors."

"Or," Theo said, "Monsieur could have been the one who did it in the first place."

Anya lowered her eyes and nodded, as if she wished she didn't agree. "That's more likely."

"But why would he reveal such a telling detail about himself to us?" I asked. "Especially after taking such care to keep his identity hidden."

"Carelessness?" Anya offered, but I shook my head. Nothing Monsieur had done thus far had shown any sign of sloppiness. If anything, he paid too much attention to detail, giving us direction before we even realized we were lost. It felt like he had a plan for us. But to what end?

"I think it's safe to assume that anything Monsieur does is on purpose," I said. "So, say he meant to give us this clue. He must have had a good reason to do so. What about that story did he want us to know?"

Dante had remained quiet throughout the entire conversation, his brow furrowed as though he were trying to fill in the gaps in Anya's story. "After the explosion, what happened to the Undead children who were on trial?"

"They escaped. The bomb had been planted by the cell where the Undead were being held. It could have been a coincidence—"

"Or that could have been the reason why he attacked the court in the first place," Theo murmured.

"To set the Undead free," Dante said, completing his sentence.

"But why?" I wondered. No one had an answer. We all suddenly became aware of the car around us; of what it meant. To fill the silence, I turned on the radio and flipped through the talk and pop and foreign commercials until the soft beginning of a symphony floated through the speakers. I sank back into my seat, letting the landscape roll past me in time with the music. It was a beautiful day. I had almost failed to appreciate the naked trees glazed with frost, the sun glinting off of the icy patches in the pavement. I pressed my fingers to the window, feeling the cold afternoon lick the side of the car. A twinge of emptiness passed through me.

My hand recoiled. "Do you feel that?"

"Feel what?" said Dante.

Death. It reached out to me from the snowy trees up ahead, its vacancy rearranging the air around the car until everything around us felt void of life. But it wasn't the Undead; no, they had a particular vacancy to them, one that coaxed me closer, that made me want to follow them and bury them. This sensation was different; I had never experienced anything like it before. It was all-encompassing, as if a shadow of death were hanging over the earth. I didn't want go toward it; I wanted to turn around and drive as far away from it as possible.

Behind me, Anya peered out the window. "I feel it," she said.

"So do I," added Theo.

In the distance stood a sign for Egmond-Binnen. Beyond it stood the rooftops of the town. But instead of driving toward it, Dante slowed just before we reached a hidden drive overgrown with trees and brush, now heavy with snow.

"What are you doing?" I said.

Dante looked at the map, then at Pruneaux's notebook. "This is it. The last residence of Descartes in the Netherlands."

I gazed down the narrow driveway. It led into a tangled thicket of naked trees that blocked out the light, swallowing the path in its shade.

Dante turned the wheel and drove us down the bumpy road. The branches of the trees tapped the sides of the car. The air temperature dropped as we drove deeper into the tangle, its cold wisps prickling the skin on my arms. We had just rounded a curve when the road came to an abrupt end.

Dante slammed on the brakes and gripped the wheel as the car skidded out over the ice, just missing a crooked tree at the edge of the path. Behind it, a chimney rose through branches.

A tattered sign printed in Dutch was nailed to the tree: VERBODEN TOEGANG.

"No trespassing," Dante translated, yet strangely, his voice sounded softer than normal.

"Now what?" Theo said. His too, was distant, as though he weren't sitting behind me but yards and yards away.

Dante turned the engine off. "We walk."

Silence filled the air. Though I could see the trees bending in the wind, they made no sound. Even our footsteps were muffled, as if the sound were being sucked away into the hollow in the trees.

We found ourselves in front of an unassuming stone house, its earthy brown color blending into the surrounding woods. It had a sloping slate roof that had long ago sunk into disrepair, and planked shutters from which the paint had all but rotted off, as though it were trying to crumble back into the ground from which it came. There was something unnatural about this place. I didn't want to see what was inside.

Snowflakes dotted Anya's red hair. *Everything is so quiet,* her lips said, though the emptiness swallowed her voice.

Frosted weeds climbed around the gate that encircled the front of the house. In one swift motion Theo jumped over it. He walked through the overgrown garden and up the front steps, which sagged beneath his feet. They must have creaked, but I couldn't hear them. He called out to us, but his voice was so muffled that I could barely hear him either. All I could make out was the shape of his lips. *There are footprints in the snow,* he was saying. *Someone is here—*

Why couldn't I hear him? Why couldn't I hear Anya?

Before I realized what I was doing, I found myself inching toward the car. "Maybe we should go back," I said, but as the words left my lips, they disappeared, the emptiness pulling them into the house. I repeated myself, this time louder, but I could barely make out the sound of my own voice before it was sucked away. The others didn't hear me either; they were already making their way toward the house.

Sound, I thought, remembering Descartes's riddle. It was the sense that marked the first point. *Sounds, they fade to the ground, the earth's music unsung . . .*

I ran toward the house as Theo opened the front door. Heat enveloped us as we walked inside, the radiators seeping in the corner, the lights still on as though whoever lived inside had just run out on an afternoon errand.

Hello? I saw Theo shout, though the sound was sucked away.

It was a dowdy house, decorated with furniture upholstered in faded florals. There was a quilt on the sofa, coasters on the coffee table. Who could possibly live here, in this strange, soundless vacuum? It had once been Descartes's house, though that was centuries ago, and he had no living relatives. I searched the walls for some clue, but except for the peeling paper, they were bare. No photographs, no artwork, no marks of identity.

The others fanned out through the house. Theo ventured off to the left; Anya wandered through the maze of little rooms to the right. Dante gazed back at me before heading down the hallway toward the rear of the house. I went to follow him when out of the corner of my eye I saw movement. The pale specter of a woman flitted past the window—or was it a girl? She almost looked like an apparition. But when I pushed back the curtain, she was gone. Maybe I was seeing things.

I followed Dante down the hallway to a small kitchen. Anya had found her way there, too, as had Theo. They were all searching the room, as though something within it had drawn them there. The floor was tiled with a faded mosaic. All I could see of it was a yellow triangle that looked like the wing of a bird. I pushed the table and rug aside, unveiling the tiles bit by bit until I saw it: a canary inlaid in the floor.

The crest of the Nine Sisters. The same symbol of a canary had been etched into each of the clues that I had followed last semester to find the chest. Had this house once belonged to the ninth sister—the same sister who had betrayed the others and hidden the chest?

Ophelia Hart, I said, speaking her name, but the words came out soundless, pulled from my mouth by an external force. I followed it across the room to the sink, where the faintest trace of my voice seemed to echo before disappearing down the drain. The copper faucet was tarnished with patches of oxidized green. Trembling, I lowered my head to the sink and spoke to the ninth sister. *Are you still alive?*

The words left me like a long exhale, the sounds pulled from my lips before I could feel the shape of the letters on my tongue. I looked up to find Anya watching me, her eyes wide as if she suddenly realized what we were looking for.

She motioned through the window to the field out back. *The well,* she mouthed.

Descartes's riddle reverberated through my mind. *The nethers first call from their hollows by dark.* Their hollow. Just like a well. *Sounds, they fade to the ground, the earth's music unsung.* Fade to the ground. Anya had to be right.

We ran outside through the snowy field, Dante and Theo on our heels. Our footsteps were silent, the woods surrounding the house so quiet they felt fake. The well was boarded up, a layer of snow packed on top. I brushed it off and pried open the lid. Stale air gusted from the hole.

The darkness telescoped into a pool of black water. My reflection stared back at me from the bottom, though as the surface rippled, my face began to shift. The Renée in the water bent over, pressing her hands to her ears as she shouted, though no sound came out.

I raised my hand to my lips, but they were shut, my other arm by my side. I bent over my reflection, confused, when a thin thread of air seeped through my lips, pulled out of me by the darkness in the well. With it, my memories began to unravel, their sounds echoing in my mind. I heard Dante's voice, its richness filling me with warmth as I remembered the way he sounded every time he had called out to me in the woods, every time he'd whispered my name under the sheets just before morning, every time he'd told me *I love you.* But as quickly as the memories passed through me, they faded, the sounds folding in on themselves until Dante's voice was nothing more than an echo in the hole in the earth.

Then I heard him again. This time he sounded younger, more cautious. He spoke in Latin. *Desiderum*, he whispered, the word rolling off his tongue the way it had when he had whisked me into the classroom at Gottfried, pressing me against the chalkboard, our bodies smudging the word until it was illegible. I tried to hold on to the memory, but it quickly faded, and before I could do anything to stop it, another memory began to unfold.

I'm Dante, his voice said, echoing in my mind. His voice was cautious, stilted, the way he'd spoken it when we'd first met at Gottfried. *No,* I tried to say. *Not this one. Let me keep this memory.* But it, too, slipped away from me, his voice growing softer until I could barely make out the trace of his breathing.

One by one, the sounds of my past unraveled, echoing in my ears one last time before dissipating into the void. The irregular beat of his heart; the way it vibrated through me while I drifted to sleep, my head resting on his chest. The sound of his feet trudging through the snow; the wind whistling through the trees in a minor key.

They coiled out of me, pulled by some invisible force. I pressed my hands to my ears, trying to hold the sounds in, but it didn't help. All I could do was listen. I heard the sound of my grandfather rustling the newspaper in his study, the sound of Dustin bustling in the kitchen, the pots and pans clinking together in a smooth rhythm. The crackling of Anya's incense as I fell asleep in her dorm room. The Chopin nocturnes that my mother used to play on the piano. My father whistling while he washed the dishes after dinner. The *shh-shh* of the ocean sweeping the California coast in the morning, until everything was gone, all gone, and I was left in silence.

I fell back into the snow, the last thread of cold air leaving me. The world around me was so quiet it felt empty. I tried to remember the sound of my mother's voice or the song my father used to hum, but drew a blank. Dante had backed away from the edge of the well beside me, squinting into the sunlight as though he had forgotten something. *He is still here*, I thought, relieved. Even if I couldn't replay the sound of his voice in my head, I would be able to hear it again soon.

Theo and Anya lingered by the well across from me, the sun glaring off their cheeks as though it had washed them clean.

I stood, about to call out to them, when something in the distance behind Dante caught my eye. I couldn't tell what it was at first, only that the pattern of the landscape looked familiar. Maybe I had seen it on a postcard before, or in a painting or some kind of engraving....

When it finally dawned on me, I caught my breath. It couldn't be.

I pointed to the landscape behind him, but when Dante followed my gaze, instead of sharing my excitement, he only frowned.

The map, I said, but the well swallowed my voice. Didn't he see it?

I took one step to the left, then another to the right, but from either position, the view was nothing more than a pastoral winter scene. I led him to the edge of the well where the hollowness was strongest, and motioned to the mountains far off to the west.

Together, we inched back until the three rivers in the distance converged into an icy blue braid. Dante opened the chest and held it up to the horizon, comparing the map to the landscape in the distance. The three interlacing lines etched in the chest between the first and second point mimicked the braid of rivers almost exactly, the water in front of us bringing the map to life. All we had to do was venture just beyond the place where their waters converged. The second point was nestled behind it. We had found the path.

CHAPTER 8

The Visitors in the Night

THE WORLD GREW LOUDER AS WE PUSHED BACK through the brush toward the car. I began to hear the weeds and branches tangling together behind us, until the house was nothing more than a chimney rising over the trees. By the time we pulled out of the driveway and onto the road, I could hear the hum of the engine, the gravel popping beneath the tires, the squeak of the leather seats as Anya and Theo shifted their weight, the steady breathing of Dante beside me.

And yet they all sounded the same—muted and dull, their sounds inspiring nothing. The screech of the brakes no longer hurt my ears, and the lull of the wheels rolling over the pavement no longer put me at ease. I could still see the black pit of the well telescoping beneath me; I could still feel its pull on me, wrenching the voices and music from my mind, rewinding my memories until every sound from my past had vanished.

"Say my name," I whispered to Dante, relieved to hear my own voice.

"Renée," he said.

I waited, hoping it would bring back all of the sounds I had lost, but when he spoke, his words lacked any emotion. I could hear each syllable forming my name, but I couldn't detect the warmth or longing in his voice, the richness of its undertones, or the subtle lilt of his Latinate tongue, a sound I could now only vaguely recall.

Dante watched me, his face pained as he realized why I had asked him to speak. "Your hearing is dulled, isn't it?"

Instead of answering, I turned on the radio. Classical music floated out of the speakers, filling the car with cello, though to me, it sounded like nothing but noise. I waited for the music to pick up, for something to click in my mind, but the notes were hollow. I fiddled with the radio knobs, adjusting the volume, the bass, the equalizer, but nothing helped.

"Can you turn it off?" Anya said from the backseat. "I can't—it . . . it sounds like—"

"Like nothing," Theo said, completing her thought.

Dante turned to me. "I—I'm sorry," he said, though he didn't sound sorry. He didn't sound like anything. This was the world he had been inhabiting for all these years, I realized. This was what it felt like to be Undead.

"Say something else," I said, trying to convince myself that with enough time I might be able to hear the richness of his voice once more. "Keep talking to me."

"I love you," he said, but the words could have been replaced with any others with no difference. I stiffened in my seat, wanting to be stirred by his voice the way I used to be, but I couldn't feel anything. Instead, a whisper rose within me. *A part of your soul is gone,* it said. *There is no going back.*

We rode in silence, not sure where we were going, other than that we had to make our way toward the braid of rivers we'd seen from the well. All we knew was that the next point was hidden somewhere behind them. In the backseat, Theo quietly flipped through Pruneaux's notes. "There isn't any information about Descartes after he left the Netherlands," he said. "He went to Egmond-Binnen in 1649. He died a year later in Stockholm, Sweden. But as for the time in between—we have no idea where he went."

While he spoke, I could feel the pull of the Undead behind us, their vacancy lapping at me in thin threads of air.

"The Liberum," Theo said. He must have felt them, too.

Anya peered out the rear window. "But how are they so close? They couldn't have known where we were going."

"They have Pruneaux," Theo said. "After our talk with him yesterday, he must have had a good idea as to where the first point on the map would be."

"And the Monitors are probably on their trail," I said. I turned to Dante. "We have to move faster."

We drove all night and through the next day, the reverberations of the tires filling the car with white noise. It startled me, how quickly sound could be forgotten. Its absence settled in around us until it felt normal. There was no direct road leading toward the braid of rivers in the distance, which peeked in and out of view with each turn. We were forced to zigzag and circle and retrace our route, with nothing to guide us but our sight. We studied the elaborate lines etched into the chest in the shape of a bird, each line mirroring the crest of a hill, the ripples of a lake, the flat line of a valley. We could only hope that beneath the pavement there was a far more ancient path rolling out before us.

We sat in a stiff silence the entire way; even Theo, who was normally so gregarious, spent most of the ride staring out the window. Anya glanced at her watch, then quietly removed a tin from her bag. Inside were dozens of vials and plastic bags filled with pills, powders, and ointments in an assortment of colors.

Theo's attention shifted toward them. "Whoa," he said under his breath. "So those are your elixirs."

Without responding, Anya searched through them until she found three bottles. From them she measured into her palm a large yellow pill, a capsule filled with a strange green substance, and a white pill the size of a breath mint.

Theo watched her. "What are those?"

"Concentrated chrysanthemum pollen, which helps enhance your hearing," she said, swallowing the yellow pill. "A mix of blossoming algae and ginseng, which restores your memory," she said, placing the green capsule on her tongue. She picked up the white pill, holding it between her fingers. "And this is just a multivitamin," she said, washing it down with a swig of water. Though it didn't look like a multivitamin at all.

Theo scoffed. "No pill can restore your hearing. Or your memory, for that matter."

Anya only shrugged. "You're free to believe whatever you want."

Theo squinted at her, as though she had taunted him. "Fine," he said. "Let me try one."

"Who said I was offering?"

"Come on," said Theo. "You have more than enough to share."

Anya narrowed her eyes, but proceeded to drop two pills in his hand, omitting the multivitamin.

"What about the third?"

Anya hesitated. "You don't need that one," she said.

Theo shrugged. "Whatever you say." He tipped his head back and swallowed them without any water.

Anya turned to Dante and me. "And you two?"

"I'll take my chances without," Dante said.

I strained to hear the fullness of his voice, but it sounded plain, like it could have belonged to anyone. "I guess it can't hurt, right?"

I reached into the backseat, feeling the two pills drop into my palm. They went down easily. I caught Dante studying me as I took a sip of water, but I ignored his gaze. I could tell he didn't approve, that he was already having doubts about me being here with him. I turned to the window and waited for the sounds of the car to suddenly grow richer. But nothing changed.

"The effects aren't immediate," Anya said, reading my thoughts.

"How long is it supposed to take?" Theo said.

Anya shrugged. "Like everything else, we just have to wait and see."

"I don't like waiting," Theo said.

I leaned my head against the window. "Me neither."

Theo leaned over the seat. "Where'd you get all this stuff, anyway?"

"My father's store. He owns a pharmacy and convenience store in Montreal."

"Sounds like an unconventional pharmacy," Theo said. "So what else is in there? Uppers? Sleeping pills? Anything that could zonk me out for the rest of this car ride to make it a little more bearable?"

"My supplements aren't for recreation," Anya said.

"What about that one?" Theo said, nodding to the corner of her tin, where a lone black pill sat in a vial all by itself. "That one looks like it could be fun."

Anya quickly closed the tin and stowed it in her bag. "It's for emergencies."

Theo narrowed his eyes. "What kind of emergencies?"

"Ones that don't concern you," she said.

I studied her in the passenger's mirror, just as curious as Theo, but the distant look in her face made it clear that the conversation was over.

The landscape changed from the windmills and rolling hills of the Dutch countryside to the sprawling farmlands of Germany. The sun dropped behind the trees, leaving us to the purpling dusk. Though we knew we were close to where the second point should be, without light it was impossible to compare the chest to the scenery outside, so we decided to find a place to spend the night. The horizon was barren except for an orange light flickering in the distance, like a fire burning in a hearth. As we approached, I could see the reflection of windows, warm light glowing behind them. A sign hung on a post at the end of its driveway: MÄDCHEN INN.

A wooden cottage stood before us, its sides buried in layers of sloping snow, which made it look like a gingerbread house. Frost clung to the edges of the windows, giving off a warm, wintery glow. Dante knocked four times, the rap of the brass hitting the door, and the patter of footsteps that followed sounded like a distant clatter of noise.

A ruddy, matronly woman opened the door, the buttery aroma of a home-cooked meal following her. She spoke to us in German, which only Dante understood.

He spoke back to her in a perfect accent. After he finished, the woman smiled. "American?" she said, with a heavy accent. *"Willkommen, willkommen."*

She didn't ask where we came from or why we were there. Instead, she shooed us around a bare wooden table in the dining room and served us a hearty German meal of pork chops, wild mushroom soup, and spaetzle sautéed in butter. I should be have been hungry, but felt my appetite fade away once the food was before me. Anya must have felt the same way, as she pushed the vegetables around on her plate, barely touching them. Theo was the only one who was enjoying himself, his napkin tucked into the collar of his shirt, lips glossy with butter.

"Do you want that?" he said to Anya, pointing to her pork chop.

"No," she said, and slid her plate over. "How do you even have an appetite?"

"What do you mean?" Theo said. "Only one of our senses in muted. Taste is just fine. And come to think of it, I'm pretty sure those pills of yours are working, because my hearing feels clearer. I can almost hear the delicious sizzle of the cook frying up another round of pork chops in the kitchen."

I frowned. "Mine hasn't gotten any better."

Anya rolled her eyes. "Neither has mine," she said. "And that's the sound of a faucet running. Someone is washing dishes."

Theo waved her away with his fork. "You have your interpretation, I have mine."

Dante sat silently beside me, the food on his plate untouched.

Theo pointed to Dante's spaetzle with his fork. "You don't have any use for that, do you?" he asked through a full mouth, winking at me, though none of us found his joke funny.

Dante's silverware was still positioned on either side of

his place mat. "No," he said, and slid his meal over. The Undead never ate.

Theo grinned and scraped the food onto his plate. "More for me."

While the innkeeper bused our dishes, I cleared my throat. "We're travelers. We've never been to this part of Germany, and we were wondering—are there any sights in particular that we should see?"

The woman gave me a confused look, then turned to Dante. He translated, speaking in German. The woman's face grew animated as she responded.

Dante listened, then said, "She's talking about local towns and shopping." He paused while she spoke, then continued, "She's telling us about all of the good restaurants nearby...and biergartens...."

"What about natural sights?" I said. "Can you ask her if there are any in particular that stand out?"

Just before Dante relayed my question to the innkeeper, Theo wiped his mouth on the back of his sleeve. "Why don't you ask her what places we should *avoid*?" he interjected. "If the second point is anything like the place we just came from, I doubt it's a tourist destination."

Dante paused, nodding in agreement, then repeated what Theo said to the woman.

She paused, and for the first time since she had invited us in, she took a long look at each of us, as if she suddenly saw something now that she hadn't seen before. *"Where the rivers meet,"* Dante translated.

"The rivers?" Anya repeated, unable to hide her excitement. Her eyes met ours over the table. "How do we—?" she began to ask, but the innkeeper backed away, shaking her head.

"I don't like to talk of such places," Dante said, translating her words.

She gave us our keys and pointed us upstairs. Before we could ask anything more, she bid us good night.

Our room had four nesting beds, each made of whittled wood, as if they belonged in a dollhouse. We dropped our bags, and while the others began to unpack and wash up, Anya pulled me out into the hallway.

"Do you remember the other night in Paris?" she said. "When I left?"

I nodded.

"I went to the Monitor Archive. They have records there for all of the cases heard by the High Court. I thought maybe they would have something on Theo. And they did. Kind of." She slipped a document from inside her coat and handed it to me.

I unfolded it and scanned the pages. Most of it consisted of Theo's physical and educational details. Height, weight, body mass index, hair and eye color, spoken languages, specialized skill sets. The year he enrolled at St. Clément; the year he dropped out. The year he was awarded his Spade, and a list of the members who witnessed it, my grandfather among them. And then I saw it. Halfway down the page, in thin red letters. *Current status: DISBARRED.*

So I'd been right. I *had* seen him sanding the red dye from his Spade that night. I felt a twinge of excitement as I turned the page, eager to see what he had done to deserve such a punishment, but the rest of the document was blacked out, the words CLASSIFIED BY ORDER OF THE HIGH COURT stamped beside it.

I flipped the sheet over, confused. "What—?" I looked up at Anya. "What does this mean?"

"I don't know," she said, biting her lip. "But you were right about his Spade. I should have believed you."

"I wasn't even sure if I believed myself," I said with a shrug. "So where can we get classified information?"

"Nowhere," Anya said. "Only the members of the High Court have access to it. Usually they only classify cases that involve major things like organized criminal attacks or plots they uncovered by the Liberum—things where the investigation is still ongoing and leaked information would compromise the case. But this—it's very odd. I don't know what Theo was doing, but whatever it was must have been bad. Very bad."

"We have to confront him," I said. "He's been lying to us this whole time."

"No," Anya said, her eyes wide. "We can't do that. What if he gets upset and leaves?"

"Then he'll be gone," I said, confused. "So what? He's been a little helpful, but we'll get by without him. It would probably be better, actually."

Anya shook her head. "I saw his cards. He has something

dark in his past, something complicated. It isn't just about right and wrong; it's unresolved. Whatever he did—that's the reason why he's here with us. It's why he wants to find the Netherworld, why he's willing to sacrifice his life for it. That's why Monsieur sent us to him. Because he knew that Theo wouldn't just be able to help us, but that he would have a stake in it."

I wanted to ask her why she, too, was willing to sacrifice her life to go to the Netherworld, but before I could speak, the door swung open.

"What's going on out here?" Theo asked, leaning on the handle of his Spade.

Anya gave me a hard look, as if to say *Not yet*, and then smiled and slipped her deck of tarot cards from her pocket. "I was trying to convince her to let me read her fortune," she said, stepping back into the room, and turned to Dante, who was sitting at a desk reading about Descartes. "But she said it's your turn."

He leaned back in his chair. "I don't think so. That kind of stuff isn't for me."

"What kind of *stuff*?" Anya said, narrowing her eyes.

"Divining magic," said Dante. "Fate. I like to believe that I'm in control of my own future."

"If you don't believe, then what's the harm?"

Dante looked to me for help, but instead of agreeing with him, I hesitated. A few years ago, I had been the sort of person who would have groaned at the idea of going to a séance or a fortune teller, and I certainly never would have elected to have my fortune read through a deck of cards. But that was before I had found out about the Undead, before I had fallen in love with Dante, before I'd realized that belief in the unknown was all we had left to cling to. Would I ever hear the richness of Dante's voice again? Would I ever be able to fall asleep to the comforting sound of the rain pounding against the roof, or to the arrhythmic beat of Dante's heart? I wanted to know if all of this was worth it.

"It can't hurt, can it?" I said.

My response surprised him. Without taking his eyes off mine, he answered. "No," he said. "I suppose not."

Anya's face brightened. She pushed her hair behind her ears, stretched her fingers as though she were about to perform some gymnastic feat, then stacked the deck and held it out to Dante, giving him the same instructions she had given Theo.

He slipped a card from the middle and held it to his forehead for us to see. Drawn on the other side was an image of a man hanging by his feet on a wooden cross. The script at the bottom read: *The Hanged Man.*

Placing it back in with the others, he shuffled, the cards fluttering between his fingers, then cut the deck three times. Anya gathered them with care, and, one by one, laid the cards.

A knot formed in my stomach when The Hanged Man came out first.

"From the beginning, suffering has carved the shape of your life," Anya said. "You are strong, but have been forced to endure much. Too much."

The next card revealed an image of a dead man stuck with swords, his insides bleeding out onto the dirt. *Ten of Swords.*

"The Lord of Ruin," Anya said, touching the edge of the card.

I caught the gasp before it left my lips.

It was followed by the *Five of Pentacles*, two men wandering through the snow in tattered clothes, their faces forlorn and shrouded by cloaks.

The Lovers came next. A nude man and woman standing at the foot of a lush garden. I tilted my head to see it better, for it was laid out upside down.

"You have fallen in love," Anya said. She traced the corner of the card thoughtfully.

I let out a sigh of relief, and smiled to myself. I was in his cards. Our love was written. I gripped the sides of the chair and braced myself for the next card, but Anya lingered. Her eyes darted to mine as if she had seen something awful and wasn't sure if she should tell me.

"But it's upside down," she continued. "Which means love lost."

"What?" I whispered. "No."

Anya bit her lip. *I'm sorry*, her eyes seemed to say, but she continued.

She laid out two more cards. *Strength*, an image of a lion with a goddess, and the *Three of Swords*, displaying a heart pierced with three swords.

"You are searching for something. You will embark on a great journey, in which you show great strength and valor. Despite this, however, you will become lost."

Up until then, Dante hadn't uttered a word. Finally, he spoke. "Lost? How so?"

Anya touched the wounded heart on the last card. "It could mean literally lost, or emotionally. Or both."

Finally, she dealt the last card. When she placed it on the table, she let out a gasp.

The Tower. A lone white tower perched atop a mountain. Storm clouds raged overhead, and a bolt of lighting stuck the top, making the tower crumble.

Anya swallowed.

"The darkest card of them all," she said. "Death and ruin."

I felt light-headed.

"I'm just an amateur," Anya said in apology. "The reading was probably faulty. You're Undead, after all, so the lifeline spread might not work on you. We could do it again. I could try a different card layout."

"It's fine," Dante said. "They're just cards." Though the way his body grew tense made me wonder if he really believed that anymore.

Anya nodded, too eager to agree with him. "No one's

future is written in stone." She leaned over the table to gather the cards, but Dante stopped her.

"Don't," he said. "I want to look at them." He traced his finger around the edge of the tower, his skin the same shade of white as the stone. "The past can be forgotten, altered and washed away by time and trauma. And the future is just a guess, a faraway point on a map. All that's certain is what's happening right now, this very moment." He slid his hand back from the cards, his eyes locking with mine. "In that way, we're no different than anyone else."

That night I dreamed of death. I was standing on the Gottfried campus once again, the frozen lake stretching out before me, its surface petrified to a deep gray. A thudding filled the air. Louder, louder, until the ice buckled, and a slick white hand rose from the gash.

Noah pulled himself up from the ice, his eyes snapping open. He gazed at me, his lips calling my name. In a flash, he was running through the woods, following a trail of footprints in the snow. Time seemed to pass quickly around him, the sun rotating over the sky as night fell. As the days passed, and the footprints tapered off into multiple directions, Noah slowed. He grew lost, wandering in circles. I watched him kneel over the snow, exhausted but unable to sleep. His throat was parched and dry; he dug his fingers into the ice and raised a handful to his mouth before spitting it out. Nothing could give him relief. His hands trembled. He studied them, his once olive skin now as white as the snow, the veins pulsing cold blood up his arms. Another flash and it was nighttime. A warm glow emanated through the trees. Noah trudged toward it until a lodge materialized out of the darkness.

He paused when he reached the front door, the light slanting out from the windows in two long bars. He ran his hands along the smooth wooden handles, then opened the door and stepped inside.

The brightness of the place dazed him, the plush furniture and wooden decor of the lobby making him look more out of place than ever before. He caught a glimpse of his reflection in the mirror on the far side of the lobby. The sight of his gaunt face and soiled clothes startled him. He pushed his auburn hair away from his face, trying to make himself look like the person he had once been.

At the front desk, the concierge studied his clothes, which were dripping water on the carpet. "May I help you?"

"I—" Noah said, his voice cracking. "I would like to make a call."

The concierge pondered his request, then lifted a telephone from beneath the desk.

While the concierge turned away, eyeing him over his shoulder, Noah dialed a Quebec number. It rang twice before a man picked up. *"Oui, allo?"* Noah's father.

Noah moved his lips as if he wanted to respond, but said nothing.

"*Allo?*"

Noah listened for a moment more before hanging up. "*Merci,*" he said to the concierge, reverting to his native Quebecois French. "I—I mean, thank you."

He rushed outside. When he was out of sight, he pressed himself against the side of the lodge and sank to the snow, his chest collapsing. His heart thudded irregularly, like a hand pounding against his ribs, trying to break free.

He looked up, his eyes dilating. "Renée," he said. "I'm coming for you."

I woke in the middle of the night, the bed creaking beneath me. I reached for Dante's arms, which had been wrapped around me when I fell asleep, but they were no longer there. I sat up. Dante was sitting at the desk, where the tarot cards were still laid out.

"Another nightmare?" he said.

"Yes," I said, wondering if I had spoken Noah's name aloud.

"About?"

I tried to shake Noah from my head, but his presence haunted me. What I'd seen had been nothing more than a dream, though it might as well have been real. He was out there somewhere, lost, searching, his life gone but his body still pressing forward, all because of me. "I can't remember."

"Those are the most frightening kind," Dante said. His eyes lingered on me, then turned to the chest, which he was holding in his hands, tracing the map inside as if memorizing its etchings.

"In case we lose it," he said, referring to Monsieur's warning.

A draft floated in from the balcony. Even beneath the heavy quilt, my arms trembled with the cold. I slipped out of bed and went to close the doors, but they were already shut. I stared out into the night. The German countryside was dark. I couldn't see anything. I held my hand up to the glass. The draft seeped through the panes and tickled my fingers, making them curl into a fist. Goose bumps traveled up my arms. I knew this feeling. The Undead.

Theo sat up in bed and immediately reached for his Spade, which was leaning against the wall. He must have felt them, too. Anya woke with him. "What's happening?" she asked, rubbing her eyes.

"They're here," I whispered.

It was too late to escape. I could feel their presence descending on us like a dark cloud rolling in on the horizon. There must have been dozens of them. I could feel their force, their desperation.

We barely had time to speak. Dante shoved the chest into his bag while I ran to the bed and slipped the shovel out from beneath my pillow. The small black box was sitting behind it. I didn't care if Monsieur thought we should let the Undead take what they wished; I wasn't letting them have anything. I stuffed it into my bag, slipping out a roll of gauze from the side pocket, and held up my shovel.

Someone pounded on the door downstairs. A chill filled the room.

Dante's face had become hard and merciless, his eyes clouding as gray began to creep over his irises. His gaze drifted to the shovel in my hand. It seemed to surprise him, as if he suddenly remembered that I was trained to bury people just like him. And even though we stood only a few feet apart, for a moment, the distance between us felt impossibly vast.

Theo waited by the side of the door, gripping his Spade. Anya stood behind him, her shovel raised. "There must be dozens of them," Anya said.

"We have to use the staircase and the hallway to our advantage," Theo said. "We wait for them to come to us so they can't surround us. Then we'll push them down the stairs and into the basement, and put them to rest."

Outside, something scurried over the balcony. A flash of white flitted past the window. Then another. I steadied myself, feeling the gauze in my pocket. A thin wisp of air beckoned me toward the window. I pushed back the curtain with the tip of my shovel, and peered out at the balcony. It looked empty. Had I been seeing things? Below, the ground was a good twenty feet away. They couldn't have scaled it, I thought. But just before I turned around, something crashed through the window.

I dove to the ground as glass shattered around me. The presence of the Undead filled the room. The tarot cards blew off the table. I heard a scream downstairs and the pitter-patter of bare feet running up the staircase. On the other side of the room, the door burst open.

I scrambled to my feet. A pair of clouded eyes appeared through the darkness in the hallway. Followed by another, and another. From afar they looked like young boys, nothing more than children. As they drew closer, I could see their eyes, vacant and clouded with gray, their hollow cheeks and skin so ghastly in color that I could almost see the veins beneath.

They swarmed inside, some so far decayed that they had gone blind. They knocked over the furniture, the fixtures, and the lamps until the room went dark.

They clawed at my legs, my arms, my clothes; they scratched at my skin, their cold fingers making me cringe. Across the room, I saw Anya whispering to the Undead boys, trying to coax them away from us as she had done back in Montreal, but there were too many for her to control. Their raspy breathing and scraping of their feet against the floor drowned out her voice.

I kicked them off, trying to press them toward the door with my shovel, but they were resilient. Three of them sprang back and tried to grab the handle from me. I swung wildly, thrusting them away, but they took hold of it, their fingers pulling the metal face until it fell from my grasp and clattered under the bed.

The three Undead rushed at me, their limbs a wild thrash of white. I made for the bed, where I tried to reach for my shovel beneath the frame, but before I could take hold of it, they knocked me onto the bed. I tried to twist out of their grip as they clawed up my legs, their tiny fingers scratching at my throat. I felt their cold breath beating against my collarbone, their hands pressing against my ribs, pushing the air out of me until my lips parted against their will. A thin coil of air began to unravel inside me. I swallowed. They were going to take my soul.

This is what I knew: the only way to kill an Undead was to bury him beneath the earth, set him on fire, or mummify him. We were on the second floor, far from a basement or a well, and I didn't have a lighter—which left only one option.

The fingers of the Undead clawed at my lips. I turned my cheek and patted at the mattress until I found a sheet hanging off the side of the bed. I swung the sheet over them, and using all my force, I twisted their bodies within it.

They kicked and grasped at the air, trying to tear the cloth off, but I held fast, and removing the roll of gauze from my pocket, I began to wildly wrap them from head to toe like I had learned in my burial classes at St. Clément. They grew weak. Their limbs slowed until I was able to push them off of me and wrap them tighter. They writhed beneath my arms. One of their fists shot out from beneath the sheet. It was half the size of mine, barely large enough to have belonged to a ten-year-old. I winced and looked away. For once I was thankful for darkness. I didn't want to see their faces; to see their eyes grow red and bloodshot before the last vestiges of life left them. They had once been children, too. When their bodies went limp, I let go of the sheet and backed away.

I grabbed my shovel from beneath the bed and braced myself to meet the others head-on, but when I turned, I was alone. A group of Undead was by the door, fighting to get past Anya and Theo, and another group was struggling by the balcony, but for some reason no more of the boys were coming after me. For a moment I thought I saw two Undead boys standing in front of me, directing the Undead in the other direction. Why weren't they attacking? One looked taller than any of the other Undead boys working for the Liberum. The other was around my height. One of them spoke to the Undead boys before him, and pointed to the balcony. "The Undead is the one that we want," I heard him say.

He was talking about Dante. I searched the room for him amidst the faces of the Undead, but they all looked the same: cold, empty, lifeless. Their pale skin was all I could see through the darkness—a face, an arm, a bare foot lying on the floor in a tangle of sheets and gauze, shuddering as the life left it. A group of Undead rifled through the dresser drawers, pulling them out of their tracks and tossing them on the floor before moving on to search beneath the beds. They were looking for the chest. Above it all I saw the glint of Theo's Spade as it cut through the air, knocking an Undead boy out of the way. I heard Anya shout to him. They were fighting off a handful of Undead, pressing them out the door and into the hallway.

"Force them into the basement!" Theo shouted over the fray.

Dante was standing by the balcony, his tall silhouette curled over as dozens of Undead boys tried to pin him down. Then one of them felt the shape of the chest inside his bag. "It's here!" one of the boys said. He snatched the bag from Dante's shoulder, opening it to make sure it contained what they were looking for, then tucked it away beneath his coat while the others pulled at Dante's hair, his clothes, his arms, dragging him toward the broken window. But why? Why were they taking him, too?

"Dante!" I screamed, and tried to run toward him when two hands gripped my arms.

I lashed out at the Undead behind me, hitting him with my shovel, only to find that it was Theo, his lip bleeding, his face glistening with sweat. Still, he held on to me.

"What are you doing?" I cried. "They're surrounding Dante. I have to help him."

"I'm trying to help you," said Theo. "There's too many. They'll kill you."

I squirmed, trying to wrestle myself free, but his fingers dug into my skin. On the other side of the room, I could see Anya pressing a tangle of Undead out the door.

"Get off of me!" I tried to twist my arms from his grasp, but Theo held tight. "They're taking him! They could kill him!"

"Don't be stupid," he said in my ear. "He's one of them. The Undead won't kill him. But they will kill you. Let him go."

But Theo was wrong. Though they couldn't take his soul, they could take him to the Liberum, who were known to kill their own kind. They could bury him or set him on fire, mummify him or force him underground. . . .

I struggled against Theo, unable to do anything while the Undead boys dragged Dante over the broken glass of the balcony window. Just before they pulled him over the threshold, Dante caught my eye. *Let me go*, he mouthed.

When I finally wriggled free, the Undead had disappeared over the railing. The ground was a twenty-foot drop away, the snow littered with tiny footprints. For a moment, I considered risking it, but quickly changed my mind. For the Undead, there was no threat of injury or death; they were already dead.

I watched them run toward the road, dragging Dante with them through the snow. And then they stopped.

Nine hooded figures emerged from the night, their bodies so dark they looked like an extension of the shadows. The Brothers of the Liberum. Their black cloaks slithered over the snow behind them. Beneath each hood I glimpsed a pair of thin blue lips and a hollow nose, which looked as if it had been decaying from the inside out. They walked toward the Undead boys, their feet barely making an imprint in the snow.

I gripped the railing. In the light from the inn I could just make out the fear in Dante's face. He twisted out of their grip and turned, locking eyes with mine. He no longer looked scared, but fierce.

The black cloaks of the Liberum swept toward him. Their shadows stretched across the snow, engulfing him in darkness. The high-pitched cry of the Undead boys sounded through the night. And like a cold gust of wind, they were gone.

I ran back inside, ready to gather my things and follow them, when I spotted a dusty handprint on the wall. Dante's handprint. Suddenly, I remembered Dante's bag, with the chest inside. Had they taken that, too? I ran to his bed, where he'd kept it, but found nothing. The tarot cards were scattered across the floor, all of them save for one. I picked it up and traced the shape of the white tower, the heavy clouds lingering above, the lightning bolt that struck the stone, sending a fissure all the way down the middle.

Anya burst into the room. "I was trying to push them into the basement, when they just stopped fighting and retreated. Did they take something?" she said. "What's missing?"

"Do you still have the chest?" Theo said.

It was gone, though I barely had the energy to tell them now. "No," I said, my voice cracking.

Anya's face sank. "And what about the black box?"

My hands trembled as I lowered my bag from my shoulder and took out the small black box. "I still have it."

Anya frowned. "But Monsieur said the Undead would take two things from us."

"Maybe he was wrong," Theo said.

The words that Anya had uttered during Dante's tarot card reading echoed in my head. *You will become lost.* Only now did I understand what that had meant.

I shook my head. "No," I said. "They took Dante."

CHAPTER 9

The Dead Earth

I COULDN'T TRY TO GET DANTE BACK. THE LIBERUM would kill me. The best thing we could do was go on without Dante, and make our way toward the second point with the hope that he would find his way back to me. That's what Theo and Anya told me as they dragged me back into the inn after I'd run after the Undead, following their vacancy through the night. "We know exactly what they want and where they're headed—toward the second point," Theo said. "The Liberum have been searching for eternal life for centuries; the only reason they've been following us in the first place is to get the chest and find the Netherworld. So it's not like we don't know where they're taking him."

"But why *did* they take him?" I said. "Why didn't they take the box instead?"

"They probably don't know about it," Anya said. "You've barely showed it to anyone."

"That still doesn't answer my question."

Theo sighed. "I don't see why any of this matters. We can't change what happened. All we can do is go forward."

"How are we even supposed to start looking for the second point without the chest?" I demanded. "You saw Pruneaux's notes on Descartes's life. There's no information about where he traveled to after Egmond-Binnen. Which means that the only way we can find the rest of the points is to follow the clues on the map."

"I practically have that map memorized," Theo said. "And I know you do, too."

"So do I," Anya said.

"See?" Theo said. "Which means we all know that the second point lies just beyond the braid of rivers we saw from the well. Once we find that, we're set."

"The major markings I have memorized, yes," I said, "But those etchings were complex. It's not like there's going to be a billboard advertising where the next point is. It could be anywhere beyond those rivers, and without the exact context of the map, we'll just be wandering aimlessly. We don't even know what we're looking for."

Theo squinted at me. "So you have a better idea, then?"

"I would have stopped the Undead from taking Dante and the chest in the first place," I countered. "You could have helped, but instead you held me back."

"Because there were too many of them. They would have taken you, too."

"I wish they had," I said miserably.

"No," Theo said. "You don't. And Dante wouldn't have wanted that either."

"Don't you dare try and tell me what Dante would or wouldn't have wanted."

"But you can't deny it, can you?"

I faltered, not wanting to admit that he was right.

"Maybe it's for the better," Anya said. "Remember what Monsieur's note said?"

"Exactly," Theo said. "Now come on, let's go inside and figure out our next move."

The inn was bustling, the other guests shuffling around the halls, talking to each other in hushed German. The local police arrived. They surveyed the scene: the broken glass, the tangled sheets still left on the floor from which the Undead boys had extricated their dead and carried them away. The police questioned us about the break-in, asking if we recognized any of the intruders; if we could describe them; if they had taken anything. "No," we lied. "No, we can't describe them, it was too dark." We glanced at each other. "No. They didn't take anything."

Downstairs, the innkeeper sobbed while the police interviewed her. She would barely notice if only three of us checked out tomorrow.

We huddled in our room and waited for the police to leave or the sun to rise, whichever came first. Theo lay on his bed, studying the black box, while Anya gathered her tarot cards from the floor and began to shuffle them. I watched her lay them out.

"What's going to happen?" I said by the balcony, where the night wind blew in from the broken windows.

Anya picked at her nail polish. "I don't know," she said, and turned over the first card.

I almost wanted her to read my own fortune, but was too scared that I would find out exactly what I had been dreading. That Dante would die. That I would live. That I would be forced to go on without him.

"Whose fortune are you reading?" Theo asked.

"My own," Anya said, turning over the second card, then the third. "Though I worry it's too biased. Many of the cards can be read both positively and negatively, depending on the context."

Theo jumped off the bed and leaned over her. "Well, I can help with that," he said. "Let me try." Before Anya could protest, he pointed to the first card. "So that one represents you, right? *The Sorcerer.* That means that you're a witch. Just like I said earlier."

He studied the second card, rubbing his chin. "You were always lonely as a child. You thought you weren't good at anything." Theo squinted at the next card. "You were depressed. You tried to kill yourself." The smirk faded from Theo's face as he looked up at her. "Is that true?"

Anya swallowed, averting her eyes, but said nothing. Quickly, she turned over the next card.

"You went to school. You were happier there." At the next card, Theo scratched his head. "And then something happened. Something terrible."

Anya bit her lip, hesitating before flipping the next card. "A woman?" Theo said. "I don't know what that means." Before he could go on, Anya flipped the next card, as though she didn't want to dwell on the one previous. "Death?" Theo studied the new image. "A plague. A woman is dying of a plague?" He furrowed his brow. "Or maybe it isn't a plague, but an illness. And it's not just a woman, but someone you know. A grandmother—no, a mother. Your mother is dying of an illness?"

Anya averted her eyes and began fidgeting with her sleeve, her chipped polish mirroring the black spades on the card. Is that why she wanted to find the Netherworld, because her mother was dying? But how would that help her mother?

Her face grew red under his scrutiny, but she quickly gathered her composure. "Of course not," she said, and swept up the cards, stacking the deck back into its box. "Your reading was totally off. That just proves how complex the art of tarot is."

Our eyes lingered on her as she bent over her bag and began packing her things. As the night sky brightened to morning, the German police filed back into their cars and started their engines. While they drove off, I felt the last of the Undead's presence blowing over the countryside with the clouds.

Anya dug through her tin, measuring out three more pills, which she threw back with a sip of water. "We'd better go," she said. "Make full use of the light while we have it."

But the sun barely rose that day. The sky clouded over,

sweeping the sun behind a gray blur. The landscape was drained of color. The air lost its woodsy aroma. Without Dante, all of the life had withered from the world, leaving nothing but a bleary sun staring down at us like the eye of the Liberum. The snow had covered the tracks of the Undead, leaving the hills a pristine white.

From where we were standing, we could see the frozen banks of one of the three rivers we'd spotted from the well. It wove in and out of the rolling landscape, its water a deep blue. "*Where the rivers meet,*" Theo said. We trudged toward it, hoping that from there, we'd be able to see the spot on the horizon where its water intersected with the two rivers to form a braid. But when we reached its shore, all we could see were more hills.

"This is useless," Theo said.

"Well, we know we have to walk either up or down the side of the river," Anya said. "We just have to pick the right direction."

"And how are we supposed to do that?" Theo said. "It could be miles before we reach the braid."

Anya peered at the horizon. "I think it's downstream. There are fewer hills there. Which means there's more space for them to flow together."

"That also means they have more space to spread apart," Theo countered.

I was about to weigh in when I saw a flash of blue. While Theo and Anya argued, I headed downstream, toward the icy brush by the riverbank. A piece of blue clothing was caught on a branch. I felt sick. I knew that fabric well. My hands trembled as I pulled it from the weeds and held it up, the wind blowing the fabric into the shape of a coat. One that belonged to Dante. It was crumpled and stained with dirt, as if he'd been dragged through the mud on his chest. I raised it to my face, breathing in the woodsy smell of Dante that still clung to the collar.

The Undead had come this way. Panic rose within me as I searched the snow for any trace of Dante. They couldn't have buried him, I told myself. The snow was too fresh for them to have done so without leaving a mound.

Behind me, Theo and Anya continued to argue.

"How are you so sure?" Theo said. "Did you consult your cards?"

"I just have a feeling about it," Anya said.

"What if your feeling is wrong? We could be walking for hours before we realize we're wrong—" Theo began to say, but I cut him off.

"It's this way," I called out to them, and held up the coat. "It's Dante's," I said, my eyes watering in the wind. "The Undead must have been looking for the second point, too. Why else would they travel by the riverbank?"

Anya examined the stains. "I'm sure he's fine," she said. "He doesn't feel the cold weather, right? He probably left it behind for you to find."

I clutched the fabric as if it were Dante's hand. I wanted to believe her. "He's trying to help us," I said. The thought warmed me; it made me feel like he was still here with us.

We left our car behind, and traveled down the bank by foot. All the while, I scanned the snow around us, searching for another sign of Dante.

"At least we haven't found his ashes yet," Theo said, watching me. "Or any trace of a burial. Without that, there's always hope."

"Don't be cruel," Anya said.

Just the mention of Dante's ashes sent my imagination into a spiral. I thought of the Undead boys dragging him behind them by the hair; I thought of the Liberum, their cloaks sweeping over the snow as they walked toward him. And then...

"I was just being honest," Theo said.

"I didn't realize you knew how," I said, still sore with him from the night before.

Theo spun around. "On the contrary, it seems that I'm the only one of us who's living in reality. You don't know that Dante is leaving things behind for us. That was just a suggestion that Anya offered to make you feel better."

"So, what—you think he's dead? That the Liberum took him just to—to—" My voice caught in my throat.

"No, I'm just saying that you should prepare yourself for the worst. He's with the Liberum, after all. I don't think they're going to be giving him the first-class treatment."

"Then why did you stop me?" I demanded. "I could have helped him. I could have fought them off."

"No," Theo said. "You couldn't have. I saw how many of them there were. They knew what they wanted. You should consider yourself lucky that they went for Dante instead of you."

But I ignored him. "You could have helped me," I said. "The three of us could have fought them off. You just didn't want to. You've never liked Dante. You *wanted* them to take him."

"Of course I never liked him," Theo said. "But that has nothing to do with this." Theo took a long swig from his water bottle. "Monsieur told us to let the Undead take him from us. So let them have him."

"I was fine with trusting Monsieur when it was all about plane tickets and rental cars," I said. "But why should I trust him when he told us to let the Undead take Dante? We don't even know who he is. He could be working for the Liberum. I wouldn't be surprised if he's been feeding them information this entire time. Maybe that's why he told us to let them take Dante. Because he's trying to sabotage us."

"That doesn't make any sense," Theo said. "Monsieur clearly knows where we are at all times, and where we're heading. If Monsieur wanted to help the Liberum, why would he wait until now to lead them to us—when it would have been a lot easier in Paris, or in Pilgrim?"

"I don't know," I said. "Maybe he's sadistic. Maybe he wants to see us slowly die off. I mean, what do we really know about him? He's rich. He's a criminal. He doesn't want anyone to know his identity. Think about it. The Undead were following us. How? They can't sense us. Some- one has to be telling them. Plus, Monsieur knew that they were going to take something from us. He couldn't have known that through intuition."

Theo didn't have an answer. "All I'm saying is that no human, especially one who used to be a Monitor, would want to help the Liberum. Even most of their fellow Undead are scared of them." He jabbed his Spade into the snow, wielding it like a walking stick. "I don't have any good reason, and I probably won't be able to convince you, but I believe that Monsieur still has our best interest at heart. Even if he is telling the Liberum where we are, it could be for our own good."

I was about to protest when Theo held up his hand. "Just hear me out. What if Monsieur knew that the members of the High Court were on our tail, that they were following Dante's presence? So, to help us, Monsieur left a note for the Liberum, telling them where we were going, and knowing that if they followed us, their presence would distract the High Court from Dante. After all, the High Court have been wanting to catch and bury the Liberum for decades. And we haven't seen the Monitors since Paris, right? So maybe it worked."

I rolled my eyes. "That's far-fetched at best—"

But Theo cut me off. "And maybe Monsieur then found out that the High Court was coming here, soon, and that when they found us, they would bury Dante. So Monsieur left a note for the Liberum, telling them to take Dante from us. But it was in our best interest, see? Because now, if the members of the High Court find us, they won't find Dante."

I let out an incredulous laugh. "Where are the Monitors, then?" I said. "If they're so close, why aren't they here yet?"

Theo turned to the hills. "Be careful," he said. "The day isn't over yet."

"And in this theory of yours," I continued, "why would Monsieur think that Dante would be safer with the Liberum than with the High Court?"

"Because the High Court would bury him immediately. They're not looking for the Netherworld or the chest; their only goal is to find dangerous Undead and bury them. And to them, Dante qualifies as that. But the Liberum could use Dante. He could help them find the Netherworld. He's like them, after all. They all want to find the same thing."

The cold made my throat burn. "Dante is nothing like them. The Liberum are lifeless, sallow, inhuman...."

But Theo only laughed. "Dante's life is already long past. He's decaying. He knows it. He told you to let him go just before the Undead swept him out the window. Remember? I was just trying to save your life."

My muscles tightened. *"Decaying?"* I threw my bag to the ground and lunged at Theo. I heard the punch before I felt it. A loud crunch, followed by a shout. Theo stumbled back, clutching his nose. Blood trickled through his fingers. My hand stung. I held it to my chest and inched away from him. Theo looked up at me with surprise, though his face quickly hardened with anger. He wiped the blood from his nose, smearing it across his face, and ran at me.

He grabbed hold of my hair and wrestled me to the ground, our bodies sinking in the snow.

"Stop it!" Anya shouted. "Stop it!"

But neither of us listened. Theo was stronger than his skinny frame suggested. I swung at him, but he ducked out of the way, then caught my arm and twisted it behind my back. A twinge of pain ran up my shoulder. I lashed back at him, trying to free myself from his grip, but he held on tight.

"You're a criminal!" I shouted at him. "Your Spade doesn't even need to be dyed red for me to see who you really are."

"Shut up," he cried.

But I didn't stop. "You're worse than the Undead. You talk about them like you're better but you're nothing. You have no friends, you barely have any family. All you have are enemies—"

Before I could finish my sentence, Theo threw me forward and, grasping my neck, buried my face in the snow. The ice burned my cheeks.

"You don't know anything about me," he said. "You don't!"

I wriggled free and jumped back, wiping the dirt and water from my eyes. I felt something trickle down the top of my lip. I licked it, tasting the metallic tang of blood. Theo stood up, a plume of red dripping from his nose. But all I could see when I looked at it was the fleck of red on

Theo's Spade. The classified file Anya had found on him in Paris. The smug look that spread over his face when I had confronted him about it. I charged him, bowling him over and pinning him to the ground.

He covered his face with his arms while I threw my fists at him. "What did you do?" I shouted, my hair wild in front of my face. "Why are you even here? What do you want from us?"

"I want the same thing as you," he said through his arms. "I want a fresh start."

I collapsed into the snow beside him, breathless. My cheeks stung from the ice; my hand throbbed from punching Theo in the nose. The rest of my body ached with exhaustion. I licked the edge of my lip where it was bleeding.

Theo sat up, brushing himself off as he turned to me. He pressed his nose to stop the bleeding. "Is that so much to ask?"

I was too tired to respond. I hoisted myself up, brushing the dirt from my pants, and then I saw a bit of brown cloth by the riverbank, half-covered by fresh snowfall. I ran to it, recognizing its weave the moment I touched it. A scrap of cotton ripped from Dante's shirt.

"You were right," I said to Anya. "He's showing us the way."

We followed the river through the valley until the hills cleared and the sight before us made us go still. Cutting through the snow in the distance were three rivers, their blue waters winding together like ropes, just like the engravings on the inside of the chest. I clutched the cloth in my hand, imagining that Dante was standing beside me.

"The braid of rivers," Anya said. "We found it."

"The second point should be just beyond the point where they meet," Theo said.

"But where?" I said. I tried to remember the rest of the lines etched into the chest, but couldn't recall all of the details. I had a vague recollection of a set of straight lines etched around the second point in the chest, like a naked forest, but there were no trees in front of us. Perhaps I was mistaken; perhaps that etching was around the third point, or perhaps it didn't refer to trees at all.

We made our way toward the point where the three rivers intersected, walking tentatively over the icy rocks that provided the only crossing over the water. When we reached the other side, what looked like a vast snowy valley was actually a white forest, the land studded with naked birch trees, their wood so ashen that I could barely distinguish them from the snow.

"Trees," I whispered. Maybe I had been right about the lines etched into the chest.

"I remember those," Anya said beside me. "They look just like the lines in the chest. The next point is somewhere in the middle."

At the foot of the woods, another scrap of brown cloth dangled in the branches of a tree. I ran to it and delicately untangled its threads. It was another shred of Dante's shirt, ice and mud caked onto it as though it had been dragged through the snow. I pressed it between my fingers, its coldness reminding me of Dante's palms, and peered through the birches. The woods were so white they blended into the ground, as though they were a mirage. A dry wind swept through them, so stale that it wicked the moisture from my lips, leaving them strangely parched. A voice within me warned me not to go inside, but I ignored it. "Come on," I said. "We're almost there."

As we crept inside, a terrible stillness filled the woods. The air grew dry and thin. There was a sour taste to it— or perhaps it wasn't a taste at all, but a lack thereof, like the starchy aftertaste of waking up after a long sleep. The deeper we ventured, the more it enveloped me, seeping through my lips until my mouth grew parched and cottony, and my tongue grew as dry as sandpaper.

Theo licked his lips and glanced around the pale trees, looking for some clue as to what we should do next. "This is taste, right?" he said. "So what are we looking for exactly?"

The nethers, they first call from their hollows by dark, I thought to myself. "A hollow," I said, remembering the next piece of Descartes's riddle. *Then taste, until food is but dirt on the tongue.*

"Like another well?" Theo said, a few paces behind me. He broke off the branches from the trees as he pushed through them.

I saw a glimmer of water in the distance, the same deep black as the water from the well at the first point. "No," I said, pushing through the brush. "But I think I found it."

My mouth was so parched, my tongue so thick that it was hard to force out the words.

A dark pool of water cut through the trees, its surface so still it looked like an abyss. I licked my lips, expecting to taste the salt of my sweat, but it was flavorless. I knelt on the bank and bent over the water until my reflection appeared below me.

The water rippled. My double licked her lips. Startled, I touched my mouth. Had I done that without realizing, or was I seeing things?

The Renée in the water parted her lips. As she did, my throat tightened. I faltered, feeling her coax my lips open, too. A thin thread of air twisted up from within me as though she were unwinding something inside of me. Slowly, the dryness on my tongue melted into something soft and moist, into the faintest memory of something I had been longing to taste. It almost wasn't a taste, but a feeling imprinted on my soul. Dante.

The warm taste of his lips filled me. I had only tasted them once, on that distant night at Gottfried, when we had first exchanged souls, and yet I could feel them against mine as though we were still lying in the grass, his touch making my eyes grow heavy and body go limp. I could taste the sweetness of his breath, the salt clinging to his skin, when the memory began to unravel. I realized it too late; the taste had faded from my lips. My reflection rippled in the water beneath me, her mouth parted, her face whitening as though something were being drained from her. I tried to bring the memories back, when a sweetness tickled my tongue.

Noah. His memory tasted of honey and jam spread over a crusty baguette, of soft cheese and late nights stained with wine. I remembered his breath, hot and muggy, the taste of coffee and sugar lingering on his lips when he'd leaned forward and kissed me. That faded, too, the memory folding into another until the taste of my grandfather's estate coated my lips with salted meats and roasted vegetables slick with butter. Then California. The greasy bite of a burger, a squirt of ketchup, a handful of fries, so salty they made my lips chap. A lick of ice cream; a thick malt sliding up the inside of a straw; the fizz of a Coke tickling my nose; the first sip of lemonade, its glass sweating in the California sun.

I swallowed, trying to keep the memories in, but it was no use. They unwound too quickly, each taste rolling into the next, each one wrenched from me by the hollow beneath me, its gravity prying my lips wider, wider, until they finally fell shut.

My reflection rippled, scrambling my face as I stumbled back from the water. My tongue felt dull. I was overwhelmed with thirst. I longed to savor the tastes I had just relived. Anya stood a few paces away, licking her lips as she stepped back from the pool. Theo blinked beside her, blocking the sun with his hand as he shifted his jaw.

I was still clutching the bits of cloth Dante had left behind. I slipped them into my pocket and turned to the horizon, trying to recall the etchings that led from the second point to the third. A set of triangles, the third point nestled in the space between? I scanned the distance, searching for anything that would jog my memory, when I spotted a familiar pattern: a rugged outcrop of mountains, framing the horizon like jaws. Beyond them stood twin peaks, their tips leaning toward each other, forming a valley.

"The mountains," Theo said, excitedly. "I remember them from the map."

"So do I," Anya said. "The third point should lie between them, right?"

I turned to them, about to agree, when I noticed a cabin, just a stone's throw away from Theo. It was made of birch, so white that it blended in with the scenery. The weathervane on top was shaped like a canary. "There's a house back there—" I began to say, when a deep voice cut me off.

"It's empty."

A pair of leather boots sank into the dirt beside me. I recognized those shoes, the way they creased at the toe in two places from walking up a set of snowy steps every winter in Massachusetts.

My grandfather, Brownell Winters, loomed over me, his face taut like stretched leather. He was dressed in a pressed gray suit and overcoat. He took off his wool hat. Beneath it, his white hair was combed cleanly to one side. Even out in the country, he kept himself groomed, ever a gentleman.

My grandfather walked to the edge of the pool and leaned over it. It happened in a flash. He blinked, his mouth opening suddenly before pressing shut once again.

He winced at the light, as if he had been standing there for hours. When he turned to me, he was unable to hide the astonishment on his face. He gave me a questioning look, but said nothing. Then he removed a handkerchief from his coat pocket and patted his lips.

A dozen elders from the High Court swept in behind him as if carried by an old, dark force that they had wielded to do their bidding. They wore red scarves to mark their distinction. Behind them stood two dozen others—Lower Court Monitors, who could be distinguished by their lack of scarves, many of whom were training for the High Court. They stopped a few feet short and waited like stone pillars, their gray overcoats barely flapping in the wind. Their faces were firm and unwavering as they watched us; they showed no sign of sympathy.

My grandfather was about to speak, when one of them broke the silence by sneezing.

Clementine LaGuerre. She was standing on the far side of the group, her father, John LaGuerre, towering over her. He had always liked me at St. Clément, and I remembered him as a jocular, even-tempered headmaster, though now his expression was rigid. He pulled a handkerchief from his coat and handed it to Clementine, shaking his head once in a quiet reprimand.

The sight of her among the Monitors of the High Court put me at ease. She met my eye, her face embarrassed. She didn't look as wild and defiant as she used to; in fact, she almost seemed relieved to see me.

"Ms. Pinsky," my grandfather said to Anya. "And— Theodore?"

My grandfather stiffened with surprise. He hadn't known Theo was here with me, nor did he seem pleased to see him.

Theo saw it, too. His eyes betrayed a hint of amusement, as if he enjoyed seeing my grandfather caught off guard. "Mr. Winters," he said softly. "I haven't seen you since—"

"Since your trial," my grandfather said quickly, before Theo could finish his sentence.

Theo looked like he was about to correct him, but then changed his mind. "Yes."

I had never seen my grandfather look so uneasy. He was about to turn back to the Monitors behind him when my grandfather spied Theo's Spade.

He tried to hide it behind his back, but wasn't quick enough.

"What have you got there?" my grandfather said. "Give it to me."

When Theo made no sign of movement, my grandfather reached behind his back and grabbed the Spade from him.

"Just like new," my grandfather said, running his hands down the handle and along the edge of the metal tip, where Theo's initials were still engraved. He tilted his head at Theo and gave him a curious look. "Imagine that."

My grandfather planted the tip of the Spade in the ground and scanned the white birches, his eyes narrowing as he turned to me. "Where is he?"

"Who?" I asked.

My grandfather shot me a threatening look, as if to say: *Don't test me.* "You know of whom I speak."

Dante. Of course I knew. My grandfather was a fool if he thought I was going to tell him anything. I gazed back at him defiantly. "It's just us three."

My grandfather sighed. "Fine," he said. "Give me your things. I want your weapons, your shovels, your luggage. Everything."

Anya and Theo slipped their bags from their shoulders and handed them to my grandfather, along with Anya's shovel. "Empty your pockets," he said to them. Theo glared but did as he was told, handing him a fistful of coins, string, wire, sandpaper, and matches. Anya gave him her deck of tarot cards. When it was my turn, I handed him my shovel, then hesitated. I felt the weight of the black box against my back. I couldn't let him have it. But what other option did I have? The Monitors had surrounded us, their gray silhouettes planted in the ground like iron bars. I couldn't run.

"Please," I pleaded, clutching the straps. "Let me keep it."

"I'm sorry," my grandfather said, though I knew he wasn't sorry at all. He twisted the bag from my grasp. I felt the canvas slip from my fingers and with it, the last remnant of hope I had left.

"He's with the Liberum, isn't he?" my grandfather said. When I didn't respond, he continued. "Just as I suspected. With or without your help, we're going to find them, and him."

Theo shot me a knowing look. Maybe his theory about Monsieur had been right. Maybe Dante was safer with the Liberum. I closed my eyes and searched for his presence on the horizon, though I wasn't sure if I should feel relieved or frightened when all I could sense was the stale winter air.

CHAPTER 10

The Castle

THE ELDERS OF THE HIGH COURT FANNED OUT over the white wood, each kneeling over the pool, their lips parting slightly before snapping shut, while the Monitors of the Lower Court held Theo, Anya, and me back. After examining the small black box from my bag, my grandfather turned to me.

"This is no map," he said. "Where did you find this?"

His words startled me. How did he know about the map?

When I refused to respond, he stepped closer to me, so that no one else would hear. I could smell the coffee on his breath. "Where is the map?"

I inched away. "I—I don't know what you're talking about."

My grandfather grasped my arm. "Of course you do. Did Mr. Berlin take it and give it to the Liberum? Or have you hidden it from me?"

I winced as he searched my pockets, but all he found

were the bits of cloth that Dante had left behind. He studied them, frowning, then let them flutter to the ground.

"I know they attacked you at the inn," he said. "We just came from there. They had some interesting things to tell us."

I wanted to pick up the scraps of cloth, but I held myself back. "They came in the middle of the night," I said.

"And yet you survived," he said. "Which means they were coming for something else. Maybe a certain map that you had dug up from the bottom of a lake?"

He must have been able to read the guilt on my face, for he clenched his jaw as though I had answered his question, then approached the elders. They huddled together for what felt like ages, their voices hushed. While they spoke, I thought I saw the pale figure of a girl peek through the trees in the distance, just in front of the birch cabin. She had a fair complexion, with long hair the color of straw. She looked almost exactly like the girl I had seen flash in front of the window at the last point on the map. The canary weathervane shifted with the wind. When I looked back at the girl, she was gone.

My grandfather turned to the rest of the Monitors of the Lower Court. "The Liberum are closer than ever," he announced. "As I suspected, the Undead that we've been tracking, Dante Berlin, has joined forces with them, and has given them what they have been searching for all these years—the Cartesian Map."

A murmur rose over the junior Monitors.

"The actual Cartesian Map?" one of them said. "The map that leads to the Netherworld?" another chimed in. "How?" another said. "Is it real?"

"Whether or not it is authentic has yet to be determined," my grandfather continued. "But what is more important is that the Liberum believe it to be genuine. They are following it now, and are after what they have always sought—eternal life. The Liberum have already apprehended Pruneaux, and attacked the Mädchen Inn. We cannot let them do any more damage."

My grandfather looked down at his feet. "I believe that we are standing very close to the second point on the map. The Liberum have already been here; their vacancy is ahead of us." He turned to the mountains in the distance. "I can sense their hollowness heading toward those mountains," he said. The elders of the High Court nodded in agreement.

I gazed at them, puzzled. I hadn't felt the presence of the Undead since early this morning. I closed my eyes, trying to tease out the slightest hint of their emptiness in the cold air, but could sense nothing.

"If we hurry, we may be able to catch them before they reach the next stop," my grandfather continued. "Then, we will put them to rest." His eyes rested on me, as if to emphasize that Dante would be included.

The elders of the High Court led the way, escorting us through the thicket. They were human, just like we were, though something about the way they moved, so steadily and swiftly, made them seem like a force that had blown in from another world. Even in their charcoal coats, they blended into the landscape effortlessly, slipping through the trees like a gray fog, striding through the snowy fields like a murder of crows. When they gathered, they stood upright and rigid, whispering in tones so low that I wondered if they were speaking at all. They seemed to communicate through a code of narrowed eyes, tilted heads, and glances over the shoulder, their gaze always vigilant.

"What do we do now?" Anya whispered to me.

My mind raced. I couldn't run for it, because my grandfather now had the box. But if I stayed, I was at his mercy. "We find a way to steal back the box."

"We'll have to do it quickly," Anya said. "What if they're planning on sending us home?"

"My grandfather wants to find Dante," I whispered. "Having us here is the best way to do it. He knows that."

"Having *you* here," Anya corrected.

Up ahead, a fleet of charcoal cars lined the side of the road, the same deep color as the suits and overcoats of the Monitors. The sight of them stunned me. It was as if the Monitors had replicated themselves in their vehicles: a vast slick of gray creeping over the landscape. The sun reflected off the hoods in a brilliant glare, each chrome ornament like the sharp tip of a Spade.

My grandfather placed his hand on my shoulder. "Renée."

I stopped walking. Had he been listening this entire time? I searched the wrinkles in his face for some hint of reproach, but found none.

"I would like it very much if you joined me in my car. And Ms. Pinsky," he continued, referring to Anya. "Would you please accompany my colleague in the car behind us?"

"There isn't enough room for her in ours?" I said.

"I'm afraid there isn't."

He motioned to the third car in the line. One of the junior Monitors escorted Anya to the car behind mine.

I opened the door and was about to step inside when I saw my grandfather grasp Theo's arm, tighter than necessary, and pull him aside. I watched them, curious, as they exchanged a few harsh words.

Our driver was busy loading gear into the trunk. Sliding across the seat, I slipped out the opposite door and crept behind the other cars until I was close enough to see their feet beneath the bumper.

"What happened with Dante Berlin?" my grandfather pressed.

I half expected Theo to tell my grandfather everything, but instead he paused. "I don't know."

"Don't be slick with me," my grandfather warned. "I saw what you did with your Spade, and I'm choosing to ignore it for your benefit."

"And I saw what you did, all those years ago," Theo countered.

In the glossy paint on the car I could see the reflection

of the clouds passing overhead. What was Theo talking about? What had he seen my grandfather do? Cautiously, I peered over the hood of the trunk.

My grandfather clenched his fist as if he were going to hit him. "You saw nothing. You know nothing. Remember that. Now, Dante Berlin was with you. What happened when the Liberum attacked? Was he aware of it? Was he working for them?"

"Why do you want to find him so badly?"

"Because he is a murderer," my grandfather said. "Not only is he an Undead, and one incredibly close to final decay, but a dangerous one at that. Only a year and a half ago, he took the soul of Gottfried Academy's headmistress, and then attempted to take my granddaughter's soul as well. It was a near-miracle that she survived."

Murderer? I gripped the side of the car, trying my hardest to keep my mouth shut. It was true, the headmistress had died that night, though Dante had been the one trying to save her. But it didn't matter how many times I'd tried to explain that to my grandfather; he only saw what he wanted to.

"Furthermore, I believe that he has information on the Liberum. And now, he has taken an unnatural interest in my granddaughter. Despite everything he's done, he has managed to convince her of his innocence. I don't know why or how, though I plan on burying him before he kills her for good."

Theo studied him. "If Dante were going to kill Renée,

he would have done it by now. If I know that, then you must. So tell me, why do you *actually* want to find him?"

I stared at Theo's shoes, the same tattered sneakers he'd been wearing at the inn, when he'd held me back while the Undead had surrounded Dante. Maybe Theo wasn't as bad as I thought. Maybe he had been trying to help.

My grandfather stiffened. "I was right to have taken away your Spade," he said. "You may have been talented at sensing death, but you were not a Monitor then, nor are you now, nor will you ever be. Now get out of my sight."

My grandfather gestured to a thick-shouldered Monitor waiting by the curb. He opened the door to Anya's car, and motioned to Theo to step inside.

Theo hesitated, as if trying to decide whether he should run.

"I wouldn't," my grandfather said, reading his mind. I watched one sneaker, then the other disappear as Theo climbed into the car. The frayed end of one of his shoelaces got caught in the door, though he didn't seem to notice or care. I smiled.

When the door clicked shut, I snuck back to my car and slid into the backseat. The car welcomed me with perfect, temperature-controlled warmth. Its interior was upholstered entirely in smooth gray leather. The driver glanced at me from the rearview mirror. I half expected to see the cheerful blue eyes of Dustin, my grandfather's estate manager, but these eyes were foreign to me. My grandfather slipped into the seat beside me and shut the door, sealing us in as if we were sitting in a hermetic chamber. I didn't hear the engine start, or realize we were driving until the landscape outside began to move past us. From the comfort of the car, the snowy countryside almost looked artificial, nothing more than a photographic backdrop we were quickly leaving behind.

We wound through the farmland, which rose into rolling foothills and forests dotted with lakes and evergreens. The sun drooped in the sky. I searched the horizon for Dante's presence. I could just make out a cool wisp of vacancy slipping away toward the mountains. Or was it just a chill?

"Where are we?" I asked my grandfather. He was busy perusing Pruneaux's notebook, which he had confiscated from Theo's bag.

Without looking up, he said, "Bavaria."

In the front seat, the driver had turned on the radio. Wagner spilled out of the speakers, one of my grandfather's favorite composers. But instead of settling into his seat, as he always used to do when he listened to opera, he winced. "Please turn that off," he said.

My eyes lingered on him, surprised. I wondered if he had gone to the first point on the map, like we had, and was suffering from the same effects.

As night closed in around us, I saw from the rearview mirror that one of the cars behind us was pulling off the road. The end of a shoelace was still dangling out the side door.

"Anya and Theo's car just turned off the road," I said to my grandfather. He had since put down the notebook, and was now jotting something down on a pad.

When he didn't answer, I continued. "Maybe something's wrong. We should stop."

My grandfather turned the page and continued writing, as if he hadn't heard me.

I could just make out Theo's hand pressing against the backseat window, as if he were trying to escape. I watched through the window while the car disappeared down a side street. "What's going on?" I said. "Where are they going?"

My grandfather didn't even bother to look. "Never mind them."

"What are you doing with them?" I cried. "Why did you have us ride in separate cars? There's plenty of room in this one."

When he didn't answer, I leaned over and tried to grab the notebook from his hands. He must have sensed me coming, because he grasped my wrist.

"Answer me!" I demanded, trying to squirm out of his grip. His palms were thick and creased like leather. They held tight, twisting my skin until it burned.

My grandfather let go and watched me while I rubbed the red skin on my wrist. He lowered his glasses. Without them he looked old and exhausted, yet as unpitying as he had on the day he walked back into my life.

"You're with me now," he said, his voice stern. "Better to not look back."

How could I do that when everything I had was in the past? I paused, then made for the door handle, but my grandfather saw that coming, too.

"Don't bother," he said. "It's locked."

His words only sharpened my anger. I tried to unroll the windows, and when that didn't work, I pounded my hands against the glass. "Let me out!" I said. "I want to go where my friends are going. I want to know what you're doing to them."

My grandfather threw his pad aside. "Calm down!" he said. The driver glanced back at us. "I am a Monitor of the High Court, not some low-level hooligan. I have not done anything to your friends other than send them home, where they should have stayed in the first place. And to be honest, I think it is an incredibly selfish and cowardly decision on your part to have ever let them come along with you on this haphazard adventure in the first place. Now shape up. It's far past time you start behaving like the Monitor that you are."

Sent them home? I wanted to tell him that I wasn't a Monitor—not at heart, at least. That I never wanted to be one. That I cared about my friends, and that I hadn't asked them to come with me; that Monsieur had invited them and they had accepted. But I realized then that I still didn't know why. Why had Theo wanted to come along, and why had Anya? The only answer I had was from her tarot reading, which intimated that her mother was dying of an illness.

My grandfather picked up his pad. "I want you to tell me everything you know about this strange black box, and the map that you so foolishly let the Liberum take from you. Where you found them, what the map said, and most importantly, to whom you have shown them."

I clenched my jaw and said nothing.

My grandfather sighed. "If this is about some sort of loyalty to your friends, then you ought to know that Theodore Healy is a delinquent and a thief. He is loyal to no one but himself. He does not do things out of the kindness of his heart. And he is not your friend. Do not be misled by his affable personality. When it comes time for him to choose between him and you, he will always choose himself, even if the consequences of such a choice are dire."

I remembered Anya's tarot reading. *You will leave your path and walk on another. You will have to choose to return or go back. The lives of those around you will be sealed with your decision.* Could that refer to this very moment? Would Theo choose to come back?

"As for your friend Anya Pinsky, she is a nice girl, but flighty and gullible. She conflates Monitoring with magic, choice with fate. More likely than not, she came along because she wanted to help you. She didn't understand the kind of undertaking you were dragging her into. Frankly, I believe it is highly selfish of you to have let her come in the first place."

I wanted to tell him how wrong he was, but wondered if there was truth to his words. "She isn't here for no reason," I said. "Someone in her family is sick. Her mother."

My grandfather scoffed. "No one in her family is sick. I saw them a few weeks ago. Both of her parents are just fine, though I doubt they're doing as well now that their only child is missing."

Her mother wasn't ill? I tried to hide my surprise by looking at my hands. So why was she here?

"Did she tell you that?" my grandfather asked, raising an eyebrow. "An eccentric girl, she is."

But Anya hadn't told us that; she'd denied it. Perhaps she had another reason for coming along, though now I would never find out.

"Now back to the map," my grandfather said. "Tell me about it."

I glared at him. Let him think what he wanted to. I was the one who had the real power here. I knew about the chest and the map etched inside. My grandfather hadn't helped me find it, nor had he helped me get here.

"Fine. You don't have to speak. But you're with me now. And you are a Monitor. Eventually, you'll have to accept that."

We rode the rest of the way in silence, our heads swaying with the motion of the car as it climbed up a winding road. It was icy and flanked by forests thick with evergreens. High at its top stood a stalwart gray castle, its stones almost the same shade as the cars and coats of the Monitors, as if they cast a shadow in their likeness everywhere they went. It was perched high on top of the hill, where even from the car I could see all around us for miles. So this was how the

Monitors traveled. They moved through the world in plain sight, making sure they always took the high road, so that when people like Dante and I crept through darkness, it was their shadows we were hiding beneath.

A young woman greeted us at the front desk. She was beautiful, with a soft figure and high rosy cheeks that were flushed from the mountain air.

"Mr. Winters?" she said. "Welcome. Dinner is waiting for you in the main dining room."

She led us toward a stately room off the back of the lobby. Before we entered, my grandfather pulled me aside and introduced me to two junior Monitors. The first was a man approaching middle age, his face set in a permanent frown. The other was a woman, thin and mousy, though her eyes betrayed a harshness that her gentle features hid.

"Mr. Harbes," my grandfather said, "and Ms. Vine will be keeping watch over you from now until we return to the States. You are to do as they say, or risk being sent home."

After my grandfather left us alone, the Monitors peered down at me, neither of them happy about their new task. They escorted me toward the dining hall, muttering to each other over my head. Before we entered, I spotted my grandfather, almost completely hidden behind a pillar near the entrance, where he spoke softly into a cell phone, his back turned. As we passed him, I bent down and quickly pulled the laces loose on my boot.

"What are you doing?" Ms. Vine asked.

"I'm tying my boot," I said, and lowering my head, I tried to hear what my grandfather was saying.

"Are you at the school?" my grandfather asked. "Did you find the boy?" I could tell from the impatient tone of his voice that he was talking to Dustin, his estate manager. But who was he talking about? The school, the boy. Was he asking Dustin if he had gone to Gottfried, and found Noah?

My grandfather clenched his jaw as he listened. He didn't like the answer. "That is not optimal," he said, his hand on his hip. "Well, keep looking. The mansion will be fine without you."

I could imagine Dustin's voice on the other line. *Thank you, sir. Of course, sir.*

"We're lodging in the Belnort Castle," my grandfather said. "Tomorrow we head up the mountain." He paused. "I've found Renée. Yes, she's safe. She was with two others. Anya Pinsky and Theodore Healy." He paused. "Yes, the same Theodore Healy. I know it's sensitive; that's why I've sent them both on a plane back to Boston. I need you to meet them at the airport and make sure they get home."

A pause.

"Well, hurry up," said Ms. Vine. "Stop dallying."

I ignored her, waiting for my grandfather to go on. "No sign of the Undead boy," he said. "My hunch is that he defected to the Liberum, though we'll find out soon enough."

Would we? I tied my laces into a knot and stood, letting

215

Ms. Vine escort me to our room to freshen up, all the while wondering what my grandfather had meant.

Dinner was served in a vast stone room, the walls the same shade of gray as the suits of the High Court. Iron chandeliers dangled from the ceiling, and a cool breeze floated in from the adjoining balcony, offering a panoramic view of the mountains. The food came, a hearty plate of breads and sauerkraut and sausages dripping in oil, but when I took a bite, I couldn't taste a thing. The meat felt rubbery against my tongue, the bread so bland that I had to spit it into my napkin. Even the water tasted strange— dry and metallic, barely able to quench my thirst. I drank it anyway, and forced a few more bites of sausage before pushing the food around on my plate and hoping that no one would notice.

I felt a pair of eyes on me.

Clementine sat across the room beside her father, her fork raised while she watched me, as if trying to get my attention. When our eyes met, she wiped her mouth with her napkin, whispered something to her father, then stood and walked toward me. She kept her focus straight ahead, as if she didn't know I was sitting nearby. When she passed, she brushed against my arm and gave me a quick glance. Her eyes darted to the balcony outside, which was lined with tall stone pillars.

Five minutes, she mouthed and walked by before anyone noticed she had spoken to me, disappearing outside.

I waited, and when the time had elapsed, I turned to the

two Monitors guarding me. "I'd like to smell the mountain air."

Irritated by my interruption, they put down their forks and got up to come with me, but I stopped them. "I'd like to go alone, if that's okay. I just want a moment to myself. I'll be right there, in plain sight."

They exchanged a glance. From where they sat they could only see part of the balcony and the sprawl of stars and mountains beyond, though even if I tried to escape, there was nowhere to go. Mr. Harbes nodded to Ms. Vine. "Don't make us regret this," he said.

Across to the room, my grandfather sat at the head of the main table, absorbed in a conversation with a Monitor to his left. While they spoke, I wove through the tables quickly, my head bowed.

The balcony looked empty. I stood beside a tall stone pillar and waited. From the corner of my eye I saw my guards watching me from the dining room. I turned and glued my eyes to the countryside and pretended to take in the scent of the night breeze. The sky was staggeringly vast, just shades upon shades of blue, cut off only by the dark silhouette of the mountains beneath it. And yet without the accompanying sound, without the crisp taste of the air on my tongue, it felt like nothing more than a backdrop painted on canvas.

I thought about what I'd overheard my grandfather say to Dustin on the phone. *We'll find out soon enough.* I held out my hand, waiting for a cold thread of air to wrap itself around my fingers, to tell me that Dante was out there, that he and the Liberum were close by. But before I could focus on the distance, a voice spoke from the other side of the pillar.

"Did anyone follow you?" Clementine asked.

"No."

"I never told anyone that I saw you and Dante that night," she said. "I wanted to. But I didn't."

I waited, unsure what to say.

"I'm telling you because I want you to believe me."

"Believe what?" I whispered.

"That something strange is going on," she said.

"What do you mean?"

"The Monitors have been following you since the day you and Dante escaped from the Liberum at Gottfried Academy. I joined them soon after with my father. We came thinking we were going to hunt the Liberum; they killed Noah, and they tried to kill you," she said, lowering her voice.

"And at first, that's exactly what happened. The elders dispatched the rest of us to search for the Liberum, while they followed you and Dante, to make sure you were safe. The elders were more secretive about it than normal, which my father thought odd. They kept disappearing for days on end, and meeting up with us looking older and exhausted, but my father didn't say anything. He's always prided himself in his loyalty. He trusted them.

"Then late one night, after everyone else had gone

to sleep, I was awake in my tent when I heard footsteps. Dozens of them, all quiet. I waited for them to pass, then slipped outside. I saw the elders walking into the forest. So I followed them, thinking they were going to have a late night meeting. But instead, they led me somewhere I'd never expected to go. The camp of the Liberum."

I had been trying to refrain from having any physical reaction to Clementine's story, lest the Monitors noticed, but her words caught me by surprise. "What?"

"We walked for what felt like miles. Then suddenly I could feel them," she said. "I could see the Brothers of the Liberum through the trees, their long black robes gathered on the ground. The Undead boys lounged around them. At first I thought the Monitors were going to mount an attack; after all, no Monitor has ever been able to track the Liberum, and most have never even seen a Brother, let alone found their camp. But they didn't attack. They waited on the outskirts of the camp, just out of sight. They kept checking their watches. Finally, two Undead boys snuck through the trees and walked toward them. I thought the Monitors were going to bury them, but instead, they started whispering to the boys, as if they had planned on meeting there. I tried to hear what they were saying, but couldn't make out anything."

I frowned. It didn't make any sense. "You're sure they were Undead?"

"Yes. While they talked, the elders seemed to get more and more angry. Eventually, two of them clamped their hands over the mouths of the Undead boys and carried them off into the woods. I watched them bury the boys, then stalk back to the tents. They didn't seem to care about the Liberum being there at all. The next morning, the elders told us they were going to track you and Dante, and that the rest of us should continue searching for the Liberum."

"But they already knew where the Liberum were camping," I said.

"Exactly."

The thought was baffling. This entire time my grandfather had known where the Liberum were, and hadn't done anything to stop or apprehend them. "So the elders have been tracking the Liberum this entire time, and not telling anyone?"

"Not just tracking them," Clementine said. "Talking to them. And not just once, multiple times. I've followed the elders a few times since. They always wait by the outskirts of the camp until a few Undead boys come out and speak to them. Then they leave. I've been racking my mind for days as to what the elders could possibly want from the Undead, but I can't think of anything. All I know is that they've been lying to the rest of the Lower Court. And the only time I lie is when I'm doing something wrong."

Multiple times? My heart began to race. "So the elders still know where the Liberum are?"

Clementine nodded. "I think so."

I remembered what my grandfather had said to Dustin on the phone. *My hunch is that he defected to the Liberum, though we'll find out soon enough.* All I had to do to find Dante was follow the elders out to the camp. "How often do they go out?" I asked.

"Every few nights. Why? Do you want to follow them?"

"Yes—" I began to say, when I heard footsteps behind me. I glanced over my shoulder. The two Monitors guarding me had gotten up and were whispering to each other while they walked in my direction. "I have to go," I said.

"My father and I sit close to the elders at breakfast," Clementine breathed. "I'll try to find out when they're meeting next. In the meantime, keep your eyes peeled. I don't know what the elders are up to, but it can't be anything good."

That night I dreamed of the lake again, its frozen surface dull like a clouded eye, the dark water seeping up through the cracks. A thudding filled the air, as irregular as a heart reanimating. The ice trembled then, shattered, a pale hand reaching out from the gash.

Noah rose from the lake, his skin glistening. His eyes snapped open. With a blink, he was running through the pines, his muscles shifting beneath the thin cotton of his shirt, his auburn hair dotted with snow. *Renée*, his heart seemed to beat. *Renée, Renée, Renée.* Another blink and the landscape behind him changed, flipping back like a canvas. He stole through the snow, the jagged peaks of the Bavarian Alps jutting up behind him like teeth. He paused, gazing up at a castle built into the edge of a cliff, its gray stone blending into the rocky landscape. A castle that I recognized. In a flash, he had scaled the cliff, his body hunched low as he crept beneath the windows lining the back of the edifice, peering inside each one until he reached a room toward the corner. He pressed his hand against the glass, his icy breath sending a bloom of frost over the pane. In the chambers within, a girl was fast asleep, her hair strewn across the pillow. *I forgive you*, he whispered.

A chill of cold shook me awake. I sat up in bed, feeling the thin wisps of air seep beneath the seam of the window and twist around my wrists. An Undead was here, though it wasn't Dante.

Noah. Could it be? I turned to the window, where I saw three words drawn into the frost on the glass. *I'm still here.*

The frost receded as the presence of the Undead shrank back, beckoning me to follow it.

On the other side of the room, Ms. Vine tossed in her sleep, but did not wake. I slid out of bed and snuck into the hallway. The hotel was empty, the attendant sleeping in the back office as I walked through the lobby and out into the night.

The air rearranged itself, forming a narrow path toward the evergreens. I walked toward it until I saw a figure standing by the foot of the woods. A flash of wavy auburn hair, now wet with snow. A swath of smooth skin, now pale in the moonlight, his cheek punctuated by a dark freckle.

Noah.

Seeing him stirred something inside me. I froze, unable

to believe that he was here, standing, breathing in front of me. A few weeks ago, I'd thought that I would never see his face again.

At first glance, he looked the same, though on closer inspection something had changed. His skin was now a clean white, and the dark constellation of freckles strewn across his face were even more beautiful than they had been before. Everything about him was more saturated, as if all of his features had been soaked in melancholy. His auburn hair seemed a deeper, darker red, just overripe, like the color of wet autumn leaves after they fall from their branches and collect on the curb. His boyish face was now mature, handsome, the way I'd always imagined he'd look as an adult.

But before I could walk toward him, I heard footsteps in the snow behind me. Noah receded into the woods. I backed through the trees in the opposite direction, watching as six elders of the High Court strode past me, their faces shrouded beneath their collars, their eyes darkened by the brims of their hats. At first I thought they had felt Noah's presence, but they didn't turn in the direction where he'd been standing.

I waited until they disappeared into the woods, then followed their tracks. They led me far from the castle, the silhouettes of the treetops standing tall against the moon. The temperature dropped. A voice rang out through the trees, first loud, then muffled. I crept toward it until I saw six more figures materialize through the trees. The others joined them. All twelve elders of the High Court. Their backs were turned to me, their gray overcoats sweeping the snow as they huddled in a circle over something lying on the ground.

I hid behind a tree and watched them, trying to figure out what they were doing, when I saw a pair of feet twitching through their legs. They were small, as though they belonged to a boy. An Undead.

"You know more," one of the elders said, his white tuft of hair blowing in the wind. My grandfather. "Tell us."

When the boy said nothing, my grandfather nodded to one of the other elders, who then began to slowly wrap the boy's hands with gauze. The Undead cried out, his body trembling as the skin on his arm turned blue.

Two other Undead boys were pinned to the snow beside him, their feet, their hands, their thighs partially wrapped in gauze.

I watched them, confused. The method in which the boys were being wrapped wasn't the proper way to mummify an Undead. Surely, the High Court knew that, which made their hasty work all the more baffling. I thought back to what Clementine had told me on the balcony. Could these be the Undead from the camp of the Liberum that the elders had been meeting with?

"You're lying to us," one of the elders said, dangling the gauze over an Undead boy's chest. "You must know more."

I shrank back. The elders weren't trying to kill these boys. They were torturing them.

CHAPTER 11

The Refuge

W E SET OUT EARLY THE NEXT MORNING, the line of gray cars waiting for us like an extension of the stone castle. While we packed our things in the trunks of the cars, my grandfather peered up into the mountains.

"The Liberum are no more than a day ahead of us," he said. "If we hurry, we may be able to reach them."

I glanced at Clementine wearily, who was standing by the car behind mine. I thought of Noah, of how his auburn hair had hung by his face in the moonlight. Had he really been there, or had I been seeing things?

Tonight, Clementine mouthed, and stepped into the backseat behind her father.

My grandfather put his hand on my shoulder. "I've brought along some gear for you, as I assumed you would not be prepared."

I studied him as he slid into the car. I didn't thank him.

Just before we pulled away, the concierge emerged from the lobby, holding an envelope. She ran up to our car, wobbling in her heels, and tapped on my grandfather's window. He rolled it down. She handed him a white envelope, his name written on the top. I recognized the handwriting immediately. Monsieur. Had he been sending my grandfather notes this entire time, too?

While we drove away, he tore it open and removed the note within. He held it discreetly, angling his body so that I could barely make out Monsieur's swooping penmanship. His face drained of all its color as he read. When he was finished, he slipped the envelope into the inner pocket of his coat.

My grandfather barely acknowledged my presence on the drive up into the Bavarian Alps, in the direction of the Liberum and the twin peaks we'd seen from the second point. He sat on the other side of the car, his eyes out of focus as they stared out the window. Every so often he slipped his hand into his coat, feeling the weight of the note within. But he never took it out.

I sank back into my seat, exhausted from barely sleeping, my mouth dry, my hearing muted. The only sound in the car was the vibration of the wheels beneath us. I closed my eyes and listened to it, wondering if my grandfather was feeling the same way I was—for he, too, couldn't taste or hear well, nor had he slept a wink last night. We had been in the woods together, though only I knew it.

"What was that note?" I asked, opening my eyes.

If he heard me, he didn't let on.

"What did that woman give you?" I repeated.

"What's that?" he said.

I sighed. I hated when he pretended not to have heard me. "The letter," I said. "It's incredible that they have mail out here."

"Mail?" he said. "Oh, yes. It was just a private matter. Nothing pressing."

I watched him turn to the window, the scenery speeding past us like a film in fast forward. Perhaps they were beautiful, the majestic Alps, but I felt nothing. "You look tired," I said. "You must have been up late last night."

My grandfather frowned. "No, I wasn't. I am merely preoccupied. There is a difference."

He was lying, though I didn't have the energy to argue with him, and frankly, he didn't look like he had the energy to argue back. "Preoccupied with what?"

He turned to the snowcapped peaks in the near distance, his cheeks sunken, his eyes tired. "With matters that don't concern you."

The road was carved tenuously into the side of the mountain, with a small stone barrier separating us from a free-fall into the rocky valley below. As we wove around it, the twin peaks that had been etched into the chest kept flashing in and out of view, growing larger, closer. The trees grew thinner, their branches starved for air. Just as we crossed the tree line, my grandfather leaned over the front seat and muttered something to the driver.

We pulled off onto the shoulder of the road. The earth outside was rocky and layered with snow, barely a tree or plant to be seen. The line of cars pulled in behind us, parking on the side of the road. The twin peaks that matched the etching from the chest jutted up through the mist in the distance.

"Why are we stopping?" I asked.

"We aren't going to find the Liberum by sitting in the car," my grandfather said. "We walk from here."

I thought back to Clementine's story from the night before, and to what I had witnessed in the woods. He already knew where the Liberum were camped; he and the elders had been tracking them this entire time. So if he wasn't searching for them, then what exactly was he looking for?

I grabbed my backpack from the trunk and slung it over my shoulder. It was lighter now without the weight of the chest and the black box. My grandfather now kept the latter in his own rucksack. He handed me a tent and a sack full of gear, along with my shovel. "This will be yours. I don't know what lies ahead," he said. "Best to be prepared."

My grandfather led the way, his Spade clinking against the ground with every step like a walking stick. Behind him, everyone followed by rank—the oldest Monitors of the High Court first, followed by the younger members, then finally by Clementine, the junior Monitors, and me.

We must have made headway with the car, for I could now feel the distant pull of the Undead on me as we trudged through the snow. The landscape was icy and stark, dotted with jagged boulders. As we ascended, the weather began to turn. The dry mountain air felt coarse against my throat, so thin that I had to take two breaths instead of one. With every step I sank up to my calves in snow, my gear weighing down my shoulders, digging into my skin through my coat.

The longer we walked, the more the landscape began to blur into one endless stretch of white. The lack of trees, of any kind of landmark, eroded my sense of depth. I couldn't tell what was close and what was far. The twin peaks in the distance seemed to waver, first growing larger, then shrinking back into the horizon. Ledges of ice and rock towered around us, balancing so tenuously that any gust could have knocked them over. My clothes were caked with ice, the snow clinging to my hair until it crystalized into heavy white strands. My lips were so chapped they stung.

I placed one foot in front of the other, imagining I was stepping into Dante's tracks, that he was just a few steps ahead of me. Every smudge of dirt in the snow I mistook for a scrap of his shirt left behind; every chill I mistook for his presence reaching out to me. I tried to remember the feeling of warmth. The kiss of the summer sun on my shoulder. The heat that bloomed inside me every time I felt Dante's lips press against my skin. I only drew a blank.

Ahead, my grandfather and the elders hiked tirelessly through the cold, showing barely a sign of fatigue. As we pressed against the wind, which whipped against my face and made my cheeks burn, I wondered what was propelling them forward. At the front of the line, my grandfather paused and closed his eyes while he teased out the sensation of the Undead ahead of us. "They are moving quickly," he said. "We must pick up the pace!"

The elders closed in around him. They weren't just the most talented members of the Court, I realized. They were also the oldest. So close to death. Maybe they wanted to find the Netherworld, too, and were using this hunt for the Liberum as a way to search for it.

I leaned against a boulder for a quick rest, when I saw the white face of a girl peer at us over the side of a rocky overhang. Her hair fluttered in the wind as she disappeared behind it. She looked just like the girl I had seen flitting past the window of the house by the well, and darting through the trees in the birch forest, and yet her face looked slightly different. Older maybe, like a sister. But when I leaned forward to get a better look, she disappeared.

I turned to the others to see if anyone else had seen her, but all eyes were on the ground or the rocky ledge of the first peak in the near distance.

Who were these girls? They haunted each point like apparitions, and yet they weren't dead; I couldn't sense them at all. I knew they were following us, watching us, and yet they never revealed themselves. I thought back to the places where I had seen them: the house near the well, its kitchen floor inlaid with a mosaic of a canary; the birch cabin with the canary weathervane. It couldn't have been a coincidence that the canary was also the sign of the Nine Sisters. Were the girls I was seeing somehow related to them, to Ophelia Hart?

I searched for them on the cliffs as we walked onward. I knew then that we had to be nearing the third point, for the girls only seemed to reveal themselves as we neared each point on the map. We had almost reached the valley in the middle of the peaks when the air began to rearrange itself.

The line of Monitors slowed. "Do you feel that?" one of them said.

A murmur rose over them as the others agreed. It didn't feel like the Undead. It felt like plain, stagnant death.

We moved faster then, walking toward the vacancy. At first, I thought it might be the pull of the third point, when I heard a shout up ahead. The elders had gathered around a patch of snow. Between them, I could just make out a leg protruding from the snow. It was clothed in a pair of wool slacks and tattered leather loafers, a sliver of skin peeking out beneath the hem of the pants.

I recognized those shoes, though they were now scuffed and soaked through from the snow. Pruneaux.

My grandfather bent over him, examining his mouth, his throat, his pulse. "The Liberum have discarded the cartographer," he said. "He's only been dead for a few hours."

While the other Monitors gathered around him, a flash of something white caught my eye. I turned to the rocky ledge in the distance and saw the face of the pale girl disappear over a crest in the mountainside, her long blond hair trailing behind her.

Ms. Vine froze. "Did you see that?" she said, her eyes glued to the same outcrop of rocks.

"See what?" said Mr. Harbes from beside her.

"A girl," she said. "She looked like an Undead, but I couldn't feel her."

"A girl?" Mr. Harbes said. "All the way up here?"

"I saw her, too," said another Monitor. "So did I," another chimed in.

"Search the area!" my grandfather said. "The elders and I will go forward toward the peaks in the wake of the Liberum's presence. The rest of you spread out across the slope!"

The Monitors dispersed, some huddling over Pruneaux while the others backtracked, taking the steep route up the mountaintop to get a better view of the horizon. Amid the disorder, I slipped away and crept behind my grandfather up the icy path.

The air thinned, its freshness fading until the mountain breeze smelled stale. With it drifted the gritty smell of the mud and debris around me, then the damp scent of my backpack, which had carried the odor of rain and snow and heat, the sweet smell of my sweat, all the cars and trains and lodgings I had stayed in—it all grew muted.

I thought back to Descartes's riddle. *The nose, it next decays, death the only stench to stay.*

The lines in the scenery began to converge into a familiar pattern, one that I remembered from the etchings in the chest. The jagged scar between the peaks of the mountains was far more terrible in person—a rocky gash that dipped so deep into the earth that it looked endless. My grandfather and the other elders gathered around its edge. I snuck to the far side, staying close to the rocky face of the mountain so they wouldn't see me, until I saw a ripple of water. It was black and still as glass. I leaned over it, my face appearing in the pool below.

The water trembled, making my reflection quiver. The Renée that stared back at me was gaunt, her expression lost. Her hair blew in front of her face in a breeze that I could not feel. She took a breath in, then another. Her chest heaved as though she couldn't inhale.

As I watched her, I felt my lungs compress. A thin stream of air curled up my throat. It seeped through the seam of my lips, through my nose, my pores. It folded in on itself, softening and rounding out until it transformed into a scent imprinted on my soul.

Dante. I could smell him, as clear as the winter morning, the woods clinging to his clothes, his hair as sweet as pine. I could smell his breath, cold like the wind in December; his skin, as clean and fresh as ice. The smoky smell of cabins and cozy wool blankets, of the wet pavement and the snow melting off the evergreens around us in the winter sun, of his scent still nestled in the bed beside me. I remembered the rustic smell of his shirt as he scooped me up from the lawn outside of Gottfried just before the Brother of the Liberum had lowered his face to mine in a kiss, and carried me through the woods, the wild scent of him filling my lungs with life.

But the memories soon faded into the autumn leaves of Montreal; the smell of thick sweaters and baking croissants and coffee brewing in the corner of a bakery. Of Noah, the waning fall afternoon clinging to his clothes and filling me with warmth. I almost believed that he was still sitting across from me, his legs tangling with mine beneath a cramped table at a patisserie.

Snap, rewind, and the scent was replaced with the crackling heat of Gottfried, of dusty chimneys and Eleanor's saccharine perfume. The aroma of steam and shampoo wafting down the hallway. Of chalk and pencil grindings, of musty books and the stillness of the library, of the pine still fresh in Dante's hair as he leaned over my shoulder...

That, too, unraveled, until I was left inhaling the salty breeze of the Pacific Ocean, the sticky scent of sunscreen and aloe vera, of charcoal crackling in the barbecue. Of California: the smell of the dew on the football field at night, of cheap beer foaming out of a bottleneck and cigarettes singeing the grass. One by one, the memories faded, stripping me of every rich smell and foul odor and comforting scent until there was nothing but a blank void.

I blinked, my reflection mimicking me, and backed away from the ravine. The air around me was odorless and thin, the wind so flat I barely registered it at all. I took a deep breath, trying to inhale the aroma of the mountains, but I smelled nothing. On the far side of the valley, my grandfather knelt over the pool. His long coat swept the ice as he stood up, his face startled. The elder Monitors of the High Court were all close by. Behind him, I spotted a pale cabin, the color of snow, nestled into the far side of the valley. It looked just like the cabin I had seen in the birch forest. The shape of a canary was etched into its door.

The last of the scents drifted past me, a swirl of memories that I would never get back. I turned to them as they swept down the far side of the mountain. And there I saw it: a circle of clouds swirling low in the sky. Jutting out of them was a lone mountaintop, which looked almost like it was floating. I recognized it from the underside of the chest, and though the engraving was far cruder, the likeness was unmistakable. According to the map, the fourth point was nestled somewhere in those clouds.

I should have felt happy. We were almost there. But there was no *we* anymore. There was barely a *me*.

My grandfather didn't say anything about what we'd found, nor did any of the other elders. The junior Monitors were busy burying Pruneaux and searching for any signs of the Liberum and the white-clothed girl, but they'd found nothing. When they were finished, the elders led them around the edge of the mountain, avoiding the gash in the earth as though they hadn't found anything there at all.

We followed the wisps of the Undead until the sun waned in the sky. A building emerged through the mist, built into the rocks on the side of the mountain, its gray stone blending into the rugged scenery. Its windows were fogged over, light flickering softly behind them. A sign hung above the door. WEILTERHÜTTE. My eyes watered with relief. An alpine refuge. A sign of life.

A burst of warmth welcomed us inside. A boy my age fed wood into a fire, making the embers crackle and dance, while a wiry man who looked like the boy's father sat at the table, peeling potatoes. He had a ruddy face, and eyes set close together like a hawk's. He led us down the hallway to the lodging rooms out back. My grandfather dropped his bag in front of the dormitory closest to the hallway. "Wash up and rest," he said. "We'll regroup again in an hour for dinner."

I shared a room with the seven other female Monitors, including Clementine, who chose the top bunk next to mine. We didn't speak while we unpacked, nor did we look at each other while we changed our clothes and washed our faces in the shared bathroom. We didn't want to draw attention to ourselves, lest the Monitors grow suspicious. Our only communication was a brief glance we shared as I slipped out the door. I motioned to the two rooms at the end of the hall, where the elders were staying. She nodded as I disappeared into the hallway.

I nudged open the door of my grandfather's dormitory with my foot. His rucksack was there, but otherwise the room was empty. The adjoining chamber was also vacant; the only sign of the elders was their gear, resting by their beds. Their Spades were gone. I ventured into the main room, where the innkeeper and his sons were busy prepping for dinner. Some of the junior Monitors were sitting by the fire, but the elders were nowhere to be seen.

My heart began to race. Where were they? Clementine had said they'd planned to meet tonight—to go to the camp of the Liberum, I'd assumed. Had they already managed to slip away? I peered back down the hallway, wondering if there was some other room I didn't know about, but all I saw were three doors: one leading outside; one to a broom closet, which was slightly ajar; and one to the bathrooms. When I turned back into the main room, Clementine brushed past me.

"Have you seen them?" I whispered.

She shook her head. "I checked my father's room, but there's only one other junior Monitor there."

I peered out the window at the white landscape that surrounded us. The snow had let up, though the wind was still howling against the sides of the refuge. "They must have already left," I murmured, and turned to her. "We have to find them."

We snuck to the back door. "Wait," Clementine said, and ran down the hall to our rooms. When she emerged she was carrying two white bath towels. "Wrap this around your shoulders," she said, handing me one. "You'll blend in better."

I did as she said, and with our shoulders draped in white, we burst out into the cold once more. I'd expected to spot them easily in the snow, but when we scanned the mountainside around us, we appeared to be alone. I spun around, shuddering as the wind thrashed about us. Dark rocks lined the slope, hanging over the trail in clusters; otherwise, everything was white and still. I searched the ground for footprints, but the ground was already so uneven with the prints we'd left hiking up to the refuge that it was impossible to tell which were new.

"I saw them last night," I told Clementine. "A draft woke me up from my sleep. I thought it was . . ." I wanted to say Noah, but was it? Or had that part been nothing more than a dream? I couldn't tell, so instead I continued, ". . . an Undead, so I followed the presence down to the woods, where I saw my grandfather and a few other Monitors doing something to three Undead boys."

"Doing what?" Clementine said. "Burying them?"

I swallowed. "I don't think so," I said. "It looked like they were torturing them with gauze."

A flash of red caught my eye in the distance. The scarlet scarf of an elder. I turned to an outcropping of gray rocks just over the edge of the hill. Unlike all of the other boulders around us, which were dusted in a healthy layer of snow, these were a little more dark and void of any accumulation.

Clementine must have been thinking the same thing I was because she stopped walking. "Were those rocks there before?"

I didn't have to respond. Pulling our towels tighter around our shoulders, we crouched low to the ground and ran toward them, using the overhang of rock and ice to shroud us from view.

I had expected that when we found the elders, they would lead us to the camp of the Liberum; but instead, they stood in a huddle beneath a ledge of snow. The lapels of their coats were flipped upward to protect from the wind. I could just make out the large ruddy nose of my grandfather while he spoke to the others. We inched closer.

My grandfather huddled over a piece of paper. "'Dear Mr. Winters,'" he read. "'You don't know me, but I know you. I know what you're doing, and I want you to know that I'm watching you. Sincerely, Monsieur.'"

"Monsieur?" one of the elders said. "He has no name?"

My grandfather shook his head and tucked the page into his coat. "I received a similar note thirty years ago, just before the incident at the courthouse."

Clementine's eyes met mine. The incident at the courthouse?

"The day before the trial for the Undead, I found an envelope sitting on my desk," my grandfather continued. "It had no postage or return address, just like this one. It said: *Dear Mr. Winters, I know what you've been doing and I cannot let it continue. Please accept my apologies. Sincerely, Monsieur.* The next morning, the bomb went off in the courtroom. I didn't show the note to anyone; I wasn't sure whom I could trust. To my relief, I heard nothing more from him after that day. Over the years, I started to hope that he had passed away or stopped caring, though now I know that I was wrong. He is still here; he is still watching us."

"If this Monsieur knows about what we've been doing all this time," said one of the elders, "then why hasn't he told anyone?"

All this time? Clementine and I shared a questioning look. Did that mean that what Clementine had seen the elders doing in the woods—it had something to do with the bombing in the courthouse all those years ago?

"Perhaps he has been waiting for the right moment to expose us," one of the elders offered.

"Or perhaps he didn't have enough evidence back then, and has been slowly gathering it," another added.

"Monsieur must have hand delivered the note to the hotel," my grandfather said. "Which means he has either been following us—"

"Or is among us," another elder said. "One of the other Monitors, perhaps."

My grandfather nodded. "We have to be more careful than ever. From now on we will only talk about our business late at night, and in seclusion."

"We are far away from the others now," another elder said. "Tell us—what of the Undead?"

"We made contact with our sources inside the Liberum last night," my grandfather said. "They didn't have any information for us about the Brothers. They said they needed time."

Sources? Clementine mouthed to me. Had the elders been

planting Undead boys in the Liberum, and using them as spies?

"Did you press them?" one of the elders said.

His choice of words me cringe. Was that what I had witnessed?

"Yes," my grandfather said. "Three of them last night. All they were able to tell us before we released them was that the Liberum are getting desperate. They've been taking souls along the way to prolong their lives."

"Should we take action?" an elder said.

My grandfather paused, as if considering it. "Not yet."

I held in my gasp. The Liberum were killing people, and my grandfather was just going to stand by and let them do it?

"The Liberum can do things that we cannot, at least not out in the open," he continued. "We'll need them when it comes to the end. We'll need someone to deal with the Keepers. They haven't struck yet, but they will. They're waiting, picking off Undead boys on the way. I've found their bodies strewn in the snow at night near their camp. It's only a matter of time before they begin with us."

Who are the Keepers? I mouthed to Clementine, but she only put a hand on her mouth, shocked. Moments later the elders disbanded and walked, one by one, back to the refuge. Clementine and I pressed ourselves against the overhang of ice behind us, wrapping our towels tightly over our bodies to make sure we couldn't be seen.

"The Keepers are rumored to protect the Netherworld,"

Clementine said as the elders disappeared down the slope. "Incredible Monitors. They work silently, blending in to the scenery around them. When they strike, you won't hear them, you won't see them, you won't feel them until the life is already leaving you. Supposedly, they're descendants of the ninth sister. There are five of them, one for each point."

I thought back to the pale girls I'd seen haunting the first three points, their hair so blond it looked as white as the snow, their complexion so fair it blended in with the winter landscape. I thought of the images of the canaries that kept appearing with them. Had I been seeing the Keepers? And were they somehow related to the Nine Sisters, or Ophelia Hart?

"That's why the elders haven't been attacking the Liberum," Clementine continued. "They've been searching for the Netherworld for years, and now that they're close, they don't want to get their hands dirty by killing the Keepers themselves. They want the Liberum to get there first and do it for them."

"And it's why they've been tracking the Liberum," I said. "Why they've been turning the other cheek, even when they know that the Liberum were taking innocent souls. The elders have been using them to find the Netherworld."

"But what does that have to do with the bombing of the court all those years ago?"

"I'm not sure," I said. "But if it's up to Monsieur, I bet we'll find out soon enough."

CHAPTER 12

Widow's Pass

THOUGH MY VISION HADN'T DULLED OVER YET, I almost wished it had. Then I would have been able to look my grandfather in the face and feel nothing. But instead, all I could feel was disdain. When he laughed at breakfast while chatting with the High Court, all I could see were yellowed teeth, hollow and decaying, like those of the Liberum. When he stood, pushing his plate aside—the food barely touched—and gathered the elders to map the route we would take toward the fourth point, all I could see were their gaunt bodies, their withered skin, their thin lips, as desperate as those of the Liberum. Even their gray overcoats recalled the long cloaks of the Brothers, their tails billowing around their legs as they led us out into the sunlight.

As we set out from the refuge, I could feel the Undead ahead of us, their presence licking my skin. We followed it west with the sun, my grandfather leading the way. With each turn, the landscape brought the thin lines of the map to life from my memory, turning a circle into a frozen lake, a swooping curve into a slope of ice, a ridged rectangle into a rocky cliff. Then finally, a diamond, into a dark tunnel leading through the middle of the mountain.

"The Undead have drifted down the mountainside," my grandfather said. "As they cannot go through the pass, they must go around it. We must catch up with them on the other side."

We crowded around the passage while my grandfather and the elders ventured inside to make sure it was safe. Their flashlights faded into the darkness.

"Widow's Pass," Clementine whispered from beside me. "Supposedly, once you're inside, if you're a widow, you can hear the voice of your dead lover bouncing off the rocks."

Dead lover. I had never used those words to describe Dante, though they were true. I peered into the tunnel, suddenly nervous. Would I hear him as we walked through it?

The dim orb of my grandfather's flashlight appeared as he walked toward us. "We stay here tonight," he said, hoisting up his pack. "It's underground, which means it's safe from the Undead, who are close. We'll be able to sleep."

Sharp black rock lined the passage through the mountain. I raised my flashlight and gazed up at the cavernous ceilings. They were so high that I couldn't see the top, only a series of jagged edges jutting down from the walls. I tried to imagine what this hike would have been like if Dante hadn't been captured by the Undead, if I hadn't been discovered by the Monitors. How would we have gotten through this section of the map together?

Dante couldn't have traveled underground, and I wouldn't have been able to hike around another mountain, like the Undead were probably doing now. They were tireless; they didn't need to sleep, and they weren't affected by the cold like I was. Perhaps Monsieur had been right about letting the Liberum take Dante. But that meant Monsieur must have known about this place. Had he traveled this path before?

We set up camp along the broadest part of the pass, no wider than a riverbed. My grandfather positioned his tent at the head of the group, with mine just a few yards away between the two Monitors guarding me.

While I put together my tent, I listened to the dull echo of voices around me. Some of the Monitors whispered to each other while they unpacked. Others built a fire at the center of camp to cook dinner. Even though they were far enough away that I shouldn't have been able to hear them, the shape of the cavern magnified their voices. But the more I listened, the more garbled the echo seemed. The sounds didn't bounce back immediately, and when they did return a few moments later, they sounded like gibberish.

I called out my name to see what would happen.

The voice that returned spoke with a mishmash of sounds, as if all the letters had gotten jumbled on the journey. It repeated itself. *Renaar—enee—entee—ante—Dante.*

I covered my mouth. Had anyone heard? I glanced over

my shoulder, expecting to meet my grandfather's watchful gaze, but he was huddled over the black box with two of the elders.

I kept hearing that echo: while we ate dinner, while my grandfather set out a strategy for what we would do if we met the Liberum on the other side of the pass. *Dante*. The cavern knew who he was. Did that mean he was still alive?

I stayed up by the fire long after everyone else had gone to bed. Tents dotted the darkness, each glowing from the lanterns within until they lit up the passage like a string of Christmas lights. When the embers died out, I tiptoed through them to the back of the camp. I could hear my grandfather murmuring in his sleep.

"Don't leave me," he said, his voice so low that had I not known which tent was his, I would have thought I was listening to someone else. He let out a snore. "Nora, don't go."

Nora was my grandmother's name. She died when I was very young. He was hearing his widow speak to him.

"I miss you," he said. "Every day I miss you."

I wondered what he was hearing, what she was saying. I wanted to listen in, to find out what she was like and what he was like with her around, but instead I averted my eyes and kept walking, ashamed for listening in on such a private conversation.

My tent was a small affair, the fabric a translucent periwinkle. It rippled in the light, making me feel like I was underwater, staring at the sun shining through the waves. It should have been lovely, but all I could think of when I saw it was Dante. The plane falling from the sky. His father praying as they hit the ocean and sank into the water; the waves a brilliant blue that grew darker, darker, until the world around him turned black.

I wrapped a blanket around my shoulders and crawled outside. Clementine's tent, which she shared with her father, was on the other side of the pass. I could see her silhouette through the fabric. She sat curled over a book, holding a flashlight while she turned the pages. I coughed, and Clementine spun around, shining her light through the tent in my direction. I pointed my beam back at her, and flashed it twice.

Clementine flashed hers back at me, and for a moment it almost felt like we were just two girls on vacation, staying up late after everyone else had fallen asleep. I had that life once, I realized, though I could barely remember what it felt like.

I turned to go back into my tent when I heard a voice. *Five more minutes.*

I spun around, but it didn't seem to be coming from one of the tents.

You saw her? the same voice said. *You're sure she's still with them?*

"Dante?" I breathed. His presence swept over me like a chill seeping in through my blanket. My eyes darted about the cavern, searching for some trace of him in the rocks, even though I knew he couldn't be there.

A pause. Was he talking about me? Who was he speaking to?

Did they hurt her?

"I'm here," I said. "I'm waiting for you." I wanted to call his name into the cavern, to tell him that I was safe, that I was going to find him. I pursed my lips to speak, but then changed my mind. I didn't know if anything I said would get through to Dante. What if my words echoed off the rock walls for all of the Monitors to hear? They would know Dante was out there. They would use me to find him and bury him.

Four more minutes. Are you ready? In exchange, I'll tell you anything you want to know about the Monitors. I can tell you about the other Monitors who were traveling with us. I can tell you about the map in the chest that they have. About the sealed box.

What? The only people he could be talking to were Undead boys. But Dante would never offer to tell them about us, about the chest and the box, about Theo and Anya. Would he?

Do you see them?

A long pause. See whom? I tried to imagine the other side of the conversation, but couldn't imagine Dante talking to any of the Undead boys like this.

All nine of them?

He could only be referring to one thing. The nine Brothers of the Liberum.

Three more minutes. This time, his voice was more urgent.

What was happening in three minutes?

Don't move, Dante said. *They're coming.*

His words made me nervous. I pulled the blanket tight around my shoulders and waited.

Did they have the boys from the village? Did they take them into the woods?

The boys from the village. The Liberum could only be doing one thing with them in the woods: taking their souls to give themselves a little bit more life.

Good, he said. *When we go in after them, we'll only have a short window of time. After they take the boys' souls, their eyes will shut while they pass into limbo. It will only last a few seconds, while their bodies absorb their new life. A minute, no more. That's when we have to take it.*

A wave of dread spread through me. I tried to piece together what Dante was talking about. Was Dante going to wait until the Liberum killed nine local boys, and use that moment—when each of the Brothers was incapacitated from absorbing their new bit of life—to take something from them? The chest. I swallowed, not wanting to believe it. The Dante I knew would never stand by and watch while the Liberum killed innocent people.

There's nothing we can do to help them, he said, as if answering my question. *If we try to save them, the Liberum will bury us. Two more minutes.*

I went still, my muscles tightening as if I were right there with him.

I don't know which one of them has it, so we'll have to search all of them. We have to be careful. Make sure your cloaks are

wrapped tight around you. We can't let them see our faces. If they
wake up while we're there and catch us, there will be no escaping.

A pause.

No, we cannot leave it behind. Without it, we will never find
the last two points.

The chest, I realized. Dante was trying to take it back
from the Liberum.

One more minute.

I hugged my knees, waiting for what came next.

Not yet, he said. *Not yet.*

I gripped the edge of the blanket. What if it didn't
work? What if the Liberum woke up and discovered him?

Wait until you hear them fall.

All I could hear was my own breath, slow and heavy. I
imagined it belonged to him, that he was sitting here beside
me. "Come back to me," I whispered.

Now!

I felt a surge of adrenaline, the mountain air whipping
against his face, the drag on his feet as they sank into the
snow. I waited for his voice to echo through the walls again,
for him to give me some sign that he was okay, but all went
still. I tried to imagine what was happening: Dante running
through the evergreens to where the Liberum were lying, half
dead, half alive, in the snow. Around them lay nine young
boys, all lifeless. I imagined Dante approaching the Brothers
and quietly sifting through their dark robes, searching for
the chest. Who was he with? Who was helping him? I didn't
know. A minute had almost passed. The Liberum would

wake at any moment. I waited for him to say he had found it. No word came. I pressed my eyes shut, wishing I could somehow transport myself there. But I was in darkness, all alone.

I didn't remember crawling back into my tent or falling asleep. All I could recall was Dante's voice as he whispered, *They're out.* I dreamed of the icy skin of the Liberum as Dante touched each of their withered hands to feel for a pulse. None. *Quickly,* I heard him say. I dreamed that he unclasped their cloaks to search for the chest within. And then...

I woke with a jolt. I heard a clamor of noise outside my tent, followed by loud voices. My grandfather's voice boomed over them. "Where is it?" he shouted.

I sat up, only to discover that my tent had been looted. Everything was gone—my bag, my clothes, my gear. All that was left was my blanket and my shovel.

"We searched everywhere," said John LaGuerre, Clementine's father. "No one has it."

"They must!" said my grandfather. "Are you trying to tell me that someone just walked into this tunnel in the middle of the night and stole all our gear?"

I rubbed my eyes, suddenly alert. Their gear was gone, too?

"Yes," said LaGuerre.

"Who?" my grandfather demanded. "It couldn't have been the Undead, because they can't go underground. So who was it?"

"I don't know," said LaGuerre.

"No," my grandfather insisted. "Whoever it was must have come into my tent while I was sleeping and taken the chest from me. Who could have done that?"

"That's what we're trying to find out—" LaGuerre began to say, but my grandfather cut him off.

"The answer is no one. Don't you think I would have woken up if someone had unzipped the flap of my tent and come inside? Don't you think I would have heard it?"

"In some other place, maybe," John said, "But here—it isn't exactly quiet."

So he had heard the echo, too.

"I don't know what you mean," my grandfather said, though I knew he was lying. I'd heard him speaking to my grandmother in his sleep.

"I'm just saying that because of the ... ambient noise ... in this passage, it's possible someone could have snuck in and taken our things without us realizing."

"Possible?" my grandfather said with a scoff. "Anything is possible, but is it likely? No." He paused. "Unless ..."

I heard footsteps approach my tent. Before I had time to sit up, my grandfather had unzipped my tent and ripped open the flap. He leaned inside, his face flushed. His eyes darted about my tent, searching for something. When he didn't find what he was looking for, his face hardened.

"Stand up."

I threw on a sweater and crawled out of the tent. Although it was morning, the only sunlight that penetrated the passage was the dim glow at the end of the tunnel.

My grandfather paced around the rocks, his white hair unusually disheveled.

"What happened?" I asked.

"Last night someone stole all of our gear and supplies. All they left behind were our Spades, burial tools, and a few cans of food."

"What?" I said, confused. "Why would anyone steal all of our things, but leave us with all of our weapons?"

"I was hoping you would have an answer to that question," said my grandfather.

"Me?" I let out a laugh. "Why would I know who took all of our things? I just woke up. All of my things are gone, too."

My grandfather squinted at me, trying to figure out if I was lying. "They took that strange black box of yours, too. You wouldn't happen to know anything about that, would you?"

"The box? Wasn't that in *your* tent?"

My grandfather gritted his teeth together, as if he had been asked that question one too many times this morning. "It isn't anymore. Now, I'm going to ask you one more time. Do you know who was behind this?"

This time, I didn't have to lie. I was just as confused as they were. "No."

My grandfather frowned. "Pack the remainder of your things," he said. "We leave in one hour."

I nodded and looked down at my empty tent, when I noticed a necklace, wrapped twice around my wrist like a bracelet. It hadn't been there before. I froze, suddenly understanding. I touched the irregular brown beads. At first glance, they looked like they were made of wood, though I knew that they weren't. They were a string of beans. And at their center hung the soft paw of a cat. For health and protection.

I bit my lip, trying to hide my excitement. Anya had made a necklace like this one for me just before I left St. Clément. She had told me it was supposed to bring me good luck and protection. I turned my wrist until I could see the clasp: a hasty knot tied into the twine. Could she have come here in the middle of the night and tied it on herself?

I realized then that I did have the answer to my grandfather's question. I straightened my face, knowing the other Monitors were watching me, but inside I was beaming. There was only one person who could have snuck into our tents without us knowing and stolen all of our things. Theo. I remembered his tarot reading. He had decided to come back. And only one person would have risked sneaking into my tent and waking me, just to tie a bracelet around my wrist for good luck. Anya.

A dusty ray of sunshine shone through the end of the pass. My grandfather held up a hand to silence us, then peered around the edge. While we waited, the Monitors closed their eyes, trying to sense the presence of the Undead. I felt nothing except for the strange sensation of someone watching me through the crowd. I peeked open one eye.

The only other person with her head up was Clementine. She shot me a questioning look. *Did you do this?* she mouthed.

I shook my head. Then smiled.

My grandfather returned, his face grim, and broke us into groups. "We'll split up and comb the side of the mountain. Whoever stole our gear couldn't have gotten far." He directed each group into opposite directions, some toward the end of the tunnel, others back the way we came from. I watched the groups depart, Clementine leaving with her father, until I was the only one left.

"What about me?" I asked.

"You stay here. That way I know you won't get into any trouble."

Stay here? To do nothing by myself while everyone else got to search for my friends? Over his shoulder, light streamed in from the end of the passage. Theo and Anya were somewhere out there. I had to find them.

Reading my thoughts, my grandfather continued, "Mr. Harbes and Ms. Vine are guarding either side of the pass, in case you get any creative ideas."

I clenched my jaw and watched the outline of his silhouette blur as he strode off into the day. With nothing to do, I sat on a rock nearby and shone my flashlight around the ceiling of the cave. I waited, hoping I would hear Dante's voice echo off the walls again, but the pass was quiet. How had it happened last night? Did the voices only come out at night, or had I done something to coax them out?

I held the flashlight up into the rocks above me and let his name slip from my lips. "Dante."

I waited for it to refract back to me, its letters jumbled and strange. *Ante—Ente—Enne—Renée.*

The echo still worked. I parted my lips, hoping I could somehow conjure his voice through the mountain walls, when I heard someone call out my name.

"Renée!"

I spun around, trying to see where it had come from. Though it belonged to a boy, it didn't have the same distant echo as the voice I'd heard the night before. It was too loud, too real, as if there were a person perched high up in the alcove.

I shone my light in its direction, scanning the rocks until a pair of eyes reflected back at me. I flicked off the light. A scuffle of footsteps. A grunt. Then a girl's voice. "Ow!"

I turned my light back on to find Theo and Anya standing before me, wincing from the brightness of the beam. They each wore a crisp new outfit: Theo in a tan expedition shirt and a pair of expensive weatherproof pants, both of which were slightly too big on him. A wool cap was pulled over his brown hair. Beside him, Anya wore black winter leggings and a thick wool sweater. I paused, taking in her outfit once more. I recognized those leggings, that sweater, even her scarf. My face burst into a smile. They were mine.

"Put that thing down," Theo said, shielding his eyes.

The yellow bruise from our fight was still visible on his right cheek.

"You've been in here this entire time?"

"Of course we have," Theo said. "And what a productive twelve hours it's been." He sat on a rock beside me. "I have to be honest, though. I was a little disappointed in you when I snuck into your grandfather's tent and found all these goodies that you had neglected to take." He patted his bag. "No, instead, we had to follow you up a snowcapped mountain, sneak into your camp at night, go into your grandfather's tent while he was sleeping, and take them from him."

Anya rolled her eyes, as if she'd been hearing that line for hours. She looked thinner than she had before, her face wan. Though perhaps it was just my clothes; I wasn't used to seeing her in clothes that weren't skintight.

"Goodies?" I said. "What do you mean?"

"Oh, just the little black box from the lake, the elders' secret caviar and champagne stock, though I was more than a little upset when I tried to eat a spoonful and remembered that my taste was dull. But this—this was the real prize." Theo slipped something out of my pocket. My grandfather's notepad. "This was sitting in your grandfather's tent the entire time you were with him. Tsk, tsk." He rapped his fingers against the pad. "Have I not taught you anything?"

The sight of it brought back all those hours I sat in the car, watching my grandfather take notes. What had he been writing?

Theo sighed. "And then, of course, we couldn't take just his things. We had to take everything, so no one would suspect we were targeting just the elders. We needed supplies, anyway. The Monitors just left us in the middle of nowhere with nothing. We let you have your shovels, though. We aren't trying to kill anyone or anything."

"Well, they didn't exactly leave us in the middle of nowhere," Anya corrected. "We left them."

Theo brushed her off. "Same outcome."

"What did you do with it all?"

"Your grandfather was right. We didn't go far." Theo gazed up at the steep rocks around us. "We barely went anywhere at all."

"You hid it all up there?" I said in awe.

"It was my idea," Anya said. "We didn't want to leave any tracks in the snow. Though Theo did most of the lifting."

"We've been playing this game for days," Theo said. "We've been following you ever since we stole the car back from our Monitor escorts."

"What?" I asked. "How?"

"Well, my first idea was that Anya should drug them with one of her famous elixirs—"

"They don't work like that," Anya snapped.

Theo acted as though he hadn't heard her. "—but apparently, they don't work like that." He tapped his finger against his lower lip. "Do they work at all? Now *that* is the million-dollar question."

Anya crossed her arms. "Of course they work," she said.

"Maybe not on you, maybe your internal chemistry just isn't right. Your body can tell when you're not taking a treatment seriously. Perhaps that's the problem."

Theo raised an eyebrow, clearly amused. "So they work on you? Your hearing, your sense of smell, your sense of taste—they're all back to normal?"

Anya frowned. "There's definitely a difference," she said. "Not a big one, but I think they're definitely getting better."

Theo rolled his eyes. "All I'm saying is that I've been taking a concoction of those pills of yours for days now, and nothing has changed."

I hated to side with Theo, but he was right; her elixirs hadn't helped my senses in the slightest.

"Anyway," Theo continued, "so my next best idea was to break out the old-fashioned way. Our escorts made the mistake of locking us inside the car while they went to the bathroom, not realizing one doesn't always need keys to start an engine."

"We followed you up to that castle," Anya said. "All we had to do was park our car behind the others. No one even noticed."

"It was pretty boring, though, sleeping in the car, so I decided to stir things up a bit," Theo said.

"Stir things up?" I said. "But nothing happened while we were at the castle."

Theo raised an eyebrow. "The letter from Monsieur that mysteriously arrived for your grandfather? That wasn't Monsieur. That was us."

"What?" I cried, a little too loudly. "But the envelope and the paper—where did you get it?"

"Snagged it from the hotel. They always have stuff like that hanging around."

"And his handwriting," I continued. "It looked perfect."

Anya beamed. "That was my work."

"I wanted to give your grandfather a little spook," Theo said.

"But how did you know what to write? Do you know what he's up to—what the elders are up to? Because I overheard them talking. They know where the Liberum are. They've been tracking them for years, and using them to find the Netherworld."

Theo tilted his head, impressed. "So you did figure something out," he said with a grin. "I have to say, I didn't think it would happen."

"But how did you—"

"That story will take all night," Theo said, and glanced at Anya.

"What we wanted to tell you," she said, "is that while we were following you, we stumbled across an Undead camp."

"Undead?" I said. "When?"

"Late last night," Theo said. "We had been following you until we reached the third point, but after that, the landscape became so barren that we couldn't risk hiking directly behind you. So we trekked a little farther down the mountain, walking parallel to you until night fell, giving us cover. It was then, when we made our way back up toward the tunnel, that we saw them."

Late last night. That must have been right after I'd heard Dante's voice echoing off the walls of the cave.

"Was Dante there? Was he okay?"

Anya wrung her fingers together the way she did when she had to tell me something unsavory. "Yes."

My chest collapsed with relief, but Anya didn't seem to share my excitement.

"The Liberum weren't there," she continued. "I couldn't feel them anywhere."

Dante had escaped, I realized, excitement stirring within me. His plan had worked. He had taken the chest from the Liberum and left their camp.

"He was sitting with a group of Undead boys. At first we thought they were keeping him against his will," Anya said. "But he looked happy. They were talking and laughing. It was like he was one of them."

My stomach tightened. Dante laughing with Undead boys? It didn't make sense. "He isn't one of them," I said. "There must be an explanation. I know him. He wouldn't do that. Maybe he had converted a few of them to his side."

But Anya only bit her lip. "We crept closer and listened to them. He was telling them about the Monitors. About where they were going and how to find you. He was helping them."

Her words made me sink back. "Are you sure it was

him?" I asked. "Because he would never do that. He could have been pretending to be on their side so that they wouldn't hurt him. Or—"

"That's an awful lot of information to divulge," Theo said. "And he wasn't lying. Everything he said was accurate. Details about me, about Anya, about Clementine. It didn't sound like he was trying to appease them."

I shook my head. I couldn't let myself believe that.

"He's been aging," Theo said. "I've noticed it; you must have, too. The way his eyes kept clouding when he was angry. The way he stiffened, his skin hollowing—"

"I trust him," I said, though my lips quivered.

Before Theo could respond, I heard a shout ripple in from the other side of the pass. My grandfather's dark outline eclipsed the sunlight pouring in through the mouth of the tunnel.

Anya backed away.

"We have to go," Theo said.

"What about the sealed box?" I asked.

"It's safer with us," Theo said. "Read this, and you'll see why." He handed me the spiral pad he'd taken from my grandfather's tent.

In the distance, my grandfather turned on his flashlight.

Anya receded into the darkness, Theo following her. "We'll find you tonight," he said, letting the darkness fold itself around him until all that was left was his echo fading into gibberish as it bounced off the rocks.

I slid the notebook into my coat and sat down on the rocks, just as the beam from my grandfather's light searched the dirt floor of the cavern.

He loomed over me, the mist of his breath vanishing into the cold air. He shone his light at the rocks surrounding us, until he let it rest on me. I winced.

"I heard voices," he said. "Who were you talking to?"

I shoved my hands in my pockets, hoping he couldn't see the outline of his notepad through my coat. "No one. It was probably just the echo." Corroborating my story, the cavern reflected my words back to us, contorting them until they sounded like they belonged to someone else.

My grandfather squinted at me. "The Liberum are drifting," he said finally. "We have to press on with the little gear we have left. I've already alerted the others."

He took one last glance at the inside of the cave, shining his flashlight just over the spot where Theo and Anya had emerged minutes before. I hoisted my bag to my shoulders, mouthing them a silent good-bye as I followed my grandfather out into the daylight.

CHAPTER 13

The Red Spade

SOURCE: *Jeremy B. Age: thirteen. Undead for five years.*

I stole glimpses at the most recent entry in my grandfather's notebook while we hiked across the alpine ridge toward the floating peak we'd seen from the third point.

Enrolled in Gottfried Academy: September 2011.

My grandfather led the way with a newfound vigor, using the pull of the Undead to guide us. Without the chest, Pruneaux, or Dante to help lead them, the Undead were slowing; I could feel the gap between them and us shrinking.

But if Dante wasn't with them, then where was he? Every few steps I searched the white expanse of mountains below us for a dark speck moving over the snow, waiting for his vacancy to reach out to me through the wind. Theo and Anya couldn't have been right. They must have misheard him. After all, their hearing had dulled, too...

I slid my grandfather's notebook out of my pocket and continued reading.

Recruited on November the 24th, 2011. Sent as source on December the 12th, 2011. Questioned on December the 22nd, 2011.

Recruited, and sent as a source? That could only mean one thing. I squinted at my grandfather's handwriting, making sure I had read his notes correctly. But before I could turn the page, Mr. Harbes glanced over his shoulder at me. "What are you doing back there?"

"Nothing," I said. "Just looking for a tissue."

He frowned, and dug through his pocket until he pulled out a crumpled bit of napkin. "Here. Now hurry up. The sooner we catch up to the Liberum, the sooner we can go home."

It wasn't until after we camped and finished a meager dinner of rice and canned beans that I was able to sneak back to my tent. But when I flipped to the second page of the notebook, someone ripped open the flap of my tent.

I slammed the cover shut and thrust it beneath my sleeping bag just as a dark, heart-shaped face appeared in the entrance. Clementine. I relaxed my grip on my shovel. "Was that really necessary?" I whispered.

She rolled her eyes. "You scare too easily," she said, and after glancing over her shoulder, she climbed inside.

"Turn off your flashlight," she said to me. "We can't have two lights on in here or they might suspect there are two people."

"You turn off yours," I said. "This is my tent."

Clementine shook her head as if she were doing me a favor. "Fine." She inspected the blue nylon of the tent. "This is where you've been sleeping this whole time?" she said with a grimace.

"It's a tent," I said. "Is yours really that different?"

"It's bigger," she said, and wiped away a bit of dirt beneath her legs. "And a lot cleaner."

I clenched my jaw, trying to hold my tongue. "So what do you want?"

"I've been watching you," she said, her eyes sharp. "You've been acting weird all day. You know something."

I slid the notepad out from under the sleeping bag, lowered my voice, and told her about Theo and Anya, about how they had visited me in the cavern and given me this. I left out what they had said about Dante. Although she had aligned herself with me now, Clementine was still a Monitor, and a fierce one at that. I didn't want to give her any reason to change her mind.

She leaned over my shoulder and together, we flipped through my grandfather's notepad.

Stephen L. Age: fourteen. Undead for eight years. Enrolled in Gottfried Academy: September 2011. Recruited on November the 7th, 2011. Sent as a source on November the 14th, 2011. Questioned on December the 1st, 2011.

Notes on the questioning:

Source confirmed that the Liberum were searching for the clues left behind by the Nine Sisters, which they believe will lead them to

the Cartesian Map. Source also confirmed that the Liberum have a
potential lead on the first clue, which they obtained through force,
and are now moving on foot to Montreal to find it.

Source was put to rest December the 5th, 2011.

Clementine furrowed her brow. "Does this mean what I think it does?"

"I think so," I whispered, a knot forming in my stomach. I flipped through the pages. Atop each entry was the name of an Undead boy, followed by a slew of similar notes.

"The elders weren't just spying on the Liberum by following them, and turning a few of their boys to their side," Clementine said. "Your grandfather was using his time as the headmaster of Gottfried Academy to recruit Undead boys to spy on the Liberum for him. He was using *students* to help get more information on the Netherworld."

I swallowed. "Then he put them to rest so they couldn't tell anyone."

Clementine flipped back in time to the earlier entries. There were dozens and dozens of them, some dating back over thirty years. "Wait," she said. "But your grandfather has only been the headmaster of Gottfried since September. So what are these from?"

"Actually, my grandfather was the headmaster of Gottfried twice," I said. "First in the 1970s."

"It couldn't possibly be 1972," Clementine said, pointing to the date of the first entry.

"That sounds about right," I said. "He was the headmaster for seventeen years. There was some sort of scandal there.

A fire. He resigned and went back to the High Court. Then last year, he returned to Gottfried Academy to resume his job as headmaster, limiting the school to Undead students only."

"Seventeen years?" Clementine said, as if that number meant something to her. When I nodded, her eyes widened in awe. "That means that your grandfather left Gottfried in 1989."

"That sounds about right."

"Nineteen eighty-nine?" she said, as if it should have rung a bell. "That's the year of the bombing in the High Court."

She searched the notebook until she found the last entries in 1989. The last four subjects were each sent as sources on the same day.

"The bombing of the courthouse took place one month after these four Undead were sent to spy on the Liberum." Clementine traced their names. *Kurt M., Henry L., Paul N.,* and *Michael P.*

"Four entries," Clementine said. "For each of the four Undead that were on trial."

However, unlike the previous subjects, these Undead had only one note for the four of them, which read:

Notes:

We were not able to question the sources. They were unexpectedly captured by a group of Monitors while traveling with the Liberum. The Monitors have brought the sources to the High Court, where they are awaiting trial for conspiring with the Liberum. They have already tried to tell the Monitors of our mission, but no one believes them. I will not come to their rescue. In a few days time, the High Court will find them guilty. They will be put to rest.

"The four Undead on trial that day were being accused of a crime that they didn't commit," I said. "That's why Monsieur blew up the courthouse. He must have known what the High Court was doing."

Clementine's eyes glimmered. "He wanted to punish them."

I nodded, the realization complicating my feelings about Monsieur even more. "And to free the innocent Undead in the process."

"But what happened to the four Undead after that?" Clementine asked.

My mind raced to put the pieces together. I thought of my grandfather, of how he'd resigned from his position as the headmaster of Gottfried not long after the trial, when a mysterious fire ravaged the school, burning half of the campus and the forest around the Academy to ash. The Second Autumn Fire, the locals had called it, for the way it had made the trees look orange.

"Those four Undead were the ones who started the fire," I realized. "They were seeking revenge on the man who almost put them to rest."

"That's why your grandfather resigned," Clementine said. "He went on to become the head of the High Court." She turned the page, but the next entry was from last September, over twenty years later. "That's why there's a twenty-year gap in these notes. Your grandfather and the elders were lying low. Without a contact at Gottfried, there was no way they could recruit new Undead boys. Until now."

That night I woke to a pair of cold fingers pressed to my lips. I opened my eyes. Anya was crouched in my tent. "Shh," she cooed.

She led me outside and away from the camp, tiptoeing through the snow like a deer. I followed her, groggy, my mind still thick with dreams.

"I can't remember him," I whispered to her. "I know I love him, but I can't feel it anymore. I can't feel anything."

"Who?"

"Dante," I said. "What does his voice sound like? I'll never hear it again."

Anya slowed, her hair blowing in front of her face. For a moment, I could almost believe that we were standing in the snowy streets of Montreal, walking back to our dormitory at St. Clément. I wanted to go back so badly, to rewind the past weeks, and erase all of the doubt I had been harboring. "Help me remember him."

"I can't," Anya said. "There is no pill for that. But you're lucky. He isn't gone yet; you still have him. Love is like any other superstition—you can't prove it, you just have to believe in it."

By the light of the moon we walked down the ridge, zigzagging through the snow until I couldn't tell which direction we had come from. A fire flickered in the distance. Theo huddled over it, a tent perched behind him.

"Did you read it?" he said.

"Yes," I said. I thought back to that afternoon in the German countryside, when I had crouched behind the line of cars and eavesdropped on my grandfather as he threatened Theo. "You already knew my grandfather was doing this, didn't you?"

"I only had an idea," Theo said. His Spade rested on the ground beside him, its varnished handle propped up on his bag.

"This has to do with your being disbarred, doesn't it?" I said.

He glanced at Anya, who gave him an encouraging nod. "Yes," he said.

"What did you do?"

Theo took a breath, as though he'd been preparing for this moment for years. "I killed my father."

"It was my first big mission," Theo said. "I had earned my Spade a year before, and was one of the youngest Monitors ever to get one. And I earned it the real way. I've never studied so hard for anything in my life. I had to show them that I was more than just a dropout and a thief. I had to prove that I was one of them." He clenched his jaw. "This is all to say that I wanted to be a Monitor, more than I've ever wanted to be anything. Do you understand?"

I nodded.

"Good," he said. "Remember that later."

Anya settled in beside me, her eyes scanning the horizon

to make sure no one had followed us. She had already heard this story.

"Prior to that, I had only gone on smaller missions in Paris and Lyon, where I, along with other newly minted Monitors, scouted for fresh Undead. We rounded up non-violent Undead and brought them to the Court to be documented and sent to an Undead school. So when the High Court told me they thought they could trust me with a confidential, high-level mission, I was ecstatic. I went before the High Court, where I received my assignment: to travel to the mountains in upstate New York, where I was to capture an Undead who had supposedly worked with the Liberum. I expected to hear the normal directions: to only bury the Undead if he threatened my life or the lives of those around me, and to otherwise secure the Undead and bring him back to Montreal, where he would appear before the High Court for trial. But those directions never came. The High Court only gave me one directive: keep all details of this mission to myself. If I ran into any other Monitors on my way, I should tell them I was on a trip to see my family.

"That was the first sign that something was wrong, but I didn't see it. I assumed that the rules were different on covert missions. They only gave me a few details: I was hunting an Undead boy, eleven years old. I remember being surprised when the Monitors told me that the Undead had only died two years before. Most Undead don't become violent until they've been dead for much longer. But the

Monitors had told me he was my target, which meant that he must have done something very bad.

"The Court told me that the Undead was somewhere in the wilds of upstate New York. This Undead was particularly vicious, they said, which was why I wasn't bringing him back to the main courthouse. We couldn't risk it. Instead, I was supposed to track him down and bury him."

Theo leaned on his knees, the reflection of the fire making his eyes flicker. "I wandered through the wilderness for days, following his presence. When I finally found him, he was hiding by an old barn. I had expected him to be dangerous, but instead, he looked frightened and confused, and very, very young. I shouted at him to raise his hands where I could see them. He did as I said without arguing. I thought he might cry, that's how scared he looked. My voice sounded so gruff in those woods. I remember feeling ashamed, standing there yelling at a child.

"Even though he didn't seem dangerous, I tied his arms together and led him outside, where I planned on doing what I had gone there to do. Sure, he looked like a normal kid, but with every step I remembered the words of the High Court: this Undead was particularly vicious. He must have realized what I was there for, because he started to whimper. He kept repeating the same thing. *They already questioned me. I don't know anything.*

"I didn't know what he meant. Who questioned him? And about what? But I forced my thoughts into silence. The Monitors hadn't sent me there to talk to him. I told him to stand still and face the trees. I pulled the gauze from my pack and was about to put him to rest, when I noticed that his knees were trembling. Then I saw his sneakers, which were the same ones I'd had when I was his age. The laces were untied. I reached toward them, my arm brushing his ankle, and he began to cry. That's when I knew that I couldn't do it. I called my contact at the High Court, and told him that I didn't think the Undead was too dangerous to transport to the High Court, and that I couldn't put him to rest.

"He told me I was going against the High Court's protocol. He said that I was letting the Undead trick me; that this was how the Undead boys of the Liberum operated. I asked him what the boy had done. He told me the boy had been working for the Liberum, and that was all I needed to know. I remember looking at the skinny outline of the boy's body. It didn't matter what the High Court said; I couldn't do it. My contact asked me for my location, then told me to leave the boy in the barn. A group of Monitors from the High Court would be there soon. I asked the Monitor on the phone if he was absolutely sure that he had the right Undead. He said yes.

"I should have left it at that, but something about his voice made me wonder. So after I left the boy inside the barn, I crouched behind a bale of hay and waited until the Monitors arrived. There were only two of them, both men. I couldn't see their faces in the dark; all I could make out were their hunched shoulders that shifted while they walked, and their Spades, which they carried low to their sides like axes.

"I knew something was wrong when I saw them in the light. Both Monitors were wearing wool face masks, which we're never supposed to do. Monitors are always supposed to make their identities known. They walked into the barn and immediately started questioning the Undead boy. 'What did you tell him?' one of them said, in a voice that sounded like he was trying to disguise his identity.

"'Nothing!' the boy said.

"'Did you tell them about your mission?' the other Monitor asked.

"'No,' the boy said. 'I did just as the elders told me to when they first sent me to the Liberum. They already questioned me about the Brothers and what they were looking for; I told them everything I knew. When I was finished, they said I could go free.'"

Theo furrowed his brow, his gaze distant as if he were still crouched by the entrance of the barn. "I had no idea what the boy was talking about. It sounded like the elders had *sent* him to the Liberum on purpose, and had already questioned him and decided to set him free. But if that were true, then why would they have sent me there to bury him?"

Beside me, Anya hugged her knees.

"The elders had sent the boy to the Liberum to find out about the Netherworld," I said.

Theo nodded. "I didn't realize it at the time, but now I'm certain that was what the boy was talking about."

While Theo spoke, Anya leaned into the tent and opened her tin of elixirs. Out of the corner of my eye, I saw her measure a handful of pills into her palm. She washed them down with a sip of water.

"The two Monitors didn't seem to care what the boy said," Theo continued. "They dragged him into the middle of the barn and pinned him down. One of the men removed a roll of embalming gauze from his pack and began to wrap the boy in cloth."

Theo threw a splinter of wet wood into the fire, making it spit. "All I knew was that whatever the Monitors were doing was wrong, and I had to stop them. So I crept into the barn and pulled the chain on the bulb, leaving us in darkness. If I couldn't see their faces, I didn't want them to see mine.

"Everything went quiet. 'Who's there?' one of them shouted, his voice gruff. All I could see were the whites of their eyes as they searched the barn. 'Take off your masks and I'll tell you,' I said to them. They both turned in my direction. 'Who are you?' one of them said, stepping toward me. 'I'm faceless and voiceless,' I said, my words throaty so that I couldn't be recognized either. 'Just like you. You don't want anyone to see what you're doing. But I saw what you did."

Theo paused. "That's when I heard one of them move toward me. I couldn't make out what was happening until I saw the tip of his Spade slicing through the air. I ducked out of the way just as it crashed into a wooden table. He swung at me again. I wove through the old furniture and equipment littering the barn. I didn't notice the other Monitor waiting for me until he was close enough for me to see his eyes through the holes of his mask. I stumbled back as he lunged at me, just barely missing my chest. When I regained my balance, I swung back at him, aiming for his Spade. I meant to knock it out of his hand, but he moved it out of the way just before we collided. I felt my Spade hit something soft. Skin. Blood splattered across the wall. He collapsed to the ground. Just folded, like he was made of putty."

Theo pushed off his wool hat and ran his hands through his hair. "I didn't mean to kill him. It just happened. I dropped my Spade. When the other Monitor saw what had happened, he turned on the light and took off his mask. I recognized him as one of the Monitors who worked with my father. That's when I got this awful feeling in my stomach. I gazed down at the man lying limp by my feet, a pool of red spreading around him. I turned the body over and pulled up his mask, already soaked through with blood. It was my father."

Anya lowered her head in respect for the dead.

"The other Monitor took me back to Montreal, where they locked me in a holding cell beneath the High Court. I thought they were going to put me on trial, but halfway through the night, the guards unlocked the bars and brought me to your grandfather. The moment I saw him, I knew that I had seen something I shouldn't have. Why else would he want to see me alone?

"He gave me some lame explanation: that they had been trying to get information about some plot the Liberum were going to launch on us. I didn't believe him, but at that point I was too shaken to care. We made a deal. I wouldn't tell anyone about what I'd seen, so as not to ruin the 'undercover goals of the mission'. In exchange, instead of putting me on trial and letting the Monitoring community know that I had killed my father, your grandfather would explain his death away as a field accident. And I would be disbarred."

"But it was self-defense," I said. "It wasn't your fault."

Theo let out a callous laugh. "Not to them. I was the one who instigated the fight. I was the one who turned off the light, and crept in like an intruder; the one who swung the fatal blow. I should have just marched in, showed my face, and told them I was a Monitor. If they had put me on trial, I wouldn't have had a chance. I was already a dropout and a known thief. It was my word against a respected Monitor. Who do you think the court would have believed?"

I looked at Theo, hunched over the fire, his sanded Spade resting by his side, his laces loose and caked with mud. I wouldn't have believed him either.

"After that I moved in with my grandfather," Theo said. "He doesn't know what happened, and I hope he never does. Since then, I've been trying to figure out what the boy was talking about that night. What the elders were doing. I had theories, but none of them proved true until now." He gazed at the notepad he'd taken from my grandfather. "That notebook fills in the gaps. The elders have been recruiting Undead through Gottfried for years. When your grandfather got into trouble at Gottfried, the other elders took over, and tried to recruit through lower Monitors like myself. Remember how I told you about my earlier missions, when I was searching for nonviolent Undead and bringing them to the High Court? I'm pretty sure that was just a way for me to bring new sources to the elders. All this time, they've been sending Undead boys to the Liberum to funnel information back about the Netherworld. When the Undead cease being useful, the elders set them free, and send a lower Monitor to bury them."

"This was why Monsieur sent you," I said. "This was why you wanted to come with us in the first place."

Theo nodded. "I want a fresh start."

CHAPTER 14

The Last Gasp

I LEFT THEO AND ANYA AS NIGHT FADED INTO MORN-ing. The tents of the Monitor camp were quiet. I wove through them, tiptoeing through the snow until I reached my grandfather's spot. Through the gray fabric I could just barely see the outline of him sleeping inside. I didn't know what I was going to say or do, only that I had to face him. With one swift motion, I threw open the front flap. But when I stuck my head inside, all I saw was a crumpled-up sleeping bag and a few of my grandfather's things. He was gone.

Footprints littered the edge of the camp: not just one set but many, each leading out from one of the elder's tents and up along the ridge. I followed them until a ring of dark specks materialized through the fog. The elders of the High Court stood huddled together. They turned to me in unison, their coats flapping in the wind.

"Renée?" My grandfather said. His white hair fluttered against his forehead. "Is everything all right?"

I surveyed the elders, then reached into my coat and removed his notepad. "No," I said. "It isn't."

My grandfather tilted his head, unable to hide his surprise. "Where did you get that?"

"I know what you've been doing at Gottfried." I took a step closer. "I know about the bombing of the High Court all those years ago. I know about Theo and why he was disbarred."

My grandfather's silence served as an admission of guilt. Behind him, the other elders inched forward, murmuring among themselves, but my grandfather held his hand up to stop them.

"Theodore was disbarred because he killed his father," my grandfather said, his face calm. "The bombing of the High Court has yet to be solved. And as for our mission, though it must be performed covertly to assure its success, that does not mean that I am ashamed of it. The work we have been doing will not only prevent the Liberum, the most vile group of Undead from our generation and generations past, from attaining eternal life; it could also restore the lives of fresh Undead and humans alike across the world."

He was completely convinced in his righteousness. "But in the meantime, you've been letting the Liberum kill innocent people for years. You could have stopped them decades ago. And you've been burying your Undead recruits right after you question them."

His upper lip curled, contorting his face into something awful. "We only bury Undead who pose a threat to others or endanger the mission, which could bring life to thousands of Undead and humans in the future. The Liberum play an integral role in our mission. They can use methods that we Monitors cannot."

"You mean they can kill people for information, and you can't. The Liberum have been murdering people to find out where the Netherworld is for years." I thought back to all of the mysterious deaths that had jarred the Monitoring community last year. "Ms. LaBarge," I continued, remembering when we had gotten the call that my old professor had been found dead on an island in Lake Erie. "Cindy Bell," I said, her name transporting me back to that day when the phone rang, telling us about another murder, of my best friend's mother. "My parents," I said. "Your own daughter—"

"You don't know that," my grandfather said, clearly pained.

But I kept going. "They were all killed by the Liberum, because they had information about the Nine Sisters and the Netherworld. You had the power to stop the Liberum—"

"Renée—be careful of what you are about to accuse me of," my grandfather warned.

But I couldn't stop. Not now. "You've known where they were all these years. But instead of burying them, you let them continue killing. Those deaths are on you now.

Because in reality, you don't really care about helping the Undead, or about giving the world the gift of eternal life," I continued. "You just want to use it to extend your own—"

Before I could finish, my grandfather grabbed my wrist with his leathery fingers. "That's enough," he said. "I do not need your blessing nor the Court's to tell me what to do. I *am* the Court."

I tried to wriggle free, but my grandfather held on, dragging me through the snow. "I would send you home, but then you wouldn't be able to watch while we bury your Undead friend," he said. "So for now, I'll send you back to the tents."

I kicked at him, thrashing beneath his grip, when a shiver rippled through the air. The fog rearranged itself, clearing a path in front of us toward the peaks in the distance. Through it, I could feel the presence of the Undead twisting around my ankles, my neck, my arms. Could Dante be among them? There were too many of them for me to tell.

My grandfather froze, his fingers loosening on my wrist. "They're here."

He turned to one of the elders. "Wake the camp. Tell the Monitors to ready themselves," he said, and pushed me toward him. "Take Renée with you. She can wait for me at the camp."

"I'm not going back—" I began to say, when the temperature dropped.

The elders gripped their Spades and turned toward the

vacancy. My grandfather thrust me toward the camp. "Go!" he said, then followed the others toward the creeping hollow in the distance, the fog folding around their bodies until all I could see of them were the handles of their Spades disappearing into the mist.

The remaining elder took my arm, his gray gloves tightening around my coat, and dragged me toward the camp. With each step, the tug of the Undead pulled me backward. I stumbled behind him, trying to wriggle free, when I noticed the tip of the elder's Spade glinting in its sheath against the back of his coat. One of the only things a Monitor would stop for was his weapon. I let my legs fold beneath me, intentionally falling into the snow. When the elder bent down to pull me up, I grabbed his Spade from its holster and threw it as far as I could. The elder spun around, stunned. I broke free and ran into the fog.

It seemed to part for me as I ran through it, the presence of the Undead carving out a trail through the mist. I could barely make out the dark shapes of the elders in the distance, when a deep crevasse materialized in the snow. I skidded toward the edge, trying to stop myself from sliding in, but the ice crumbled beneath my feet. I dug my fingers into the ground, searching for traction, when someone grabbed the back of my coat and pulled me to safety.

I fell back into the snow with a thud, my legs tangled with those of another. Theo groaned beneath me. "You're heavier than you look," he said, and pushed me off him.

Anya stood beside him, her chest heaving as though

she couldn't catch her breath fast enough. She leaned over, clutching her chest.

"Are you okay?" I asked.

Anya took a moment to gather herself, then nodded. But she didn't look okay at all. Her face was exhausted, her shoulders hunched as though she didn't have the energy to hold them upright.

"When you left, I had a feeling that something bad was going to happen to you," she said. "Then Theo felt the Undead coming."

"You're welcome, by the way," Theo added, picking up his Spade, and glanced over the edge. The crack in the ice was just wide enough for me to jump over, and so deep that I couldn't see the bottom. A bit of snow crumbled off the edge and fell into the crevasse. I waited for it to hit the bottom, but heard nothing.

"Thanks," I said.

I watched as Theo stood up, dusting off his bag. I eyed it. "Do you still have it?" I asked.

Theo hesitated, then lowered his pack and took out the black box. "Of course I do," he said. "I steal from other people. No one steals from me."

"Give it to me," I said.

But he didn't move. He gripped it tighter, as though he wanted to keep it for himself.

Anya nudged him in the side. "Give it to her," she said, her eyes wide.

At her urging, Theo reluctantly dropped it in my hand.

I stuffed it in my bag, suddenly uncomfortable. "I meant it," I said quietly. "When I thanked you. I don't know what I would have done without you."

"Died, is what," Theo said, wiping the snow from his hands. "But don't get too emotional. I didn't do it for your sake. I just need you to get that chest from your boyfriend."

I rolled my eyes, telling myself that he was joking, though his eyes weren't teasing at all.

A shout sounded through the fog. I stared at the mist with apprehension, wondering what I would meet on the other side. Though I couldn't sense Dante's presence, the prickle beneath my skin told me he was there. "I have to find him."

"I know," said Anya. "We're coming with you."

Deep crevasses cut through the ice like scars. We maneuvered around them, the silhouettes of the elders growing larger, clearer, until we could see them gathered beside a jagged crack, the ice beneath their feet so thick it looked blue. I could feel the Undead before I could see them. The atmosphere was still and frigid, as if all the life had been hollowed out of it.

"Force them toward the crevasse!" my grandfather yelled.

The air around us rippled, as if the entire world was shuddering. A blur of white billowed over the crest in the mountain like an avalanche.

"Form a line!" my grandfather shouted to the elders. "Don't let them surround us."

We reached them just as they collided, the Undead boys tumbling into us in a flurry of hands and hair and snow, our shovels pressing them back. They clawed at our feet and hands, their tiny bodies slipping between our shovels. I felt the shock of an arm, ice-cold against mine. A pair of dulled eyes stared up at me, their pupils so clouded the boy must have been close to blind. I twisted out of his grip only to see a set of yellowed teeth biting into my leg. I kicked him off, swinging my shovel wildly as I pushed forward against their weight with the rest of the elders, trying to force the Undead closer to the crack in the earth. Theo and Anya fought beside me, their shovels clinking as they peeled the Undead off of their limbs and pushed them toward the opening.

My grandfather cleared a path before us, knocking the Undead aside with his Spade. With his other hand he wielded a roll of gauze, wrapping their legs, their arms, anything he could get his hands on. I scanned the fray, searching for Dante. The sight made my stomach sink. Undead crowded the mountainside, so many that I could barely pick out one from the next. They outnumbered us ten to one, their tiny bodies surrounding the elders, who struggled to stand amidst the swarm.

I ran toward them, thrusting the Undead aside and searching their faces for Dante's, when a sunken face, so sallow that I could barely believe it once belonged to a child, appeared through the fog in front of me. He grabbed my shovel, pulling me to the ground. I couldn't see what was happening; I could only feel the weight of his bony body on top of mine, an elbow in my ribs, a knee in my thigh, four nails scratching at my shoulder.

We wrestled in the snow, his fingers scratching at my throat. I kicked him off only to be pinned down by two more, their hands as cold as ice. They knelt over me and clawed at my cheeks. I thrashed, trying to wriggle free from their grip. Through their fingers, I saw an elder clutching his face, his cheek nothing more than a mess of pulp and blood. An Undead boy leaped onto the elder's back, biting his neck, his shoulder. Beside him, another elder fell. The Undead boys swarmed him like insects, pushing each other aside to suck out his soul. They were overpowering us.

The Undead boys leaned over me, ready to press their mouths to mine. I felt the gravity of their lips pulling a thin cord of my breath toward them. My head grew faint. Then a voice bellowed through the wind: Clementine's father, John LaGuerre. He bounded toward us holding a Spade and a torch, the rest of the Monitors from our camp trailing behind him.

The Undead's grip on me loosened as they looked up. I flung them into the snow, watching as they flew across the ice and into the dark pit of the crevasse.

The junior Monitors rushed toward us in a force of fire and metal, pressing the Undead back with their torches. Clementine fought beside her father, her eyes wild and ruthless as she struck one Undead into the crevasse with her left hand, while warding off two others with a torch in her right.

She thrust her shovel into the ice and, with both hands, plunged the torch into the chest of an Undead boy, her face devoid of any mercy. Black smoke coiled up around her. She stood, her chest heaving. After wiping the sweat from her brow, she continued into the fray.

On the periphery, I could just make out an Undead leaping toward me. Just before he made contact, a Monitor knocked him into the snow. I looked up, startled, to see my guard, Ms. Vine. Her mousy figure was far stronger than it looked as she swept him into the crevasse. *Thank you*, I mouthed. She nodded before ducking under a Spade and pressing forward.

Behind her, Theo shouted and sliced his Spade through a crowd of boys while Anya kneeled over one fallen Monitor, then the next, her tin open as she wiped their foreheads with a bit of cloth and dabbed ointment on their wounds.

A shiver ran through the air.

"Another throng of Undead, coming up on the rear!" my grandfather yelled. "Spread out!" he said. "Guard the back!"

As they grew closer, an icy thread uncoiled through the air and wrapped itself around my fingers like a hand grasping mine. It sent a prickle beneath my skin, so familiar that it made my chest swell.

Dante.

A cluster of dark figures emerged from the fog. I didn't know whom he was with, though I was certain he was there. But before I could run toward him, a chill settled in over the mountains, colder than I had ever felt before. I spun around to see nine black dots move across the horizon, so quickly that they seemed to be carried on the wind. The Liberum. With them came a foul gust, so cold that it made the air around us grow brittle. One by one, the elders looked up. They felt the vacancy, too.

"The Liberum are coming!" my grandfather shouted, throwing an Undead into the crevasse. "Prepare yourselves."

The nine Brothers swept toward us like a dark fog, their black cloaks dragging through the snow. I backed away and watched as the Monitors surrounded them, trying to ward them off with torches, but the Brothers moved smoothly, soundlessly, slipping just out of reach as if they were made of nothing more than robes.

All the while, I felt Dante's presence behind us, getting closer, closer, his vacancy prickling up my skin like frost. I heard a Monitor near the back shout that more Undead were upon them, but beyond that I couldn't make out his words; I could only sense Dante, his hollowness tickling the back of my neck.

I caught glimpses of him. An arm reaching toward me through the fog. A flash of brown hair, wet with snow, as he ducked beneath a Spade. His hands, grasping the tattered shirts of the Undead boys and pulling them away just before they attacked the Monitors. A pair of lips, frosted red, parting to call out my name. I pushed through the bodies between us, trying to make my way to him, but the sway of the fight kept pushing us apart.

Out of the corner of my eye, I saw a pair of Undead boys

run toward me. I swung my shovel toward them, but before they reached me, an Undead with blond hair thrust them in the opposite direction. Beside him stood a tall Undead with broad shoulders and a frame that bespoke someone my age. Together, they scooped up another Undead that ran toward me, and then another, tossing them aside until the snow around me was clear.

Their vacancies felt familiar. I thought back to the pair of Undead who had directed others away from me at the Mädchen Inn in Germany. These boys must have been the same ones that had protected me that night. But why?

The taller one must have noticed me staring because he touched the blond boy's arm and pointed at me. I held out my shovel, ready to attack, when I felt someone come up behind me. I spun around, slicing my shovel through the air. Clementine ducked out of the way, the metal tip barely grazing her hair. When she stood, she patted her head, making sure her barrette was still in place. She let out a sigh of relief. "You're lucky," she said. "If you had cut off any more of my hair, I would have had to send you into the crevasse with them."

I felt my chest deflate. "You're lucky I didn't aim a little bit lower," I said, and together we turned to face the two Undead through the fog.

"You take the blonde," Clementine murmured. "I'll take the tall one."

I nodded. But they didn't come any closer. Instead, they backed away, disappearing into the mist.

I blinked. "What was that?"

Clementine didn't respond. Before I heard the footsteps behind us, she whipped around and struck an Undead in the jaw. Blood splattered across the snow. She wiped the blade of her shovel on her pants, unfazed, and turned to the fog where the two Undead had stood, her face just as perplexed as mine was. "I have no idea."

But I didn't have time to linger. I had to find Dante. His presence reached out to me in icy tendrils of air, leading me through the Monitors and the Undead boys, over the bodies strewn across the ground, contorted by death. Now that Dante was closer, I could feel the life coming back to me. The colors grew vivid, the filth of the fight brightening until it almost looked surreal. Warmth returned to my hands as I gripped my shovel.

The Brothers of the Liberum loomed over the fight, their hooded silhouettes casting dark shadows over the snow. They scanned the snow, as if searching for something. An Undead boy beside them whispered to one of the Brothers, then pointed in my direction. The Brother turned; his empty visage rested on me. One by one the Liberum broke free and followed him.

"Are they coming toward us?" I asked, a wave of dread passing through me. "They saw Dante rescue me at Gottfried Academy. They know I know him. They must think I have the chest."

"I call the two in the middle," Clementine whispered. "Which ones do you want?"

I steadied my arm. "I—I guess the two on either side."

Clementine's eyes met mine, a mischievous smile spreading across her face. "What do you think is under those cloaks? All I can picture is more cloaks."

I let out a nervous laugh. "Aren't you ever scared?"

"Of course I am," she said. "The trick is to never show it. So what do you think is under there?"

I thought back to that awful day at Gottfried, just after Noah had died, when one of the Brothers had swept through the snow toward me. All I had been able to make out of him was a crinkled sliver of white beneath his hood. I tried to extend that hint of white to the rest of his face, but it withered into mist. "A cavity of wrinkled skin and bones."

Clementine shook her head. "See, that's what you're doing wrong. You have to think of them as what they actually are: kids, just like us. The only difference is that they've gone on living long past their expiration date. Which is why there's nothing to be afraid of. Watch them," she said. "Their senses are dulled. The Monitors know it; you can tell by the way they're attacking."

The nine Brothers pressed their way toward us. The Monitors crept around them, striking with stealthy, sudden movements, before receding back. With each blow, the Brothers lashed out, but always a few seconds too late.

"They act like they can see and hear us, but they can't, at least not that well," Clementine said. "It's a weakness that we can manipulate to our gain."

I hadn't even realized that my fingers were trembling

until Clementine reached out and put her hand on mine to make them go still. When she removed her hand from mine, a roll of gauze was wedged between my fingers.

"If I don't get a chance to see you before the end," she said, "then good luck. I hope you find what you're looking for."

My eyes stung in the cold. "Thanks," I whispered. "Maybe in another life, we'll run into each other again."

"I hope so."

Together we crouched low to the ground and crept forward, our feet barely making a sound, as if we were carried by the wind. The Liberum were just yards away, their hooded heads leaning forward as if they were trying to see where we were. I stole to the left, Clementine to the right. We raised our shovels. The Liberum tilted their heads, as if they had seen a flash of something move, but before they had time to turn their heads, we struck. A glimmer of metal. A clean swish through the air. A low wheeze as our metal hit their sides. Once, twice. A blow on either side, stunning two of the Brothers, followed by a quick turn of the wrist. I looped a roll of gauze around one of their arms, catching a glimpse of the sallow skin beneath. Clementine did the same. Then we both ducked out of the way, their heavy robes grazing my forehead as I crouched low to the ground and went still.

I tried to silence my breath as the Brothers searched for us, their long hoods swooping to the left, the right. Clementine and I mirrored each other like we were two hands on the same body; she doled out the strikes while I wrapped the gauze around their ankles, their hands, weakening them bit by bit.

One of the Brothers must have heard me breathing. He lunged at me, his withered wrist reaching out from beneath his robes. I fell back just as his icy fingers grazed my skin. Grabbing my shovel from the snow, I scrambled to my feet and backed toward the crevasse as two Brothers swept toward me. Over their shoulders I could see Clementine fighting off two more, her slender body weaving through them like a shadow.

I swung at them, once, twice, trying to knock them into the crack in the earth, but they were too quick. I stumbled, feeling the cold wisps of their breath lick at my throat as one of their hooded faces came dangerously close to mine. The crevasse was inches away, the ice beneath my hand crumbling into the abyss. I would only have one chance. I gripped my shovel by my side, hiding it behind the folds of my coat, and waited for the Brothers to lower their faces to mine. One of them leaned in, his hollowness wrapping itself around me, compelling my body to his. I let him lean closer, until I could feel the breath within me curl into a thin stream of air and force its way up to my lips. My body grew weak, the colors around me dulling, darkening. Just before the Brother's hand closed around my throat, I summoned the last bit of energy I had left and thrust my shovel into his chest.

I heard a dull crunch as it broke through his ribs. The Brother keeled over, letting out a raspy breath of air. I pushed the shovel deeper until his flesh compressed in on itself, making him shrink back. I was about to swing him into the crevasse, when his arm went rigid. His hood slid back. I could see the reflection of the sky in one of his dull gray eyes. The handle slipped from my hands. He pulled the shovel from his ribs and threw it into the snow, pausing while his flesh repaired itself.

"Find me," I said, hoping the wind would carry my voice to Dante. In the distance, I heard a shout. Footsteps running toward me. A white silhouette materialized through the fog.

Dante collided with the Brother, tumbling with him onto the snow. I backed away as they grappled close to the edge of the crevasse, their bodies a snarl of black cloth and pale skin. My heart raced as I watched Dante throw the Brother into the hole, then tackle the Brother that had cornered Clementine.

My shovel lay in the snow just a few feet away. The temperature dropped as a Brother grew closer. Just before he reached me, a torch hurtled through the air. I rolled to the side as the second Brother collapsed beside me. Fire engulfed his cloak.

My grandfather burst through the fog. He swung his Spade over the Brother's chest and threw his smoldering remains into the abyss. His movements were swift, controlled, concise: the result of a trained hand. With his right arm he sparred, with his left he unwound a roll of gauze, looping it around the Brothers as if he were knotting a necktie.

A handful of Undead boys strayed from the fight and

ran toward him. I grabbed my shovel from the snow and intercepted them, thrusting them, one by one, into the crevasse. I wiped the edge of my shovel in the snow and started to search for Dante, when I heard a shout.

My grandfather's scarf had come loose from his lapel, its crimson tails unraveling in the snow beside him like a trickle of blood. I heard a loud rip as one of the Liberum circling my grandfather caught hold of his sleeve, tearing the seams from his overcoat.

His arm trembled. He didn't make a move toward the Liberum; he waited, his chest rising and falling. They closed in like a long black shadow. One lunged at his Spade. My grandfather barely ducked away in time. He was tired. His reflexes had slowed.

They were closing in on him when the fog parted. Dante charged through the circle, knocking two of the Liberum to the ground. My grandfather stumbled back, stunned, as Dante wrestled with the Brothers, the muscles in his arms flexing while he pressed them into the snow.

His intervention gave my grandfather a second wind. He fought beside Dante, using the last bit of his strength to knock another Liberum aside. But it wasn't enough. Another slice through the air and he stumbled back. I saw his Spade fall. He tried to pick it up, but the hooded figures closed in around him.

"No!" I shouted, fighting toward him. He removed a roll of gauze from his pocket and held it in front of him, his final attempt to ward them off.

My grandfather didn't run when one of the Brothers came up behind him and took hold of his arms, nor did he stop fighting when the other approached him from the front.

"Stop!" I cried.

His legs buckled. He dropped to his knees.

For a moment, it no longer mattered what he'd done or why he'd done it. I pushed through the Undead boys before me, tangling their arms in the gauze to clear a path. But when I looked up, my grandfather's eyes met mine.

"Stay where you are, Renée," he said. He never looked the Brother of the Liberum in the face as his robes swept over the snow toward him; my grandfather's eyes were fixed on me. There was no sign of fear, just regret, as if to say, *This my fate, not yours.*

I saw my mother's face in his. Though she had once been his daughter, they were so different that I always felt they belonged to separate incarnations of my life. My mother, to the bright California sun rising up over the trees; and my grandfather, to the gray wintry skies rolling in over New England. But now his eyes were a watery blue, like the swells of the ocean on a rainy summer day. He missed her too, I realized as he took me in one last time. Just like he would miss me.

I saw Dante lean back into the snow as the last of the Liberum around him tumbled into the crevasse. He turned, ready to fight off the others, but my grandfather stopped him. "Leave me!" he shouted to Dante, his voice wavering. "Take her away. Keep her safe."

The shadows of the Liberum eclipsed his body until all I could see of my grandfather was his hand lying in the snow, his fingers still closed around the roll of gauze. They quivered as the life left him, their grip loosening until the cloth unraveled between his fingers and flapped in the wind like a flag of surrender.

An icy hand wrapped around my waist. A tingling sensation crept up my skin. I spun around to see a pair of thin lips; an ashen cheek, cut at a harsh angle, like ice; a pair of melted brown eyes, now clouded behind a thin film of gray. Dante.

I saw another hand wrap around Theo's mouth. One more over Anya's. Before I could call out to them, Dante lifted me in his arms and carried me away from the fight, the snow billowing around us until my grandfather, the Monitors, and my friends all faded into white.

CHAPTER 15

The Monastery

THE COLORS OF THE LANDSCAPE GREW BRIL-liant and saturated as Dante carried me through the snow. The mountains that layered the horizon brightened into vivid shades of blue and purple, and the snow glittered in the sunlight. It felt like a lifetime had passed since I had last seen color, since I had last felt the comfort of his arms as he held me to his chest, the thin fabric of his shirt soft against my cheek. Gray clouds rolled in from the east, the shade of my grandfather's coat, as though they were mourning for the Monitors, too.

"You're okay," Dante said. "I have you now."

I waited for his voice to envelop me in its richness, to bring back all of the memories I had lost, but all I heard were words, the sounds flat and dull. I listened to him breathing, to the unnatural rhythm of his heart beating against my side, waiting for the sounds to stir something within me, but they inspired nothing. I had the vague recollection of smelling the woods on his skin, but no matter how deeply I breathed him in, I sensed nothing.

So instead, I used the senses I had left. I studied the porcelain white of his skin; the frosted red of his lips, just a shade away from turning blue; the rich brown of his hair, its ends caked in snow. I slid my hand down his arm, remembering the smooth feeling of his muscles beneath my touch; the familiar shift of his shoulders as he trudged through the snow; the way his brown eyes seemed to melt, the gray haze clearing, when he looked down at me.

Dante pushed the hair away from my face. "I found you," he said, as if he was referring not only to this life, but to all iterations of our lives in the past, and all that lay ahead of us in the future.

"What about the others?" I said. "Theo and Anya?"

"Don't worry about them," said Dante. "They're fine."

We zigzagged around the crevasses, scaling the final slope of the mountain. Slowly, the landscape began to look familiar, though I couldn't place why until I felt the chest thudding against Dante's back. When we were far enough away from the Undead that their chill began to recede, Dante slowed.

He let my feet slide to the ground, then took the chest from his bag and opened it. A sweep of lines and shapes, etched into the lid, stood between the third and fourth point. Dante held it up to the landscape before us. As he did, the map came to life before our eyes. Its thin stack of triangles mimicked the crooked staircase of mountains in front of us; its swirl of circles mimicked the low-hanging clouds that the ridge disappeared into, the fog engulfing everything but the peaks of the mountains as if they were suspended in the sky. The fourth point was nestled some-where within the mist.

As we walked toward it, the snow lost its brightness, the blinding white losing its shimmer until it looked faded and old. I looked back at Dante, wondering if he noticed the difference, but his hair distracted me. Its rich brown seemed to be fading, as though the color was washing out with the wind.

The next verse of Descartes's riddle echoed in my mind. *The eyes follow, the jaws of the mountains a colorless gray...*

A weathered red temple rose through the clouds. It had a hollowness to it, as though its windows and doors had sucked up the air around us, making everything go calm. A wooden terrace wrapped around it. At its center stood a heavy wooden door. Dozens of crooked steps led up to the entrance, each brushed clean of snow. A broom rested on the wall as if someone had just finished sweeping. Dante turned to me, the dye in his clothes draining with every step.

"It must be inside," he said.

He paused, as though I, too, looked different. He took my hand in his, turning it in his palm. My skin looked paler than ever. I curled my fingers around his, the feeling of his hand in mine giving me comfort.

We found ourselves in a vast room, warm and dark. Tea

candles lined the walls. Their flames danced in the draft from the door, their trails branching off into dozens of tiny paths, revealing a labyrinth of passageways leading deep inside the monastery.

The floor was tiled with pieces of glass, glimmering in the flickering light. At its center lay a mosaic of a canary, its golden wings spread in flight. The Keepers.

As I walked around the image, venturing deeper into the room, the color drained from the tiles. The golden luster seeped out of the bird's wings, and the red and blue glass around it faded until it looked like a gray film had been laid over the floor. I peered down the hallway. Despite the candles lining the walls, it looked impossibly dark, as though the rooms beyond were absorbing all of the color.

"This way," I whispered to Dante.

I led him toward the end of the hallway, where the darkness looked most drab. Dante's body changed shapes beside me as the shadows from the candles shifted over him. The smooth contour of his arm beneath the cuff of his shirt grew dull as he held me back while he inched forward to make sure it was safe. The loose strand of hair falling across his cheek as he leaned around a corner, glancing left, then right, seemed to lighten, losing its rich color. The glimmer of his eyes as he looked back at me grew dimmer until they looked lifeless.

"Wait," I said, touching his wrist. "Let me look at you."

It was the last time I would be able to see his beauty, to

appreciate the tilt of his nose, the melting brown of his eyes, the muscular contours of his shoulders shifting beneath his shirt.

"I'll still be here on the other side," he said, reading my thoughts. "You'll still be able to see me."

"I know," I murmured. "But not in the same way."

At the end stood an open-air courtyard lined with columns. I blinked and the scene darkened, as though my vision were fading. Startled, I squinted into the light. Though I could tell that the wood had been stained in the same shade of red as the rest of the temple, the columns in the courtyard looked dull, as though all of their color were being drained into the ground. Likewise, the Alps rising behind them lacked the luster they had held just moments before; the sky above them was now flat, the clouds stagnant.

I blinked again, and the world went darker still, spots forming in my eyes. I strained to focus, until I spotted a girl's face peek around the column on the other side of the courtyard, her long hair fluttering through the mist. She looked like the girls I had seen at each of the points before. But when I looked again, all I could see were clouds. They hung low around the courtyard, folding in on themselves.

Beneath them stood a reflecting pool. It was asymmetrical in shape, and looked wild and jagged, as though it had been a natural feature of the landscape, the monastery built around it. It grew blurry, its details darkening, slipping away from me. I froze, steadying myself, before pressing my eyes shut. When I opened them, I could just make out the black water of the pool. I stepped toward it, letting the clouds surround me, and leaned over the pool until my face appeared on the surface.

The Renée that looked back at me seemed drained of all her color. Her hair looked brittle, her skin pasty, as though all her pigment were in grayscale. The water rippled and her eyes rolled back in her head. She grasped her face, her arms moving without mine, and clutched her eyes, her mouth opening to cry out in pain. As she did, I felt a cold stream of air whirl up my throat, the clouds around me coaxing it through my lips.

The memories swirled out of me in textures and colors so rich they made my eyes water. A brass bell. The chrome frame of a bicycle. A mess of auburn hair, the same color as the autumn leaves. A freckle, then another. Spinning wheels. Then soapstone, the clean lines of the Gottfried dormitory. A blond ringlet. A green slated chalkboard. The crisp cuff of an Oxford shirt. The outline of his chest beneath as the rain matted the thin cotton to his skin. A strand of brown hair falling loose from a knot. His eyes, so soft they seemed to melt. Gone, all gone.

I rubbed my eyes, trying to bring the monastery back into focus. All looked the same as it had before, though now the shapes looked flatter, the colors muted as though a thick film had collected over everything around me.

Dante stood beside me, the gray haze creeping over his eyes. I watched his irises contract, struggling to focus on me the way they used to. Was he still beautiful? His features looked the same as before, though their arrangement seemed somehow less vivid, less alive. All I had left was the prickle his touch sent up my arm, the curvature of his arms, his chest, his neck, as I ran my hand over him; reassuring myself that he was still here, that he was still the Dante I knew.

Dante took my hand as if I were slipping away from him. "Look," he said.

I followed his gaze through the columns of the courtyard to the east, where I could make out a familiar collection of shapes on the horizon. Three lakes in the valley below. Dante opened the chest and held it up. On the map within, three circles marked the path, the fifth point circumscribed within the third circle. It was inside the lake. Someone else may have called the sight beautiful. I could no longer see anything but lines and shapes, the colors monochrome like an old photograph; and yet, it made my chest swell with hope.

I turned to go back through the monastery when a draft of cold air lapped against my neck. Two Undead swept down the passageway, pulling Anya and Theo behind them. I recognized their silhouettes: they were the Undead who I had seen diverting the other boys away from me during the fight.

"Renée," one of them said.

How did they know my name? I stepped toward them, studying the shorter of the two. Though I remembered that his hair had been blond, I could barely make out its color now.

The candlelight flickered off his face, giving me a glimpse of his button nose, his lips, and his cheeks, so full they looked like they belonged to a girl. But no—could it be?

"Eleanor?" I whispered, recasting what I thought was a boy's figure into the slim profile of my roommate from Gottfried Academy.

Her lips spread into a smile. "It's me."

I dropped my shovel and ran to her, throwing my arms around her slender frame. I knew it was her when I felt her hair against my cheek, as soft as silk. "Why didn't you tell me?" I whispered.

"It was for your safety," said Eleanor, her sweater soft beneath my touch. "It was important that you didn't try to leave the Monitors and find us. If you did, and the Liberum found you, they would have killed you. We didn't want to show ourselves until the last possible moment."

Suddenly I understood why she and the other Undead had been diverting the boys away from me during the fight on the mountainside, and during the attack at the inn. They'd been protecting me.

I turned to the boy standing behind her. He was taller than she was, his broad shoulders filling the passageway. But there was something more than just his height that looked familiar. A draft blew through the corridor, making the light from the candles dance across his face.

"Noah?"

He stepped toward me until I could just make out a freckle beneath his eye. I reached out and touched his arm to make sure he was real, but the shock of it made my hand recoil. His skin was ice-cold, as if he'd just surfaced from the depths of the frozen lake at Gottfried. I still remembered the way he used to feel, like the first perfect day of autumn, his soft hair tangling around my fingers, his arms smooth and strong as they wrapped around me, warming me in the evening breeze. All of that was gone now.

I wanted to tell him how much I'd thought about him, about how much I'd missed him. I wanted to tell him about my dreams, about how I kept reliving that awful day, about how his death had haunted me. With every step, I could feel the guilt reaching up through the earth and pulling me down by the ankles, as though it were trying to bury me in his stead.

I wanted to tell him about my regrets. If only I had done something differently. If we had missed our train down from Montreal; if we had run out to the lake five minutes earlier. Or the one that hurt most of all: if I hadn't let him come along with me in the first place. Maybe then, things would have turned out differently; maybe then I could have saved him.

He spoke first, his voice so lifeless that I barely recognized it. "The Undead have followed us. We have to leave."

They each stepped into the courtyard, their eyes bleary and unfocused as they emerged. We ran down the mountain toward the three lakes in the distance, each larger than the next, until we spotted the first sign of life. Trees. Dante and I led the way, weaving through the snow until we were under the cover of the woods, when a shout rang out behind us.

"Wait!" Theo said. He was far behind us, huddled over Anya, who was lying in the snow.

I ran to them. Her face was ashen, her hair tangled with ice. The clothes hung limp around her frame, which looked astonishingly thin. She had lost weight. Her chest heaved, her breath so quick it frightened me.

"What happened?" I asked, but Anya didn't answer. Her eyes fluttered shut, as though she were struggling to keep them open.

Theo shook his head. "I don't know," he said. "She started to slow down. I turned to ask her what was wrong, and she collapsed."

I knelt over Anya. "What's wrong?" I said.

She pressed her lips together, still trying to regain her breath. She took my hand and placed it on her heart.

I didn't understand why until I felt it beat, its rhythm quick and irregular, like the heartbeat of an Undead.

My arm recoiled. "What—what is that?"

"Is it still beating?" she asked.

I nodded. "Though not like mine."

"Good," she said. "It's hard for me to tell anymore if I'm alive or dead. The line is so thin these days."

"But it feels like..."

"An Undead," Anya whispered, finishing what I couldn't bring myself to say. "Ironic, isn't it?"

"I—I don't understand."

"I'm dying," she said. "I've been dying."

Her words struck Theo in the face. He shrank back into the snow, stunned. They knocked the breath from me as well. I sat back on my heels, feeling a pit form in my stomach. I finally understood why she had carried around a tin of elixirs, why she had always reserved a few pills only for herself, why she frequently looked tired and breathless. I thought back to her tarot reading, to the card of the woman dying of an illness. It hadn't been referring to her mother; it had been referring to Anya.

"Of what?" I asked, trying to steady my voice. I wished I had already lost my sense of touch, for then I wouldn't have had to feel so overwhelmed with guilt, with sadness. Why hadn't I noticed? All of the clues had been there, but I had missed them. I had been too wrapped up in Dante, in my own quest.

"Cardiomyopathy. A disease of the heart. The muscle is wasting away. It has been for years."

That was why Monsieur had sent her with us, why she had been willing to come in the first place. "Tell me what to do."

"You can't do anything," she said. "No one can. Eventually my heart will stop, though now it seems it might be sooner rather than later."

While she spoke, Theo rifled through her bag until he found her tin. He sifted through the bottles and salves inside, measuring out five different kinds of pills. "These are the ones you normally take, right?" He took a bottle of water from his bag and offered it to her. "Take them."

Anya gave him a weak smile. "You've been paying attention," she said, and with some difficulty sat up, taking the water from Theo. "I never realized."

"Neither did I," Theo said, studying her. "What about the black pill?" he said, holding up the thin vial with a single tablet inside. "You said it was for emergencies."

Anya shook her head. "Only the bad kind of emergencies," she said. "If I'm in pain and want to end it."

Her words startled Theo. He dropped the vial back in the tin, as though he no longer wanted to touch it. "I didn't think anyone could surprise me," he said softly. "But you always prove me wrong."

Dante stared up at the mountains, where I could see the small figures of the Undead moving toward us. "Can you make it a little bit farther?" he said. "I can help you."

Anya shook her head. "I can walk," she said. With Theo's help, she stood. "Though I have to go slower."

We pressed onward until a vast frozen lake came into view: the first of the three circles that led to the final point. When Noah saw it, he stopped. His eyes lingered on the frozen ripples, which looked eerily similar to the ice he been pulled under at Gottfried. His bag slipped from his shoulder but he made no move to pick it up; his gaze was distant, as if he were staring back into the past.

Watching his shoulders curl forward and his hand tremble by his side, I wanted nothing more than to stand beside him and tell him that I would fix everything that I had done, that I would give him his life back. But I didn't know if those were promises I could keep.

While Anya rested, I peered through the trees at the mountain in the distance. The Undead were closer; I could feel their wisps licking at my skin, beckoning me toward them. They looked like a group of dark silhouettes trailing behind us down the slope. Yet one by one, they began to vanish. I scanned the mountainside, wondering if they were splitting up and trying to surround us, when I saw something white dart through the snow in the distance, like a fist of wind and ice billowing toward one of the Undead boys. It knocked him off his feet and dragged him out of sight.

I squinted. What had I just seen? It happened so quickly that the other Undead didn't notice.

After a moment, another Undead boy fell to the ground, and was pulled by some invisible force into the woods. A person, or a white specter of the woods? I thought back to each of the points, and how I'd kept seeing the white faces of girls watching me through the snow.

"The Keepers," I whispered.

"What about them?" Eleanor said from behind me.

"They're up there," I said. "Taking the Undead."

If Noah heard me, he didn't let on. When he finally turned, he lowered his eyes to the ground so that we couldn't see his face. He hefted his bag onto his shoulder. "Let's go."

I glanced at Anya, who was leaning on Theo's shoulder. "I'm ready," she said.

The second lake was wider and deeper than the first, and covered in a thin layer of ice, through which I could see the water pressing against the surface. I felt the presence of the Undead fade behind us.

The sun was setting over the trees when we stumbled upon a sleepy mountain town. The snowy roofs of the houses blended so perfectly into the landscape that at first, I thought my eyes were betraying me. There was only one main street, laid with cobblestones, and so quiet it looked deserted. It was lined with wooden houses, their rooftops blanketed with white.

"Where is everyone?" Anya said.

One of the buildings bore a sign that read: BOULANGERIE. We were back in France. Through the window, I caught a glimpse of a woman rolling out dough on a table. She stopped working when she saw me and watched us as we passed.

Dante looked up at the darkening sky. "We should stay here tonight," he said.

I scanned the houses. Each door had a large metal knocker and was studded with iron rivets like the entrance of a fortress. They looked like they hadn't been opened in decades. Rising over the houses stood a steeple topped with a metal cross. I followed it down to see a simple stone church. Dante must have seen it, too, for he nodded and walked toward it.

The church greeted us with the calmness of a place that hadn't changed for centuries. It was modest in size, with bare wooden beams vaulted beneath the ceiling. The waning light shifted through dusty stained glass windows, though the colors looked monochrome to me.

We settled near the pulpit, gathering prayer candles for light. Anya nestled in by the front pew, her breathing thin and weak. She closed her eyes, trying to steady herself while Eleanor lit the candles one by one, their flames making our shadows stretch over the walls. Eleanor curled up beside me. Even Undead, her face was like a burst of sunshine, her rosy cheeks now pale but just as full, her blue eyes now faded but just as warm. Her ringlets were sheared off into a boy's haircut. I wrapped a lock around my finger.

"It was the only way to blend in with the Undead boys," she said, touching a curl by her ear. The length still seemed to startle her. "I wish you had been there."

I shook my head. "What happened?"

Eleanor looked to Noah. "You should start," she said. "It's your story."

He adjusted his glasses. They were the same pair he'd worn at St. Clément, though they seemed more fitting now; more mature. "I rose from the lake. Everything was bleary and dull. I was so cold. The last thing I remembered was being pulled under the ice by the Undead. And there I was, wet and cold, yet no one else was around me. I didn't know what had happened or how much time had passed. I didn't know I was dead." He let out a breath, as if he still couldn't believe it.

"I looked for you," he said, gazing at me. "But the lawn

was empty. At first I thought the Undead had taken you. Then I saw her." He looked to Eleanor. "She found me."

"I saw everything," Eleanor said. "I saw the Undead pull him into the lake; I saw them chase you in the woods, the Monitors following them. But I didn't know what happened after that. I thought the Undead might have taken you. But there was nothing I could do alone. So I waited, watching the lake. All of the professors had gone to track down the Liberum, leaving us in the care of the school groundskeepers. I figured they would come back for Noah in a day or two, but no one did. It was too chaotic; they each must have thought that someone else was tending to him. I wanted to help him. Every day I watched the lake from my bedroom window, but I was too afraid to fish him out. If I got caught, I could be buried. So I waited. Nine days passed. On the tenth day, I went outside. After he got over the shock of how everything looked and felt—the muted colors, the dullness of the smells and sounds..." She let her voice trail off, as if she were trying to remember what the world had been like before, too. "I told him everything."

Noah stared at the floor. "I thought she had made a huge mistake."

Eleanor swallowed. "But I hadn't."

My dreams of Noah hadn't been true, I realized. They had been a creation of my guilt, of my imagination. All that time, Eleanor had been with him. She had helped him. The thought put me at ease.

"We tried to figure out what to do," Eleanor continued. "We could stay at Gottfried, where Noah could be taken care of for the remainder of his time on earth, but I already knew what that existence was like. It was bleak and empty, with nothing separating one day from the next. We were all wasting away. And then Noah told me about the chest. I knew then that there was only one thing to do. Leave."

"That's when we got the note," Theo said.

"A note?" I said. "From whom?"

"A man named Monsieur," Eleanor said. "He told us that we didn't know him but he knew us. He instructed us to go to the Liberum and join them. That they would help us find you. He told us where they were headed, and where we could find their camp. So we went."

"You joined the Liberum?" Theo said with a laugh. "What, did you just walk up to them in their camp and ask if you could join them?"

"Yes," Noah said, his face grave. "After we cut her hair," he said, nodding to Eleanor. "The Liberum only use boys. We had to make her blend in. Finding them was the hardest part. I can't sense the Undead anymore like I used to be able to." He let eyes drift to the shovel by my feet. "We searched the woods for days, looking for their tracks in the snow. I was ready to give up. We couldn't just wander around the East Coast for weeks, hoping to stumble across the Liberum. After all, the Monitors were roaming the woods, too. What if they found us first? Then Eleanor had an idea."

"I decided that we had to find the Monitors," Eleanor

said. "They would be easier to locate; they have to sleep and eat; they can't just stay outside all day. They leave more of a trail. I thought if we found them, the Undead couldn't be far away."

"We don't have to sleep or eat, and we don't get tired, so it was easy to catch up to them. We traveled all night and all day, walking through the woods. We searched all of the inns and bed-and-breakfasts until we found them," Noah said. "And just like Eleanor predicted, the Undead camp was there, too, just a few miles into the woods."

"We tried to think of a good strategy," Eleanor continued, "but there really isn't any great way to approach the Liberum. So in the end, we took our chances and walked in."

"They could have buried you," Anya said, her face aghast.

Eleanor hung her head. "When you're like this," she said, gazing down at her pale skin, "risks don't seem as risky."

"The Undead boys seized us before we even made it into the camp. They dragged us in and brought us before the Liberum," Noah said. "I told them we used to be Monitors. That we knew everything about how the Monitors worked and thought; that we could help them, if they would only let us. I told them I was an outcast. I could never return to the Monitoring community. They would put me to death. I still believe that." Noah paused and looked at me. "All the while I was looking for you, wondering if you were somewhere in their camp.

"They said nothing while they listened to us. When we finished, they left to confer. A few hours later, they returned, telling us we could join. They needed us."

"Why?" Anya said.

Noah tilted his head and gave her a funny look, as though the answer was obvious. "To get to all of you. To find the chest."

"It was you that night in Bavaria," I realized. "Both of you. That's why the Undead didn't surround me. Because you were guiding them away."

Eleanor nodded. "We didn't want them to take any of you," she said. "But we knew we couldn't prevent that without blowing our cover. So we led them toward Dante."

"As an Undead, we knew he was the best one for the Liberum to claim," Noah said, though his voice was so cold that I wondered if part of him liked the idea of separating Dante from me. "They wouldn't be able to take his soul."

Still, I had to admit that he was right. I thought back to the night at the castle in Germany, of how I had run out to find Noah disappearing into the night.

"I was looking for you," Noah said. His eyes darted to Dante.

"The Liberum wouldn't let me go on any of the night raids," Dante said. "They left me under the watch of a group of Undead while we hiked up to the refuge. I asked them to find you. I wanted to make sure you were still here, and that someone was protecting you if the Liberum came."

I remembered the voice I'd heard in Widow's Pass. *Was*

318

she there? Was she safe? I'd heard Dante say to an Undead boy. I realized then that Dante hadn't been consorting with the Liberum or the Undead boys. All that time, he'd been talking to Eleanor and Noah. I turned to Dante. "I heard you speaking to them," I said. "I heard your voice echo off the walls of Widow's Pass."

"We were planning to find you," Eleanor said. "We were trying to steal the chest back from the Liberum."

They'd done so much for me, and I hadn't even known it. "I—I don't know what to say. You put yourselves in so much danger for me." I looked up at Noah. "I don't deserve it."

Eleanor shifted her weight. "We didn't just come for you," she said. "We came because we want to find the Netherworld, too."

CHAPTER 16

Good-bye

WHEN THE CANDLES HAD DRIPPED DOWN to stumps, Noah made his way to the stairwell that led up to the bell tower. Just before he disappeared into the corridor, he met my eye. *Follow me*, he seemed to say.

"I—I have to go," I said to Dante.

He hesitated, as though he had known this moment would come. "Then go."

I tiptoed after Noah, climbing the winding staircase, his presence coaxing my feet forward, cold and still like the first breath of winter. He stood by the stone barricade, his back turned to me as he gazed at the alpine view that stretched out before us, his outline dark against the night sky.

"Thank you," I whispered.

Noah said nothing. He didn't even move.

"I'm sorry," I said.

He turned. "Sorry for what?"

"It's my fault, what you are," I said. "If it weren't for me you'd be alive."

He studied me, his face void of any warmth. "You don't like what you see. You're afraid of what I am now."

"No," I said. "I'm not. I just—"

"Liked me better as a human," Noah said, his face betraying the smallest hint of sadness. "But not enough to stay and find me."

"I couldn't," I said. "Dante—he took me away. I couldn't go back; the Monitors were there."

"You could have," Noah said, his face softening. "But you chose Dante over me."

I shrank back. He was right.

"And yet, I still choose you," Noah said. "All those days I spent wandering the woods, all the nights I couldn't sleep when I stayed up thinking about my parents and sister, about our house in Montreal and how I could never return there again—the only thought that gave me hope was you. I can never see my family again. I can never be a Monitor, nor can I go back to St. Clément or even to Montreal, with all the High Court there. All of my training, all of the hopes I'd had before are gone. I can't feel cold or warmth. I can't taste food, nor can I smell the air around me, nor can I hear the softness of your voice, and yet every time I try to remember the feeling of happiness, my mind drifts to you."

I had been prepared for Noah to be angry, but I hadn't been ready for this.

"I helped him," Noah said, glancing at Dante. "I helped

321

him for you. Because I knew it was what you would have wanted. I came to you in the night at the castle in Bavaria; I watched over you. I wanted you to be safe. And when the Liberum attacked, I protected you."

"I didn't know," I said. "If I had I would have—"

"You would have what?" he asked.

I waited for him to continue, but he said nothing. "I—I don't know."

My admission struck a silence between us. Noah understood then that nothing he could have done would have changed this outcome.

"I gave up my life for you once," Noah said. "I would do it again. Everything I've been doing is for you."

"Why?" I asked. "I have nothing to give you. My soul is just as parched as yours."

"It's not," Noah said. "You make me feel alive. As alive as I can be. I won't ask you to come to the Netherworld with me; I would never have asked you to give up your life to help me find mine. I just ask that you wait for me. When I take a new soul, I'll find you. We can pick up our lives where we left off."

"I—I don't understand."

"Choose me."

The problem was that I didn't want to continue this life. I wanted to start a new one. There was nothing left for me here—no beauty, no sadness, no hatred—just a steady numbness. My parents were gone, as was my grandfather; all of my friends were either living normal sunny lives or wallowing as Undead, and as a Monitor, I would eventually be tasked with ending their lives, a calling I never wanted in the first place. I couldn't help but feel like I had one foot in the underworld and one foot on earth. How could a person go on living like that?

Although I couldn't remember the scent of Dante's hair or the taste of his skin or the sound of his voice as he whispered to me while I fell asleep, I knew that every part of him was imprinted on my soul, breathing life into my past, my present, my future. He was the only person who made me feel alive. Who made me want to be alive.

I inched away from Noah. "Dante never asked me to give up my life for him. I wanted to. Without him, there's nothing here for me," I said, my voice cracking. "He *is* my life."

My words struck him. He moved his fingers, as though he wanted to reach out and touch me, though he held himself back. "And you are mine."

Though I knew he meant what he said, his words were void of emotion. His coldness frightened me. This wasn't the same Noah who had run into me with his bicycle in Montreal, his crooked smile making me melt; or the Noah who had stacked my arms full of food at the grocery store, making me laugh for the first time in months; or the Noah who had brought me to his childhood bedroom, where I'd sat on his twin bed and tried to imagine what my life would be like if I chose to spend it with him. This Noah frightened me.

"I'm sorry," I whispered. "I can't give you what you want."

Noah let his hands drop to his sides. "No," he said, his voice dead. "I am."

I shook my head. "I didn't mean it like that—"

But he cut me off. "You want to leave," he said. "So go. Go!"

I backed down the stairs.

Dante was waiting for me in the front pew. I ran to him, trying to will my hands to stop trembling. "My answer is you," I said. "It's always been you."

He eyes drifted to the stairway, wondering what had shaken me so, but he didn't ask any questions. "And mine, you," he said. "Come on."

He led me to the back of the church, where he pulled me into the shadows. But as he reached for my hand, I noticed something strange.

The skin on his wrist looked different, as if it belonged to man twenty years older. It looked so pale that I could almost see the veins running beneath it. Dante must have seen me staring. He pulled his arm back into the shadows.

"What did they do to you?"

Dante curled his fingers, studying them. "They dragged me into the woods, where they wrapped my arms and legs with gauze. The nine Brothers surrounded me. They asked me questions about the chest and the Netherworld, about the Monitors. They told me that if I didn't help them find the next point on the map, they would find you and take your soul."

He lowered his eyes to the ground. "For days I tried to escape, but it was no use. The gauze had made my hands and legs so weak that I could barely move them. All I could do was think of you."

I took his hands in mine, tracing my fingers along the insides of his wrists. "How did you get away?"

"I didn't," he said. "I don't know how much time passed before they came back, but when they did they set up camp nearby. I could hear the Undead boys talking through the trees. I listened for your name; it was all I could think of. Had they found you? Had they taken your soul?" He ran a hand through his hair. "Then, one night, two of the Undead boys approached me. They were some of the oldest Undead in the army. So tall. I thought they had been sent to burn me. But instead, they turned out to be Noah and Eleanor."

He glanced back to the front of the church where I could hear Eleanor whispering. "They told me that you were still alive. I felt like they had given me my life back. They watched over you. They helped me plan my escape and steal back the chest from the Liberum. I owe them everything."

I shrank back against the wall, feeling the dust stick to my fingertips. "Not everything," I said.

Dante leaned his forehead against mine, his breath tickling my lips. Then he slid his hand around my waist and inched back toward the pews until I could see the last of the candlelight dance across the angles of his face. He lowered me onto the bench, the wood creaking beneath us as he traced his hand up the back of my thigh.

I felt the warmth blossom beneath my skin. My chest felt hot and flushed. His hands grasped at my clothes, sliding beneath the layers of fabric until I felt his cool touch graze my skin. My body moved without me, my neck arching back, my legs wrapping around him as he pulled me to the floor beneath the pews. I felt the cold stone against my skin, the weight of Dante pressing me deep into the ground.

His breath was thick and cold as it beat against my neck. I felt his hand tangle itself in my hair, coaxing my head back as he kissed my collarbone, the nape of my neck, my chest.

Theo murmured in his sleep from the front of the church, but I didn't care if I woke him.

"Make me feel something," I said. "Please."

Dante's eyes were barely visible beneath the cloud of gray. Slowly, he unbuttoned my cardigan. The cool air of the church lapped at my chest as he peeled my clothes off of me, first my sweater, then my shirt, his fingers sending a shiver up my skin as he counted each of my ribs. My lips trembled as I grasped at his shirt, twisting it over his head until all I could see was the pale curvature of his chest expanding and contracting in the darkness.

I pulled at his sides, kissing the muscles in his arms, his shoulders; I pressed my hands into his shoulder blades as if I were trying to rip them apart. His lips flitted over my skin, sending a prickle of cold up my back. Everything within me ached for him.

My eyes drifted over the vaulted ceilings of the church, at the chipped paintings adorning the stone. Images of burial and the afterlife, of angels ascending into the clouds. Everyone had to face death one day. I ran my hand through Dante's hair as if it were the last time I would ever touch him, as if it were the last day of our lives.

"I choose you," I whispered. "I choose you."

He hovered over my mouth, the tendrils of his breath tickling my lips. A part of me wanted to press my mouth to his, to try and taste the salt on his tongue as it melted into mine. But Dante tightened above me, his grasp strong around my hands to hold me back. "We're almost there," he said.

I collapsed back against the dusty floor. Dante lowered himself to the ground beside me and wrapped his sweater around my shoulders. I rested my hand on his chest and felt the vibrations of his heartbeat. Its rhythm had grown even more irregular. It lagged behind as if it were tired, then sped up in an attempt at recovery. What I didn't want to admit was that my heart was slowing, too. I'd noticed it over the past few days, the occasional palpitation in my chest. I closed my eyes and counted along with his heart. *One, two, three—one—one, two—one.* Mine skipped in tandem, filling in the beats his heart missed, until I fell asleep, our bodies rising and falling as one.

I woke to the sound of paper slipping beneath the door. The morning sun shone through the stained glass windows, dimpling the floor in light, and though I imagined it was beautiful, all I could see were the scuffed panels of glass, their colors monotone. The candles had all burned out, their wax in hardened puddles on the floor. Dante sat beside me, turning the small black box over in his hands.

"Did you hear that?" I said.

"Hear what?" he said.

I ran to the entrance of the church, where an envelope lay halfway beneath the door. I swung it open, letting the sun spill inside. Monsieur had been here just moments before, I could feel it; though when I looked in either direction, the street was empty.

It had been so long since we'd heard from Monsieur that I almost wondered if it was a fake. But the paper and the handwriting were perfect, exactly the same as in the letters before. I ripped it open.

Dear Ms. Winters,
You have their protection. Show it to them.
Sincerely,
Monsieur

"Whose protection?" I asked, but before Dante could respond, a chill descended over the church. I pressed my finger to his lips and froze. A dark cloak swept past the windows, blocking out the light. The Liberum.

The others stirred in the front of the church. They must have felt it, too, for they grasped their shovels. Theo rubbed his eyes and peered out the window. "The Brothers are here," he said. "Three are heading toward the front door. Two to the back." The door rattled, punctuating his sentence.

Anya swallowed, supporting herself on a pew. "Is there any other way out?"

"No," said Theo. "I've already checked."

I peered through the window, feeling the long wisps of the Liberum curl toward me. A black cloak swept past the panes, its shape warped by the uneven glass. The remaining Undead boys followed, surrounding the church.

"We'll have to face them," Theo said. Gripping his Spade, he turned to Anya. "You stay inside. I'll take the front." He nodded to Dante, Eleanor, and me. "You take the back."

"Where's Noah?" Eleanor said.

I scanned the church. I didn't see him anywhere. Before I could answer, one of the Undead fell to the ground. A thrash of legs, a muffled scream. Then a wave of long pale hair swept past the window.

"What was that?" Anya asked.

"The Keepers," I said.

One by one, the Undead on the other side of the window fell, and were dragged through the dirt and snow, pulled by something soundless, faceless.

Eleanor inched back. "Noah?" she called, his name echoing off the ceilings like a voice of a ghost. "Noah?"

As she repeated it, a terrible feeling crept over me. Had he left because of what I'd said?

Outside, everything grew still. Dante inched toward the door, ready to turn the knob, when a cry stopped him.

I lowered my shovel and ran toward Eleanor's voice. I found her standing in a doorway that led down into a cellar, her body trembling.

No, I begged, inching closer. This couldn't be happening again. I already knew what I would find, and yet I still hoped to find an empty hallway. The light from the windows shone into the stairwell, illuminating an arm, its skin turning gray. The bottom of the stairs was dark.

Everything inside me collapsed. He had put himself to rest. I backed away, my hands muffling my sob. This had happened because of me.

I heard footsteps behind me. "Get him out!" Dante said. Theo ran down the stairs and dragged Noah back aboveground. His body was limp, his face hollow with death. I turned away, unable to look any longer. Dante and Theo carried him through the church, bursting through the front doors and into the sunlight.

Outside, the church grounds were quiet, but they weren't empty at all. Five women stood around us, their hair fluttering in the wind. They each held a Spade, the metal tips glinting in the sunlight.

Theo and Dante slowed, laying Noah in the snow, his head facing the sky. Seeing him in the light was startling, his lips the same muted shade as the clouds, as though he were already fading back into the folds of the universe. I wrapped my hand around Eleanor's, feeling the cool touch of her skin as I squeezed her palm.

The Keepers looked almost identical, though I could see the difference in age. The first woman's cheeks were far more sunken than the others, her youth sucked from her too early. The second woman had withered lips, her mouth falling into a wrinkled pout. The third woman's face had hollowed into a pinch, her nose spotted with sun splotches. The fourth woman had clouded eyes, her irises now a foggy white. And the fifth had gnarled and knotted hands, her fingers wrinkled as she gripped her Spade.

There was something about their faces that looked familiar, beyond having seen them over the past few days, though I couldn't place how I recognized them.

"What do you want?" Theo said, pointing his Spade at them.

Instead of answering, the first woman spoke, reciting a line from Descartes's riddle.

"Sounds, they fade to the ground, the earth's music unsung," she said, then turned to the woman on her right.

"Then taste, until food is but dirt on the tongue," said the second woman.

"*The nose, it next decays, death the only stench to stay,*" the third woman said.

"*The eyes follow, the jaws of the mountains a colorless gray,*" the fourth said, then turned to the fifth women.

"*Touch, the noblest, is last to decline,*" she said. "*The final remainder of life in this soul of mine.*"

The five Keepers. One for each point. That's why their faces had aged so differently—they each occupied a separate point on the map, one sense decaying while the others lived on. I remembered Monsieur's note. *You have their protection. Show it to them.* The five women in front of us, the Keepers, were supposedly the descendants of Ophelia Hart, the ninth sister, the one who had hidden the chest in the lake for us to find. Which meant that they could only want one thing. "The box," I said.

Dante squinted at me, his thoughts meeting mine. "*In its world it is dust, in the hand it is coal,*" he said, reciting the final lines of Descartes's riddle. "*At long last I found it, the ephemeral soul.*"

He lowered his bag and took out the small black box. The Spades of the Keepers wavered.

"In the hand it is coal," he said to himself. "Does that mean that this is—?"

"A soul," I whispered, completing his sentence. Was that what the final lines of the riddle meant: that in the Netherworld, the soul took on the form of dust, and in the hand, it solidified into a rock, just like the one we'd found in the chest? Was that how Descartes had taken a soul to use on his deathbed?

Anya had been right, back in Paris; it had never been a box in the first place. All this time we'd already had an extra life with us, and we'd had no idea.

The Keepers didn't answer. They lifted their Spades, and speaking in harmony, they each whispered, "A soul is not given; it is earned. It is yours to use." Their white figures shrank back.

Ours to use? An itch inside me wanted Dante to press it to his lips and take a new life. But where would that leave everyone else? Where would that leave me?

The others were thinking the same thing; I could tell by the way they eyed it, their faces greedy.

"Give it to Noah," Anya said finally. "I don't have any elixir that can bring him back," she continued, looking at Dante, "but you do."

None of us spoke as she stepped toward Dante and took the black box from his hands. I could see its weight tugging against her as she knelt over Noah. She pushed the hair away from his face. His lips parted slightly at her touch. She held the black box over him, its heaviness making her arms tremble. When she lowered it to his mouth, its black edges began to dissolve. The dust swept itself into a thin black thread that seeped between his lips, twisting down, down, until there was nothing left in Anya's hands but a smudge of black.

Noah's muscles twitched, the veins in his arms lifting as the blood began to pulse through them. His chest heaved. His lips parted. He gasped.

Anya backed away, so startled that she stumbled over herself.

The Keepers swept over Noah. "Go," they said to us in unison. "Go."

But I couldn't move; I was too stunned. Was it real? Had it worked?

I felt Dante's hand on my arm. "We're almost there," he said. "We have to go."

As Dante pulled me away, following the others toward the valley, I turned and watched over my shoulder as Noah's hand, which had lain lifeless in the snow, curled into a fist. He was alive.

"Good-bye," I whispered to him.

Following the etching on the chest, we made our way down the valley toward the third lake, inside of which lay the fifth point. The path cut through the surrounding hills like a dry riverbed. The snow on the ground grew spotty, revealing dry and rocky earth.

A twinge of pins and needles prickled the underside of my skin. It traveled down to my fingertips, where Dante's hand was interlaced with mine. His palm felt suddenly distant, his touch no longer familiar, his skin no longer cold. Though I could see the wind blowing the dirt in swirls over the snow, I could barely feel its icy sting against my face, and though I could see the sun, I could no longer feel it warming my face.

Touch, the noblest, is last to decline, the final remainder of life in this soul of mine. We were nearing the end of Descartes's riddle.

The landscape broke open into a vast lake, its shore crusted with ice, its water black. It was so serene that it almost looked like it wasn't a lake all, but a strange extension of the land around us, reflecting the clouds and the French Alps like a world inverted.

I bent over the surface. I felt Dante, Theo, Anya, and Eleanor kneel beside me. The water rippled, shifting my reflection until the Renée that appeared before me had changed. She stared up at me, bewildered, as though she could see me, too. She reached up, her hand trembling as it neared the surface, trying to touch me.

As it came closer, the memories spilled from my fingertips, so tactile that I felt the smooth texture of Dante's shoulder blades beneath my hands; the chalkboard, dry and dusty against my neck as he pressed me against it. His sheets, rough against my cheek as I nestled into his bed in Attica Falls all those years ago, and his body, heavy beside mine while I fell asleep next to him. His hand wrapped around mine as he guided my pencil across the page in Latin. The first time we touched, his hand sending a spark of electricity under my skin beneath the desk in science class.

The memories dissipated like dust, replaced with the

scratchy knitted blanket that lined Anya's couch; the squish of the beets that the fortune teller made me peel before reading my fortune; the velvety texture of Eleanor's cashmere sweater as she wrapped her arms around me. The sticky feeling of sunscreen and tanning oil; the salt of the ocean clinging to my hair. The warm breeze as I held my hand out the window, letting the summer sun kiss my skin.

I tried to cling to the last part of my soul, but it slipped from my grasp, unwinding until I couldn't remember what it felt like to be chilled to the bone, to be warmed by the sun, to feel the grass beneath my feet or Dante's fingers tangling with mine.

I felt nothing as the last bit of touch left me. The ice beneath my hands no longer felt cold, the bag on my shoulder no longer felt heavy. My hair blew in front of my face. It should have tickled, but I registered nothing.

I stared down at the Renée in the water as she reached up and broke the surface, disturbing the glassy reflection of the lake. The water sloshed out, and when it did, I caught a glimpse of something straight and long beneath, like a beam of wood. I leaned closer, following the beam as it slanted down into the shape of a roof.

"What do we do now?" Theo said beside me, but I didn't respond.

I threw a rock into the lake, and then another until the houses beneath began to appear. There were dozens of them deep beneath the surface.

"There are houses under there," I said. How many were

there? I scanned the perimeter of the lake. It spanned almost the entire width of the valley.

The others gathered around me.

Anya's eyes widened. "The lost city," she said. "I've heard stories about this place: an ancient city of Monitors who were protecting a secret. But it soon became overrun by Undead. The Monitors flooded it, washing it clean of the Undead and burying them for good at the bottom of the lake. I always thought it was just a children's story."

"Washed clean," I said to myself. "Like the soul."

This was it, I realized. The Netherworld. It was somewhere beneath us; we just had to find the way in.

"It's at the bottom," Dante said beside me, reading my thoughts. "We have to swim."

"Underwater?" Eleanor whispered. "But that will kill me."

She knew just as well as I did that the Undead couldn't sink; their bodies naturally had to float. And for good reason: sinking beneath the earth had the same effect as burial. It would put them to rest.

"I think that's the point," I said.

"But what are we even looking for?" Eleanor asked. "How will we know what to do?"

I bit my lip. The riddle said nothing about this part of the journey, nor did the chest. I had no idea.

Anya dropped her bag. "Not everything is guaranteed," she said. "We just have to take a leap, and hope that we're right."

Eleanor fell quiet. "But how will we even get down there?" she said. "We can't swim against the force of our bodies."

"But we can," Theo said. "Hold on to us." He dropped his bag and began to strip down, as did Anya, quickly slipping off all of the gear that might hinder any ability to swim. While they prepared themselves, I turned to Dante. His eyes reflected the sky and the clouds, as if he was already drifting to another world. Was this good-bye?

Gently, he unbuttoned my coat and let it slide off my shoulders. "Don't worry," he whispered. "This is just the beginning."

Though his eyes were clouded, behind them I could still see the softness of his irises, the pupils sharpening as they took me in. He was a part of me, and I a part of him.

His hand slid down my arm. I could barely feel it. Still, I laced my fingers through his.

"Are you ready?" he said.

"No," I whispered. I knew now that there were some things in life I would never be ready for. Our eyes met. I could see my reflection in his gaze. I didn't say good-bye. I had to believe that there would be time for me to say it later.

"Don't let go," I said.

I took a deep breath, feeling my chest expand with air, and before I could change my mind, I dove beneath the surface.

I waited for the shock of the cold to make my muscles seize, but I felt nothing but numb. The weight of his body pulled against me as we plunged beneath the earth. I spread my arms wide and pushed harder, dragging him deeper into the lake.

I didn't know where I was going; I only hoped that when I saw it, I would know. Beside me, Theo and Anya pulled Eleanor underwater. Dante's grip loosened on my hand, threatening to slip away. I tightened my fingers around his and swam faster, leading us toward a slant of rooftops. The houses looked centuries old; their walls were covered in a film of algae. The windows looked in on abandoned rooms, the furniture covered in a thick layer of sediment.

Dante's body grew weak, his arms beginning to quiver. *Not yet*, I pleaded. We were close. We had to be.

A white stone steeple stood tall over the houses. The tower, I realized, remembering the last card Anya had placed on the table during Dante's tarot reading. Beside it stood a thick stone gate. I swam toward it, pulling at the handles of the doors, but they wouldn't budge. Theo swam beside me, tugging at them until they cracked open. Clutching Dante's hand, I pulled him inside.

The water from the lake gushed in, carrying us with it into a dry cavern. I gasped, my lungs starving for air, while the others slid in behind us, the press of water pushing the door shut. I scanned the rocky enclave for the others. Anya was coughing on the floor. Theo helped her up, then slung Eleanor's arm over his shoulder. She was barely conscious, her body trembling from the weight of the ground above her. The last bit of life was leaving her. There was no time.

I stumbled through the water toward Dante, who was lying against the rock, almost lifeless, each rise and fall of his chest slighter, weaker. "Dante?" I said. "Don't leave me yet. We've almost made it." I waited for him to speak, but he said nothing.

Unsure what to do, I scanned the cavern around us, searching for an answer. Around us loomed a vast underground cave, the walls made of a hard black stone, the same as the sealed box. Inside, it was dry. There was no end to the ceiling, only darkness as far as I could see. A swirling black lake lapped at the rocks by our feet, its waves made of dust rather than water. I reached down and touched it, watching as the dust hardened in my hand like a black stone.

In its world it is dust, in the hand it is coal,
At long last I found it, the ephemeral soul.

I could hear the soft murmur of voices rising from the surface: laughter, whispers, shouts of pain, of joy.

The waves twisted and looped up, contorting up into shapes. They shifted into a face, followed by a narrow set of shoulders and a pair of skinny legs. The thin frame of a boy materialized before me like a shadow. I recognized him. "Nathaniel?" I whispered. One of my first friends at Gottfried. He pushed his glasses up his nose and opened his mouth as if he were going to speak, but no sound escaped his lips. Had he been put to rest? Is that why I was seeing him here? I reached out to touch him, but before I could, he shattered, the dust dispersing around me. Out of it emerged others, friends and family, all long-dead, each of them dark and grainy. Black memories.

I saw my grandfather, his shoulders stooped into a hunch; my father, his calloused hand shielding his gaze, the wrinkles on the corners of his eyes smiling as he took me in; and my mother, her long hair pinned back in a loose chignon. I felt my breath go thin. I couldn't help myself. I reached out to a tendril of her hair, wishing I could touch her just one more time. But before the dust met my fingers, it dissolved, until my mother, my father, and all of the shapes in the dust around me had dispersed.

I turned to Dante lying beside me on the rock, his body weakening as the life left him. I folded to the ground next to him and slipped my hand in his. "I'm still here," I said, searching his face for some sign that he could hear me.

Then his fingers tightened around mine. He opened his eyes, his irises struggling to focus on me. His breath was thin. "So am I," he whispered. His heart slowed. I waited for mine to fill in the beats his had missed, but mine was fading, too. This was the end. Just before our lips touched, his eyes fluttered shut. "I love you," he said.

His hand tightened around mine, pulling me toward him one final time. I saw his lips, lifeless as they pressed against mine in a cold last kiss. A real kiss. The dust from the lake lapped against our mouths, surrounding us in a swirl of dust until everything around me faded to black.

I felt the last of my mind unravel. I watched all of my

remaining memories fade to black as each day, each year, each face reversed itself in unbeing, the lake washing my soul clean.

Dante. It always came back to him. I saw him stalking along the shore of the frozen St. Lawrence River, waiting for my silhouette to appear through the snow. I saw him searching for the secret of the Nine Sisters; I saw him following the Liberum through the woods while they chased down Cindy Bell, Miss LaBarge, and finally, my parents. I blinked and I was there with him on the sunny afternoon when he snuck out to the side of my childhood house and tried to warn them that the Liberum were coming. I saw my mother in the kitchen, washing dishes with my father. They had no idea what was about to happen to them. Finally, I saw myself, my freckled cheeks still kissed from the California sun. We were in our first class together at Gottfried Academy. Our professor had just called out our names, pairing us together. Dante walked toward me from across the room, his dark eyes a clear, startling brown. I waited for him to speak, for the moment when our hands were supposed to touch beneath the table, sending that first prickle of cold up my skin, but the memory faded away before he had a chance to sit down. His face blurred. I squinted, trying to bring it back into focus, but I could barely remember what he looked like. I tried to reach out to him. "Don't go," I cried, when I heard his voice echo in my head.

I'll find you, he whispered.

CHAPTER 17

A Boy

I WOKE UP IN A SOFT CANOPY BED. SUNLIGHT streamed through the windows. It stung my eyes. I winced and looked down at the coverlet. It was made of thick downy satin. I touched its smooth surface with my fingers. It felt so familiar, but when I tried to figure out why, I drew a blank. My mind was bleary. I sat up against a pile of pillows and took in the room. It was a lovely bedroom, decorated with books and posters, shelves stacked with knickknacks and jewelry boxes. Was this my room? It seemed I had been here before, and yet I couldn't place where or when or why.

A photograph was propped up on the nightstand by my bed. It was tinted yellow from age. A man and a woman smiled back at me from a grassy lawn, their fingers splayed on top of each other in a comfortable kind of love. Did I know them?

I kicked off the sheets and stood up. My legs wobbled beneath me. When I took a step, a deep sadness weighed me down. It was a strange sort of melancholy; it almost felt like I was missing something, and I would never know what. I looked at my face in the mirror. The girl that stared back startled me. She looked young and crisp, her cheeks dotted with freckles and her hair pale from the sun. I didn't feel as young as I looked, and I couldn't remember the last time I had been outside or felt the warmth of the daylight on my skin. On the shelf beside me stood a photo of a girl who I could only identify as myself, though something about her looked different than the girl in the mirror. I touched my cheek, tracing the collection of freckles scattered across it. None of my features had changed, and yet the entire arrangement of my face looked off, as if everything had switched sides. As if I were an alternate version of myself.

The door creaked open. I jumped back toward the bed as an old man slipped inside, carrying a silver breakfast platter. He was bald, his face heavy with wrinkles. He wore a three-piece suit, black and tailored short, as if he were a butler. He looked familiar, though I couldn't place who he was.

He smiled. "Ah! You're awake," he said, and carried the platter to my bedside table, as though this were a daily routine for him. "Good morning."

I furrowed my brow and watched him with suspicion. "Thank you."

He set the platter down on my bedside table and lifted

the lid. A plume of steam rose up from the plate. The smell of it startled me, first sweet and syrupy, then a sharp zing of an orange, followed by a thick salty smell melting with butter and oregano. I took a deep breath, savoring all of the subtleties, as though I hadn't smelled food in years.

"Eighteen items in total. One for each year."

I had no idea what he was talking about. I frowned, suddenly remembering that I was standing in a strange room with a man I didn't know. I stepped back from the platter. "Who are you?"

"My name is Dustin," he said. "I'm the estate manager of the Wintershire House. Your house."

I paused. *My* house? I gazed out at the topiaries lining the crescent driveway, the maintenance workers meticulously grooming the lawn. Impossible.

"Do you know who you are?" Dustin said.

I laughed. "Of course I do," I said. Surely I knew my own name, but when I tried to recall it, my mind went blank. "I—I actually can't remember."

Dustin clasped his hands behind his back. "Your name is Renée Winters," he said quietly.

"Renée," I said, rolling the letters around in my mouth. Yes, that did sound familiar.

"Do you know how old you are?"

My eyes darted to the coverlet, as if the answer lay somewhere in the embroidery. My hands looked young and soft. Perhaps I was sixteen. My hands looked sixteen, though part of me felt much older. "I'm not sure," I whispered.

Dustin's face dropped. I had disappointed him. "What about today?" he asked gently. "Do you know what today is?"

I glanced out the window to the manicured yard outside. The garden around it was lush and colorful with flowers, the trees splayed out in brilliant shades of green. It must have been summer, I thought, though I couldn't recall how I had gotten here. The most recent weather I could remember was ice and snow. I shook my head. "No."

"Today is your birthday," he said. "You're eighteen years old."

I had to be dreaming. I didn't see how any of it made sense. How could I wake up on a strange bed that a strange man claimed was my own, and not even know my own name or birthday?

"Are you all right?" Dustin asked.

I narrowed my eyes and peered around the room, looking for some sign that it was mine, but everything within me felt blank. I didn't know what I liked or didn't like, or what kind of person I had been. It felt like I hadn't been anyone before this.

"Ms. Winters?" he continued. "Maybe you ought to sit down."

I listened for the sound of heavy footsteps down the hall, as if they were a natural part of the house. But none came. "Who's missing?"

Dustin lowered his eyes. "Your grandfather. He was killed trying to save you."

My grandfather. The word came with a flash of white

fluffy hair, of broad shoulders stooped beneath a tweed suit. Yes, I had a grandfather once.

Dustin studied me, his face riddled with worry. "I'm so sorry. According to his will, I'm your guardian now. Though I suppose since you're eighteen, you don't need one."

But I barely heard him. Who had my grandfather been protecting me from? Why couldn't I remember anything? My eyes drifted to the photo on my nightstand.

"Your parents," Dustin said.

The apologetic tone of his voice told me that they were dead, too. Though strangely, I didn't feel upset. I felt a distant sadness, as though a previous version of myself had already mourned for them, and now I could go onward, unencumbered by the past.

"What happened to me?"

Dustin hesitated. "You went on a long journey," he said, carefully selecting his words. "A dangerous journey, though you didn't know it at the time. Your grandfather did. He and his colleagues followed you there. They tried to protect you." He frowned. "But I suppose they were the ones who needed protecting. You were found alone in the French Alps, washed up on the shore of a mountain river. You were barely alive."

His words brought back vague slivers of memories that felt more like pieces of a dream than reality. A white swath of snow. A blue lake reflecting the clouds. A terrible dark mist lapping against my face. "Who found me?"

"I did," Dustin said, somewhat sheepishly. "With some

help. I brought you home, where I've been caring for you. We do this every day, you and I."

"Every day?" I said. "I don't understand."

"You've been here for six months. Every morning you wake up and you cannot remember. Or perhaps you remember a little bit more every day. Only you know the answer."

"Six months?" I said. It was an impossibly long time. How could I have not remembered?

"Do you recall anything now?" Dustin ventured.

I blinked and was being washed down a black river that carried me away beneath the earth until I saw a white burst of sunlight. But that version of the past felt like a dream. "I was looking for something."

"Yes," Dustin said, his eyes brightening.

"But what?"

Dustin lowered his head. "I cannot pretend to know the desires of your heart. My sole job here is to help you."

"Do you think I found it?"

"Only you can know the answer to that."

My heart sank. I had been alone here for six months. I knew then that whatever it was I had been looking for, I had lost it.

Dustin was about to turn, when he ventured one more question. "Do you remember who you were with that day?"

Had I been with someone? I closed my eyes and went through all of the fragments of images still floating in my head. I tried to fill in the blanks between them, to summon a face amid the snow and rock. I saw a bit of red hair. A tin of pills. A necklace made of beans.

I opened my eyes, the images forming one word. "Anya."

"Yes," Dustin said, startled. "She was your friend. We recovered her, too. She is safe at home in Montreal. She is healthy. I spoke with her parents the other day; they said she called out your name."

I repeated his words to myself. She was my friend. I believed him, and yet I could barely recall knowing her. I closed my eyes, trying to remember more. Shoelaces. A bit of sandpaper. Red dust collecting on the floor. A crooked grin. Then an arm, lifeless. A swath of auburn hair. A constellation of freckles. A handful of blond curls. A pair of thin arms wrapping around me. Candles flickering in a church.

"Theo," I said. "Noah. Eleanor. They were my friends, too?"

Dustin beamed. "Yes, they were. We found Theodore and brought him back to his grandfather's house." Dustin chuckled to himself. "He picked the lock of my car twice before we got him home. I had to go gather him from the countryside, where I found him wandering about aimlessly, but he is back now, and safe. As is Noah. He is at home in Montreal; his parents are incredibly glad to have found him in one piece. He will be returning to St. Clément in the fall. Eleanor is still recovering, though her father and brother are taking care of her."

His words made me glad, though I didn't know why. Though I knew they had been my friends, they now felt like people I had known in a different life, people who didn't belong in this one.

Dustin shifted his weight. "Do you remember anyone else?"

Was there another? I thought back, but the most I could see was a pale sliver of skin, and a dull gray eye, like the sun obscured by a cloud. I tried to complete it, but it slipped away from me.

I opened my eyes. A single image lingered. "Blue lips," I whispered.

Dustin fell quiet. My words seemed to startle him.

"I—I don't know where that came from," I said.

"That's all right," he said softly. "Keep thinking. It will come to you."

I swallowed. The tone in the room had suddenly become somber.

After a moment, Dustin spoke. "Perhaps this will help you."

I wanted to protest, to say that I didn't know him, that I didn't even like presents, but Dustin held up his hand before I had a chance to speak.

"Don't worry, it's not a gift," he said, reading my thoughts.

I looked up, surprised. Maybe he did know me after all.

He handed me a sealed plastic bag. Inside were a pile of dirty clothes and a white canvas bag.

"The clothes you were wearing when we found you."

I slipped the bag out from the bottom of the pile, and as I did, a sprinkling of black dust billowed up around us. Instead of scattering across the rug, for a second it seemed to pause and hang in the air as if suspended.

I gasped, partially out of surprise, but also because it looked oddly familiar. I felt a warm breeze come in through the window. It picked up the dust, swirling it around and carrying it back outside. I blinked. Had I been hallucinating, or had the dust just moved on its own?

I turned to Dustin. "Did you see that?" I asked.

Dustin merely shrugged, as if nothing out of the ordinary had happened. "A bit of dirt from the mountains, perhaps. Don't worry, I'll get one of the cleaners to clean it up later."

Maybe I had been seeing things.

"How did you find me?"

Dustin paused. "I've worked for your grandfather for thirty years," he said. "Before he left to follow you, he asked me to look after you should he pass away. So I did just that."

I looked at him curiously. I had an inkling that he wasn't telling me the entire truth. "Well, thank you," I said.

He nodded and backed out of the room. "Enjoy your breakfast."

I lifted the cup of tea. Beneath it was a thick white envelope. *Ms. Winters*, it said, in a sprawling cursive that seemed somehow familiar. Instead of a card inside, there was just a note. I unfolded it.

Dear Ms. Winters,

Only the pure of heart deserve a second chance. A soul is not given; it is earned. To many more birthdays to come.

Sincerely,

Dustin

A soul is not given; it is earned. I heard someone say that to me before, though I couldn't remember whom. I stared at the handwriting, at the way a hand had smeared the blue ink just after the word *Sincerely.* It looked startlingly familiar, as if I were holding something I had only seen in a dream. The only part that didn't fit was the word *Dustin.*

A memory flashed into my mind. A thick envelope with plane tickets. A letter slipped beneath the door of a church. They had helped me, those letters, though I couldn't remember why. A single word rose to my lips.

"Monsieur?"

Dustin froze. He had his back to me, his hand resting on the knob. His shoulders relaxed, as if my words had lifted something heavy from them. He turned. "Yes."

As I studied his face, I began to remember. *Descartes. The Nine Sisters. A long-lost secret, and a hidden map leading to it. Eternal life. The Netherworld.* That was what I'd been looking for. But why?

"You—you were the one who was helping me."

Dustin took a step forward. "Yes. With the help of my granddaughters."

Granddaughters? I blinked. An image of a pair of small, gentle hands flashed through my mind. I felt them lift me from the river. Bright yellow light filtered in and out behind my eyelids. I cracked them open to see the pale cheeks of a woman, her blond hair fluttering around her shoulders, her eyes a watery blue. Though she was young, she had the face of someone old and wise. She looked so familiar, like a kind man I had once known. I reached out to touch her cheek, but she gently pushed my arm away. "Shh," she cooed.

I remembered the five women, one disappearing behind the window of a old house, another stealing through a birch tree forest, another peering down at me from the mountains, still another materializing through the fog in a monastery. The Keepers, their blond hair the same color as a canary, the bird that had been etched into each of their houses. Their faces had been so familiar, though I hadn't been able to place from where.

I saw their features in Dustin's, and suddenly remembered who he was. I remembered him carrying my luggage to the car and holding the door open for me when I first left for Gottfried Academy. I remembered him standing in the dining room behind me, listening as my grandfather lectured me about school. I remembered when he took me duck hunting in the woods out back; when he told me about my mother and what she was like when she was my age. All along, it had been him.

"You're the descendent of Ophelia Hart, the ninth sister," I said in awe. "That's why there were canaries in each of the houses. That's how you found me. You always knew where I was going. You're the protector of the Netherworld."

Dustin pursed his lips and nodded. "Yes." His eyes twinkled as he studied me. "We protect it, but never use it. We've never had to. We believe that its powers should be reserved for those whose lives are cut off far too soon. Fortunately, I've been blessed with a long, wonderful life, as have my daughters and granddaughters. And that's more than enough for us," he said. "I wanted to show you the way, though I first had to make sure that you didn't merely want a second life, but that you were choosing it. Through every point, you had to make the decision. I couldn't make it for you."

"Thank you," I whispered.

He smiled at me, crinkling the creases by his eyes. "You're welcome." He clasped his hands together. "Well," he said. "It's your birthday. What would you like to do? We can do anything."

"I'd like to go for a drive," I said.

"A drive?" Dustin clasped his hands together. "Wonderful. I'll get my coat."

"Alone," I said softly. "If that's okay." I don't know what made me say it, though once it came out, I knew it was the right thing to do.

Dustin paused. "Are you sure?" he said.

"I'll be fine," I said.

Dustin clasped his hands together. "Very well. I'll fetch you the keys."

After eating breakfast, I picked up the white canvas bag and slung it over my shoulder. It felt so natural, as if I'd been naked without it.

Dustin led me downstairs to the driveway, where my grandfather's Aston Martin was still parked. He held open the front door and handed me the keys. "It's yours now."

I paused on the front step and shielded my eyes. Everything outside looked so vibrant and bright, the grass a lush summer green, the sky an almost electric shade of blue. I was eighteen years old. I had looked up at that same sky for years, and yet it felt like I was seeing in color for the first time.

"Is everything all right?" Dustin said.

I wasn't sure. I walked to the car and threw my bag in the passenger's seat. "I'll find out soon," I said, and shut the door.

I drove down the winding driveway lined with trees until I reached the main road, where I took a left. I didn't know why I chose that direction or where I was going, only that I would know which way to go when I saw it.

I drove for hours. The road meandered in and out of the countryside. Trees arched over the pavement, forming a canopy of green. Sunlight flickered through it. I opened my window and let the warm summer hair blow in my face. The ends of my hair flitted in the wind. I ran my hand through it, surprised by its length. Had I always worn my hair this long? I couldn't remember.

I caught a glimpse of a clear gray eye in the rearview

mirror. I gasped, only to realize it was my own. It was pale in color, with hints of blue like the sky on an overcast day. Why had it startled me so much? I gazed at my reflection, trying to grow accustomed to my nose, my cheeks, my mouth.

I turned on the radio to fill the emptiness of the car. An announcer spoke about the weather, about September approaching. My gaze drifted to the seat beside me. I half expected to see someone sitting beside me, but all I saw was the white canvas of my bag. Who had I been looking for? I didn't know when I started crying, only that it felt like the tears had been building up inside me for years. The past was gone.

A road sign approached. What did it say? I wiped my eyes, but I was too late. It had already passed. And yet when I saw the road it led to, I knew it was the right way. I swerved, and pulled onto a bumpy street that led toward a small town perched by the side of the ocean. The road was lined with restaurants and shops. Families gathered on the streets, chatting and laughing and licking cones of ice cream. I parked and stepped out into the crowd.

I kept my head down as I slipped through them. I didn't want anyone to see that I was crying. I walked along the marina to the far end of the street. Seagulls circled above. My gait was light and quick without the weight of the bag on my shoulder. The afternoon sun streamed down over the ocean, making the ripples in the water shimmer. I slowed. I was standing in front of an old house, a sign creaking over the door. THE OLD SOUL. I peered through the windows. An old man was wiping down the bar inside. I cupped my hands over the glass. Did I know him?

Sensing my presence, he turned around. I ducked out of the way and turned back toward the road when I saw the outline of a boy in the distance. He stood by the curb and stared out at the ocean, the hazy light glowing around his silhouette. There must have been dozens of other boys in the marina, and yet the sight of him seemed to paralyze me. He must have seen me, too, for he turned, his head tilted as if he were studying me. He ventured closer.

As he approached, I could just make out the short brown locks of his hair, his broad shoulders and the smooth contours of his arms. The sunlight blinked around him. Did I know him?

He inched closer. He said nothing as he studied me, his eyes curious, searching, as if he were trying to relearn my face. I had never seen him before. None of his features looked familiar, and yet when put together, they formed an expression that I knew from a lifetime ago.

A thin white scar cut through his upper lip, the same exact mark I had, though his was on the opposite side. Without realizing what I was doing, I lifted my hand to his face and traced the scar over his lip. His skin was so warm. When we touched, the flash of a memory barely registered in my mind. *A cave. A swirl of dust. A kiss.* I closed my eyes, trying to fill in the spaces, but the memories kept slipping away.

I let my hand slide down his arm, where it rested at his wrist. Gently, I pressed my thumb into his skin until I felt the steady *thud, thud, thud* of his pulse. He was alive.

He laced his fingers through mine. The world around me came into focus. I gasped, realizing now that I knew him, that I had always known him.

His lips parted, as if he were just as startled as I was. "You," he said.

My chest swelled. I felt my heart. "You."

ACKNOWLEDGMENTS

Ted Malawer, for being as good an agent as you are a friend. Tracey Keevan, Christian Trimmer, Ricardo Mejías, Abby Ranger, and Laura Schreiber, for your invaluable editorial advice. I feel so lucky to have been able to work with all of you. All of my copy editors, for sharpening my writing. The entire team at Hyperion, for taking such good care of me all these years.

Lauren, Shirin, and Rahia, for getting me out of my apartment, and reminding me how friends can be soul mates, too. My mom, for every trip to Aussois, clock included, and for giving me an appreciation for mountain life. Claire and Luc, Roland and Josette, for your incredible hospitality, home cooking, and mountaineering skills. Claudia, for schooling me in everything German. My brother, Paul, for getting me through all those family vacations. Vicky, for her generous help with my French translations. My dad, for sending me books and packages while I was writing, and for being a real-life Monsieur. Akiva, my soul mate.

Thank you.